MW00364222

JACK OF DIAMONDS

'Til death do us part...

All Jack Stratton wants to do is get married to the woman he loves—and make it through the wedding. It seems like he is finally getting his wish until he responds to a police distress call and discovers his old partner unconscious in an abandoned house. Investigators insist it was just an accident, but Jack fears there may be more to it. Sketches of women cover the walls, and among them is one sketch that makes Jack's blood run cold—a sketch of Alice, pinned up beside an invitation to a very special wedding—his own.

Locking horns with law enforcement, Jack digs deeper. What did his old police partner see in the house? Who's been creating these sketches? More importantly, what do they want with Jack's bride-to-be?

When he identifies two of the women in the sketches, only to discover that they are both missing, Jack finds himself thrown into one of the deadliest cases he's ever worked. Jack comes to a terrifying conclusion—there's a serial killer on the loose... and Alice is his next target.

As their wedding day looms closer, Jack and Alice must work together to solve the murders and put an end to the killer. Will they catch the psychopath in time, or will their loved ones attend a funeral instead of a wedding?

This time, "till death do us part" might just be a bit too accurate.

Also by Christopher Greyson:

And Then She Was Gone

Girl Jacked

Jack Knifed

Jacks Are Wild

Jack and the Giant Killer

Data Jack

Jack of Hearts

Jack Frost

Jack of Diamonds

The Girl Who Lived

Pure of Heart

The Adventure's of Finn and Annie

A DETECTIVE JACK STRATTON NOVEL

JACK OF DIAMONDS

WALL STREET JOURNAL BESTSELLING AUTHOR

CHRISTOPHER GREYSON

GREYSON MEDIA

JACK OF DIAMONDS
Copyright © Greyson Media 2019

The right of Christopher Greyson to be identified as author of this
Work has been asserted by him in accordance with sections 77 and
78 of the Copyright, Designs and Patents Act 1988.

All rights reserved. No part of this publication may be reproduced,
distributed, or transmitted in any form or by any means, including
photocopying, recording, or other electronic or mechanical methods,
without the prior written permission of the publisher.

This book is licensed for your personal enjoyment only. This book
may not be resold or given away to other people. If you would like
to share this book with another person, please purchase an additional
copy for each recipient. If you're reading this book and didn't
purchase it, or it was not purchased for your use only, then please
purchase your own copy. Thank you for respecting the hard work of
this author.

Find out more about the author and upcoming books online at
www.ChristopherGreyson.com.

ISBN: 1-68399-093-5
ISBN-13: 978-1-68399-093-2
Jack of Diamonds v 1.0 12-14-19

This book is dedicated to my wife—my Alice. I'd marry her again in a minute and my love and respect for her grows every day.

CHAPTER

1

"Help . . ."

The one-word plea over the speaker was little more than a faint groan.

Jack turned up the volume on his police scanner as all of his emotions dialed down. No longer on the police force, he still listened to calls while he drove and now the habit could save a friend's life. The check-in had started out as routine as they come, but like any first responder, Jack knew that a boring call could turn deadly in an instant.

"Officer Pugh, what is your status?" The dispatcher's words were crisp, clear, and filled with fear.

Jack sped up, and the trees along the road became a blur of green. His former partner, Donald Pugh, had been on patrol up on Buck Mountain, and noticed the front door of one of the rentals was open when he drove by at the start of his shift. After he looped around the peak and saw the door still ajar, he stopped to perform a simple welfare check. Folks in these parts—where a foraging raccoon or a hungry bear could do a lot of damage—might leave their doors unlocked, but not open.

"Ten-thirteen," Donald gasped.

Officer down.

Jack's knuckles turned white as he gripped the steering wheel. He jammed the gas pedal to the floor and the engine of the Dodge Charger roared as the car surged forward. In the backseat, Lady, his one hundred and twenty pound king shepherd, barked excitedly.

The dispatcher was trying to get Donald talking, but there was no response now. Jack could picture the flurry of activity inside the dispatch room. No other code brought more distress to emergency responders. "Backup is on its way, Donald. Stay with me."

Jack grabbed his phone and called 911 as he pumped the brakes and took a sharp turn.

"Nine-one-one. What is—"

He recognized her voice instantly and grit his teeth wishing any other operator had picked up. "Marilyn, this is Jack Stratton. I'm three minutes out from Officer Pugh."

"Okay, ah . . . Jack, you're *not* a cop anymore." Marilyn sounded like she was spitting nails into the phone. Most women liked the handsome, hometown hero with a heart of gold, but *not* Marilyn.

"Let the other units know I'm en route. I'll leave this line open." Jack dropped his phone into his cup holder as he turned onto the unpaved road on his right, racing over the rough gravel, the cacophony drowning out all other sounds.

He didn't need to be reminded that he'd lost his badge. He lived that harsh truth every day. But this far out of town, the nearest backup unit was fifteen minutes away. Jack was all Donald had.

"Hang on, Lady."

Lady settled back in the seat against her restraint, panting loudly. Jack had tricked out the rear of the Charger to keep his new partner safe, installing a safety harness for the enormous dog.

Rocks pinged off the undercarriage as the Charger raced up the dirt road. At this speed, avoiding potholes was Jack's biggest challenge. Whenever he clipped one, the muscles in his forearms flexed as he struggled to keep control of the car.

He reached for his body camera and turned it on. He had been a big fan of the device while he was on the force, and as a bounty hunter, having a video recording of his apprehensions of bail skips was invaluable. But that wasn't why he was turning it on now. If something were to happen to Jack, the camera could help the police find whoever was responsible.

He tried to shove the morbid thought aside as the Charger slid onto the main road. He was almost to the remote address and had to be careful to avoid missing the driveway.

"Jack? ETA?" Marilyn called out over the phone.

"One minute out." Jack jammed on the brakes and turned in at the long driveway.

Marilyn didn't let her dislike of Jack affect her professionalism. "Backup is still ten minutes away."

"Understood."

Jack rounded the last turn and the house came into view, a two-story, cherry-red farmhouse with white shutters. Donald's police car was parked out front. The driver's door hung open and the engine was running.

Jack picked up the phone and slid it into his shirt pocket. It would have to act as a makeshift police radio. "Arrived on scene. Donald's cruiser is out front."

As he opened his car door, the dome light clicked on and Jack's eyes locked on the black-and-white photo clipped to his visor. Aunt Haddie was old-fashioned and had convinced Alice, her foster daughter, to have an engagement picture taken. The photographer had captured something special in that moment, and Jack's fiancée had never looked so beautiful. In her favorite dress, which he'd bought her in Hope Falls, she seemed to be smiling just at Jack. He'd cut the wedding announcement out of the newspaper and hung it up as a reminder of what was at stake. He had always been, and still was, willing to put himself in harm's way to help someone in need. But he had more than himself to consider now.

Closing his eyes, he prayed. *God, please help me.*

He pressed the release switch on the console. Lady's harness unlatched and the back door swung open.

"To me," he whispered as he unholstered his Glock and stepped out of the Charger.

Lady bounded to his side and shook out like a sprinter preparing herself for the big race, her bulletproof vest clinking softly. To some, the protective gear may seem like overkill, but not to Jack. His four-legged partner had proven herself loyal, rushing into harm's way to protect him time and time again.

Jack scanned the windows and open doorway as he silently climbed the five stairs to the porch, sticking close to the edge. Lady's claws tapped against the wooden porch, then she stood still beside him. The house was pitch-dark within, all the shades drawn and the curtains pulled closed as well. Jack's military breach-and-clear training clicked into gear.

He pressed his back against the wall and swept the inside of the house with his flashlight. The interior of the house was as dark as a cave, and silent. A narrow staircase on the right led to the second floor. The sparse living room, furnished with only a couch and a TV, was deserted. Jack's flashlight beam reflected off the TV screen and several mirrors. All the doors were closed except for the one in the far-left corner, which was slightly ajar.

Lady lifted her head and sniffed; her ears laid back on her head. Growling, she pushed against Jack's leg. "Easy," Jack whispered, his own heart pounding in his ears. It was a stressful enough task to enter an unknown residence when he had the authority to do so as a cop, but as the dispatcher noted, he wasn't a cop anymore.

"The police are on their way!" he yelled. "I'm coming in!" Pushing the legal ramifications aside, he started forward, but Lady barred his entry. The dog was not only enormous but very strong, and when she braced her feet and pushed against him, she stopped him in his tracks.

Jack pushed back. "Easy, girl."

Lady's senses were a thousand times more attuned than his, and it was clear that she didn't want him to go into that house. What the dog didn't understand was, Jack didn't either, but he had to.

Keeping his flashlight focused on the partially open door to the rear, Jack crept across the living room toward it. Lady whined in protest, but the sound of her paws sticking close to his side brought him some relief. She had saved his life a few times already, and they were turning into a great team.

It's always good to have a partner.

Jack pressed his shoulder against the doorframe on the hinge side and listened. The house was quiet save for the breeze rattling the windchime outside.

Lady growled, a low rumble that slowly built up to a snarl.

Jack used his foot to open the door wider and made a slow arc with his flashlight. The room was empty, not a stick of furniture, but there was a gleam on the floor. He angled the light down, illuminating a pair of heavily polished shoes. He immediately recognized the police uniform and knew the body lying on the floor was Donald's.

Forcing himself not to rush to his former partner's side, Jack methodically swept his light across the rest of the room, which was empty, though dust floated in the air, now mixing with dog hair. At the back was a closed door.

"Anyone home?" Jack whispered to Lady as he shined the light on the door.

Lady skittered around Donald and trotted over to the closet. Alice had been training the dog, and although Jack didn't agree with her choice of commands, he couldn't argue with the results.

Jack's fingers tightened on the grip as he kept his gun aimed at the door. Lady sniffed the air but neither growled nor clawed the floor. As far as the dog was aware, no one was behind that door. She looked at him expectantly.

Jack quickly crossed the room and jerked open the door. All that greeted him was an easel and a few art supplies in a corner on the floor. Turning back to Donald, Jack exhaled when he heard the fallen policeman groan. But his relief was short-lived as he noticed blood pooling beneath Donald's head, a mosaic of red being painted on the wood.

Laying his flashlight on the floor, Jack knelt beside Donald and grabbed his phone from his pocket. "Marilyn, this is Jack. Are you still there?"

"Jack? Two units are still four minutes out."

"Roger that. Notify the ambulance that the officer is breathing and suffering from a head wound." Jack winced as he examined Donald's head. A gash ran down the back of his scalp, and a huge lump was already cresting out of his bald spot. "Looks like blunt force."

Donald drew in a ragged breath.

"Help's on the way, buddy." Jack laid his hand gently on Donald's back.

The door behind him creaked open a little wider. Jack pivoted around, his gun raised and prepared to fire, and Lady also faced off against this new threat, the fur on her back standing on end, making her appear even larger than usual.

A cold breeze wafted across Jack's cheek. In the shadows beside him, a paper rustled as Lady shifted her weight. The wind died down and the door creaked back to its original position.

Pinned to the floor beneath Lady's large paw was a sheet of paper, smeared with blood. The sketch of a smiling young woman was beautifully done. The artist clearly had a gift—the lines, the proportions, even the shading was impeccable.

Jack had paid little attention to the papers taped to the walls when he first swept the room, but now he lifted his eyes and the flashlight beam. All were pencil drawings of women of various ages. They were high-quality portraits on thick art paper, and Jack wondered briefly why they weren't matted and framed.

A much smaller piece of paper drew his eye. He couldn't read the words on the gold-and-green embossed card, but he didn't need to. He'd seen a hundred of them in the last month.

It was an invitation to the wedding of Jack Stratton and Alice Campbell.

Next to it was another pencil drawing. Jack's breath caught in his throat as a swell of fear he'd never known rose from the core of his being. The sketch was a larger-scale replica of the very photograph he had hung on the visor of his car.

It was a portrait of Alice wearing her favorite dress.

CHAPTER

2

The rough bark of the oak tree digs into the palm of my hand as I watch the lights from the emergency vehicles reflecting off the wet lawn. Blood pounds in my ears, my palms sweat. Safely hidden in the shadows of the thick trees, I still feel exposed. The thrill at being this close to so many people who want to catch me is almost overpowering.

But I won't let them.

There is still so much for me to do.

Stupid policeman. Because of him I've left so many of my drawings behind. Part of me wonders if I did it on purpose. Do I want them to stop me?

Not yet. I'm too close to the ultimate prize.

The silhouette of the man I've been waiting for appears once more on the porch. Even this far away I can pick out Jack Stratton. Tall. Muscular. He moves with the easy grace of a born athlete. The people who circle around are in awe of him, too. You can see it in their body language. They come close to him, but not too close. They hover like moths around a flame.

Jack speaks, and they listen.

I can't make out his words. I know he's upset. Because of me.

I didn't think he'd get in my way so soon, since he's not on the force anymore, but now he might jeopardize everything. I only want to capture Alice the way I see her—fun, beautiful, kind, and loyal. She's perfect. Listen to me—I sound like I'm writing her dating profile. But it's true.

They're taking away the policeman now. He's on a stretcher with an oxygen mask over his face. He's still alive. I thought he was dead. I should have killed him. A mistake.

I wonder what he saw?

I hurriedly snap photographs of the ambulance as it rushes down the dirt road, the red and white lights reflecting off the trees like fireworks, but the photographs won't capture the essence of the scene. They never do. I'll have to sketch it later.

My sketches . . .

Slipping behind the tree, I chance a quick peek at my phone. I made certain to photograph each sketch as soon as I finished it so I could look at them whenever I want. I stroke the screen, caressing one face after another; there's still graphite beneath my fingernails. I may have lost the originals, but at least I have my copies.

My invitation. I've lost that, too. And I didn't take a photograph of it. Another foolish mistake.

Jack and Alice were so very kind to invite me to the wedding. It made me feel wanted. They wouldn't have invited me if they didn't want me to be in attendance at the most important day of their lives.

And their greatest day will also be mine.

They will know the utmost joy.

And poor Jack Stratton will know the pain of losing everything.

CHAPTER

3

As Jack paced at the bottom of the steps, Sheriff Robert Morrison stood on the top stair with his arms crossed and a sympathetic look on his face. The tall African-American man in his late fifties used to be Jack's boss—and was still his friend. He wore the tan uniform of the sheriff's department, minus the hat. His curly black hair was short and graying at the temples.

Jack stopped pacing and glared up at him. "I just want to go in and see if there's anything on the back of the invitation."

"I can't do that, son. Not until Castillo is done processing the scene." Morrison's voice lacked conviction, but Jack knew he would hold firm.

"Technically, it's my invitation." Jack was grasping at straws. "I'm retrieving stolen property."

"It's a crime scene. Period. You know the deal, Jack."

"There's a picture of Alice in there, Bob. My Alice!" Jack was close to yelling. He wasn't angry with his friend. He knew Morrison was doing his job. But seeing the sketch of Alice's smiling face inside that room had sent a surge of fear through Jack that still held him in its grip.

"I'm aware of that, and right now Detective Castillo is working on figuring out why."

Jack ran his hands through his thick, dark hair, turned, and marched toward his car. He didn't stop, though Morrison called out after him. He could just about tolerate Ed Castillo on a personal level, but professionally . . .. The man tried hard, but Jack always felt he was not so much an actual detective, more like a man playing the part of a detective, wandering around in a costume with a badge. It didn't help that Castillo had been harboring a grudge against Jack ever since Jack caught the man known as the Giant Killer.

Being sidelined with Castillo in charge only added to Jack's fears; he felt the knot in his stomach tighten. He had to do something and was wondering what that would be as he slid into the Charger. Lady stood up in the backseat and laid her head on his shoulder. Jack scratched behind her ears as she whined. She pointed her muzzle at the house and barked.

"I know, girl. I want to get inside, too. But what am I going to do? Push Bob out of the way?"

Lady's head bobbed up and down.

Jack stopped rubbing her fur. If he didn't know better he'd swear she understood him. "You know"—he grabbed the sides of Lady's face and gave the top of her head a kiss—"that could work. Let's go." He opened the car door and Lady hopped out. He whispered in her ear, and she trotted for the house.

Morrison's eyes widened. "Hey, Lady. Whoa. Stop. Lady, stop."

Jack beamed as Lady trotted straight up the steps to the porch.

"Get your dog, Jack!" Morrison backed up as Lady climbed the stairs.

"Sorry, Bob. I don't know what's gotten into her."

Ed Castillo emerged from the open front door, took one look at the enormous dog coming up the stairs, and slammed the door shut behind him. His light-gray suit looked as if it would've cost a month of Jack's pay, and his brown hair was gelled and styled.

Morrison continued to back away until he was standing beside Castillo. Both men had their backs to the door as Lady stopped on the porch and faced them.

"Hey, Jack." Castillo waved and cast a nervous eye at the huge dog. "I need to ask you a couple of questions."

"Great." Jack nodded. "Let's talk inside."

Castillo shook his head. "No can do." He pointed at Jack. "Civilian." Then he jerked his thumb at the house. "Crime scene. End of story."

"Get off your high horse, Ed," Jack snapped, jaw clenched. "I was first on scene and I'm a witness. I've already been in the crime scene, so I won't be introducing DNA that isn't already there. Besides, I can point out details when we go inside. You're not violating any rules."

Castillo shrugged. "You can give your statement right *here*."

"Lady," Jack said.

His furry partner pinned her ears back and growled.

"This is not funny—or fair, Jack." Morrison kept his voice light, for Lady's sake, even as he glared at Jack. Morrison and Castillo both remained pressed against the house.

"Lady is very protective of Alice, Bob. You know that." Jack crossed his arms, standing his ground, a smirk threatening to tug the corners of his mouth up.

"Jack wanted to see the back of the wedding invitation," Morrison explained to Castillo. "It's a good idea. There could be something written on it."

Castillo scowled, but Lady growled again. "Fine. But no dog."

Jack nodded and climbed the stairs. "Lady, sit. Stay." He patted Lady's head.

Morrison and Castillo went inside, and Jack turned his body camera back on and took out his phone as he followed the men through the living room and into the room where Jack had found Donald.

"This is a huge overreaction on your part, Stratton," Castillo said, stretching out Jack's name. "There's nothing sinister going on here."

Jack opened his mouth to retort, but Morrison cut him off. "I have an unconscious officer on his way to the hospital, Ed. Explain to me how exactly Jack's overreacting."

Ed stopped in his tracks. "I did not mean to make light of the situation with Officer Pugh, but I don't think it was an ambush." He cleared his throat and pointed to an object beside the door. The lights had been turned on and now it was easy to see the metal kettlebell on the floor amidst the dust floating in the sunlight. "It's a five-pound kettlebell," Castillo continued. "They use them in CrossFit."

"I'm aware of what a kettlebell is, Ed. What I don't know is why you think this wasn't an ambush of one of my officers."

Castillo pointed to a nail sticking out of the wall about seven inches above the doorframe. "See that nail? They call this setup a 'redneck alarm.' You rest a weight on the door. When Donald opened the door . . . *bam*! The kettlebell hit him in the head. I'm not minimizing what happened, but that's just what it was."

"And what fairy tale did you come up with to explain the Charles Manson art wall?" Jack said. He slowly turned, his camera capturing the sketches taped to the wall, and at the same time, he held his phone low, covertly snapping pictures like a crazed paparazzi. He would have liked to check out the rest of the house, too, but there was no way Castillo would allow that.

Castillo bristled. "You know what your problem is, Stratton? You love drama. It can't ever be anything ordinary to you. The guy's obviously an artist. There's art stuff all over the house. Maybe he likes to draw women, simple as that. Creepy and strange, but not illegal."

"The guy has a sketch of my fiancée taped to his wall, with an invitation to my wedding pinned next to it, and I'm being dramatic? Look at all the empty spots! He had three dozen pictures up there but rips half the sketches down and just runs out of the house?"

Castillo held up his hand. "We're trying to locate the homeowner now so they can identify who rented it. The tenant probably panicked when their kettlebell trap ended up clobbering a cop. Once they calm down, I bet they turn themselves in."

"That still doesn't explain why there's a picture of Alice on his wall."

"Isn't that a copy of the picture that was just in the paper? Maybe the guy thought she was . . . particularly attractive."

Jack pressed his lips together. He wasn't buying Castillo's theories, but he knew that letting his own fear turn into anger wouldn't do anyone any good. "Can I see the invitation?" he asked as calmly as he could manage.

Castillo pulled on a set of gloves and removed the pin holding the invitation from the wall. "Don't touch it." He held it up and turned it around so Jack could see the blank back. "Nothing. No name."

Jack scowled. "We didn't put names on the invitations, just on the envelopes. Erica insisted it wasn't necessary."

"Erica?" Castillo asked.

"The wedding planner."

Castillo raised an eyebrow.

Jack was about to point out that having a wedding planner and a lavish wedding wasn't his idea, or Alice's for that matter, but their billionaire friend Pierce kept insisting and gifting . . .

"We're going to find the homeowner," Morrison said. He placed a restraining hand on Jack's shoulder. "As soon as we get an explanation, we'll let you know."

Jack was about to protest when a police officer called from outside, "Hey, Sheriff. You'd better come out here."

Morrison strode out onto the front porch, followed by Castillo and Jack, who was suddenly grateful for the fresh air. A news van was parked behind the police cruisers, and a brunette reporter strutted forward. A harried-looking cameraman, wearing a red baseball cap turned backward, hurried to keep up with her, despite her cumbersome heels.

"Sheriff, Paula Thompson, Channel 5 News."

Morrison smiled but held up his hand. "Nice to see you again, Paula." He pulled the front door closed. "I'd be happy to give you a statement in just a moment. Over there, please." He pointed toward the cruisers. "There's no need to broadcast this address, you know that."

"I'm just covering the facts." Paula ignored Morrison's request and stopped at the bottom of the stairs. The cameraman handed her a microphone and stepped back as she positioned herself to film in front of the house.

Morrison looked incredulous, but the last thing the sheriff's department wanted was to be accused of stepping on press freedoms.

Jack leaned down to Lady and whispered, "Meany face."

The huge dog bared her teeth and barked ferociously, spit flying from her mouth as she clawed at the porch.

Paula almost bowled the cameraman over in her dash for safety by the news van.

Morrison covered his laughter with a coughing fit. Jack patted Lady's back, and the dog gazed happily up at him.

Morrison lowered his voice. "Thanks for the assist."

Jack smiled as he clicked Lady's leash onto her harness. He had started the practice of wearing the leash around his shoulders like the K-9 handlers. Alice liked the look, an added bonus. "I wish I could have gotten you out of it altogether, Bob. You're still going to have to give a statement."

Jack understood his friend's reticence. Channel 5's reporting on the sheriff's department was not always the fairest, and they had just recently run a story on the department's increased training expenses, with extra spin that made Morrison look bad. The story had failed to consider that the increased training was to get accreditation for the department—which would, in the long term, lower equipment costs across the board as well as cut down on expensive lawsuits.

"Pray I don't put both feet in my mouth this time," Morrison said.

Jack gave him a sympathetic salute.

Morrison started down the steps, stopped, and turned back. "Look, Jack, believe me, I think the world of Alice, and I would never let anything happen to her. But right now, until we talk to the homeowner and get in touch with the renter, it looks like Castillo's theory is the most likely. A redneck alarm and a spooked artist. Nothing more." Jack started to protest, but Morrison cut him off. "As soon as I have anything, I'll tell you about it. Okay?"

Jack nodded. He didn't agree with Castillo, but he knew Morrison was doing all he could. "Thanks, Bob. Do me another favor? Let me know when I can talk to Donald. As a friend," he quickly added.

"Will do. Time to face the press." Morrison rolled his eyes and headed over to Paula Thompson and the cameraman, who had now taken up a position that would show the police cars and not the house.

Jack walked Lady over to the Charger and let her inside. He stood staring back at the house, his heart thumping wildly, the knot in his gut twisting further. He closed his eyes and took three long breaths, but his heart refused to yield.

Slowly, he opened his eyes and focused on the front door. A feeling of dread washed over him. His fingers tightened into a fist. Castillo was wrong. He was sure of it.

The weight over the door might well have been a do-it-yourself alarm, but whoever had been living in that house had left behind more than sketches. It was as if their presence had contaminated the home . . . and it felt evil.

CHAPTER

4

Jack let Lady stretch her long legs in the newly fenced-in backyard while he hurried upstairs to talk to Alice. He had no clue how he was going to break the news to her that some psycho had drawn a picture of her and taped it to his wall and might very well be coming to their wedding.

He stopped on the second floor, hesitant to enter the apartment. The stress of wedding planning was weighing on Alice and she was unusually skittish. She wanted a simple wedding, but when Pierce Weston learned they were getting married, he insisted on paying for the nuptials—and the boy billionaire could not be talked out of it, no matter how hard Alice tried. Jack and Alice had saved Pierce's life—and his company—and he wanted to repay them. Finally, they'd agreed, but neither of them had foreseen what it would entail—the best wedding planner in the Northeast, a custom-designed bridal gown, a photographer recording Alice's every move, menu tastings . . . Pierce spared no expense.

With the lavish wedding only a week away, Alice and her small, motley entourage found themselves being whisked all over town by Erica, the wedding planner, who was an odd mix of army staff sergeant and football cheerleader. The woman's high-pitched voice, ever-present grin, and brisk efficiency grated on Jack, so he'd taken to avoiding the peppy dictator at all costs.

Jack hated to add to Alice's burdens. But he had no choice. She had to be aware of the situation and start taking precautions for her safety. Deciding on the direct approach, he stepped forward, opened the door—and froze.

He hadn't expected to see her again—ever. Yet here she was, standing in his living room, admiring her own artwork. Marisa had her back to him and her arms crossed as she gazed at the painting hanging above the couch, which she had given Jack and Alice after they had saved her life. It was a painting of a young girl running through a field, her long hair flowing out behind her, her arms outstretched. You could just make out her face and a hint of her hidden smile. The only color in the piece was the blue in the girl's eyes. It was truly stunning.

Jack had seen an early sketch of the painting on a cocktail napkin the night he first met Marisa. Her raven hair was dyed blonde now and somehow the tattoos that had covered her arms were gone, but Jack would know that voluptuous body anywhere.

"Hello, Jack," she said without turning, her voice warm and smooth.

"Are you out of your mind?" Jack shut the door behind him.

As he marched across the room, she slowly pivoted to face him. Marisa Vitagliano was tall for a woman, at five-ten, and her four-inch heels brought her to eye level with Jack. Her green dress showed off her curves and fit her impeccably.

"It's not safe for you to be back here." He had to stop himself from rushing over to the window and drawing the shades. "I thought you were safe and hiding in plain sight in Hope Falls."

"It's good to see you too," she whispered as she studied his face. "The last time I saw you, I didn't know if you would live. You sacrificed yourself for me."

Jack's brows knitted together. "Which is why I'm *really* confused that you're back in Darrington."

Marisa's Mona Lisa smile rose on her lips. "Alice needed gloves for the photoshoot."

Jack rubbed his forehead. "You're not making any sense."

"It's simple, really." She reached for his hand but stopped with her fingers a breath away. "I'm tired of running. I have no plans to move back, but I'm done hiding. This is my life and I will live it. Besides, *you* invited me to your wedding."

Jack opened and closed his mouth. The truth was, he hadn't invited anyone to the wedding. He'd rattled off a short list of people to Alice, who relayed it to the wedding planner. He was quite certain there was no way he'd mentioned Marisa's name.

"I would have invited you, but . . ." Jack cleared his throat. Marisa possessed an uncanny ability to get into his thoughts like no other. As a result, he found himself being more truthful with her than anyone. Even Alice. He felt a pang of guilt at that thought.

"Inviting you wouldn't be safe for you," he finished. "I kept you away to protect you, and . . . ."

"And?"

"And Alice. I thought it would be really awkward having you, my . . ." Jack wanted to say "ex-girlfriend," but the word was such a poor expression of what Marisa had meant to him.

"Ex-lover? Ex-soulmate?" Marisa leaned in. Jack took a step back, but she followed, her face only inches from his. "Is that possible?"

"Is what possible?" Jack swallowed.

"For two souls that were entwined like ours to ever really come apart?"

Jack started shaking his head, then changed it into a nod. "You know that . . . what we had was . . . I'm getting married in a week. I'm in love with Alice."

The Mona Lisa smile reappeared. "And that's why I'm here. To help Alice."

Jack exhaled and took another step back. "I still don't think it's safe—wait. Where's Alice now?"

"She's getting fitted for her bridal gown. The photographer insisted she get her gloves, and I offered to come back to get them for her. She gave me the key to let myself in."

"How did you even find her?" Jack asked, instantly wishing he had asked why she had tracked Alice down. "Even I rarely have any idea where she is these days."

"You do know that your entire wedding itinerary is online, right? The wedding planner has a detailed calendar of events on your wedding web page. You should check it out."

Jack shook his head. "No, I should shut it down, especially now. If you could find Alice, anyone could."

"I wouldn't worry, Jack. The wedding site is only accessible to invited guests." Marisa's lovely eyes clouded with concern. "Wait. Is something wrong? Why are you concerned about someone finding Alice?"

Jack told her everything, from responding to Donald's call, to finding him unconscious on the floor, to seeing the wedding invitation pinned next to a sketch of Alice. It was a relief to share this heavy burden with someone he trusted. "It was a pencil sketch, high-quality. Almost as good as yours."

Marisa pressed her lips into a thin line. When it came to her artistic ability, she was as proud as she was insecure.

"I said *almost*," Jack stressed.

She nodded. "Well, you know what they say about artists." She drew the pause out for effect. "The best ones are insane."

Jack frowned. "This isn't a time for joking." Though he had to agree to some extent.

Marisa grabbed his hand. "I'm not. I'll never forget that Alice helped to save my life. I'm indebted to her, too, and I consider her a friend, Jack."

Jack squeezed her hand; it felt familiar in his own. "We'd better go find her so I can break the news to her."

He turned to go, but Marisa kept hold of his hand. "I do need you to understand something about us," she said. Her face had turned serious. "And I explained all of this to Alice."

"You talked to Alice about us? Me and you? You and me?" Jack pointed back and forth between them in utter disbelief.

She closed her eyes and her finger stroked the back of his hand. The simple gesture made Jack start to sweat.

"What we had . . . I can't just forget."

She opened her eyes, and Jack's breath hitched in his throat. Marisa's eyes drew him in and it was like snuggling down in a warm bed under a velvet blanket.

"I was very honest with Alice," she continued. "I told her that my feelings for you are unchanged, but I won't act on them. I promise that I will do nothing to interrupt your wedding. However, if Alice changes her mind . . . or if you do . . . I want you both to know that I'm still in love with you, Jack Stratton."

Unable to look away, Jack fought the urge to bolt for the door. He gave Marisa's hand another squeeze and let go. "You know there was a time when you and I had something very special. You kept me alive then. If it wasn't for you, all the pain I was going through would have killed me. I'll never be able to thank you enough for that. The last thing I want to do is hurt you. But . . . I must be completely honest, Marisa. Your telling me this doesn't change anything. I love Alice, and I'm going to make her my wife. I still love you, but I haven't been *in love* with you for a long time."

Her expression gave away nothing. He waited for Marisa's reaction, unsure if she was going to kiss him or slap him.

"Tu sei il bello mio," she whispered at last.

Jack didn't speak Italian but he knew what the phrase meant. Marisa used to say it to him often. *You are my beautiful one.*

"I wouldn't expect any less from you, Jack. You're the most loyal man I know." She smiled. "Part of me wants you to be happy. I want you and Alice to have a long life together in wedded bliss. But . . ."

she stretched the word out, "you can't blame me for letting Alice know that if she gets cold feet . . . well, mine are hot."

She angled her leg as she talked, and Jack found his eyes traveling from her open-toed high heels, up her toned calf, over her thigh, before locking eyes with her once more.

"Do you want to catch a ride with me?" Marisa grinned as she picked the gloves off the coffee table. "Or would you prefer to follow?"

Jack watched as she sauntered toward the front door. Marisa was the kind of woman who could wear an old sack with holes cut in it and still be the sexiest woman in the room. When she reached the door, she picked up her handbag and slung it over her shoulder. The strap moved her hair to the side, and Jack noticed that she left one tattoo uncovered: a heart, closed with a golden combination lock.

The combination was 2614.

My old badge number.

CHAPTER

5

J ack elected to follow Marisa, and he parked behind her car outside
the photography studio. Several cars filled the parking lot,
including the silver BMW that Jack had learned to hate the sight
of—Erica's car.

"I thought it was weird that Alice had a dress fitting so late in the
evening," Jack grumbled as he joined Marisa on the sidewalk. "And
why is it taking place at the photographer's studio?"

"Erica thought the space in the dress designer's studio was too
drab, so they created a small set for the photoshoot. According to
Erica, it's a 'gorgeous Italian villa, absolutely to die for'!" Marisa did
a spot-on impression of the wedding planner, waving her hands
excitedly and mimicking her high-pitched voice.

Jack chuckled—until he saw that Marisa wasn't smiling. "You're
kidding me, right?"

"No." Her chocolate eyes fluttered. "Whoever this Pierce is,
Erica certainly enjoys spending his money. She must be racking up
quite a commission."

"Wait a second." Jack stopped. "What do you mean, 'whoever
Pierce is'? I thought you were going to show him around Hope Falls.
He said he was going up there."

Marisa shrugged. "He never showed. I got a polite email from
his assistant saying that he had a 'scheduling conflict.'"

Jack stared in disbelief. He'd gone out of his way to set Pierce up with a woman most men would kill to have a chance with, and he stood her up?

"I'm sorry," he muttered.

"Don't be. I had no expectations. And from the way he's throwing money around, I doubt we'd be a fit for one another."

That much was true. Marisa was a rare breed; her father, Severino Mancini, was the head of the Mancini crime family and worth millions, but money didn't move her at all. Still, not many people would shrug off a date with a billionaire. Even Jack had to admit, Pierce was handsome as well—but he wasn't going to tell Marisa that.

"You're one of a kind." Jack gave her a wink, and she lit up. "His loss."

"Is he coming to the wedding?"

"I assume so, since he's paying for it all. He's overseas right now."

Jack held the door open and followed Marisa inside. He immediately felt like he'd walked onto a movie set. Lights blazed down on the opulent scene. Large flash stands with shades behind them flanked both sides of the realistic photo backdrop of sun-kissed Tuscan hills and ancient olive trees through a mullioned window. The set was adorned with snow-white veils, roses and a small altar. He caught only a glimpse of the top of Alice's head as she walked behind a huge spray of flowers.

Jack spotted Shawna Hammond bustling about with a clipboard and a pen. Today her hair was in a thousand glistening black braids gathered in a topknot, which added five inches to her petite five-foot frame already raised higher by her iridescent four-inch platforms. She'd managed to pack her ample form into a sunflower-yellow spandex jumpsuit, but in several places it looked ready to break at the seams. Jack was glad to see that Alice had included Shawna in the bridal party. Not only had she proved to be extremely efficient— bossy as a mother hen—in Titus's office, where Jack worked now, but she was also a good friend to both Jack and Alice.

He heard a grating voice coming from one corner and saw Erica ordering around the photographer's assistant and rearranging the drapery on the altar at the same time. Catching sight of the new arrivals, she beckoned them over, waving both arms. "Marisa, do you have the gloves?"

Jack groaned as Erica bore down on them.

"Is that Jack?" Alice's voice rose high. "He can't see me!" She ducked down and disappeared between some potted palms and Roman columns.

"Oh no you don't! Out! Out!" Shawna marched over, grabbed Jack, spun him around, and started shoving him toward the exit.

"I don't buy all that superstition—" Jack started, but she cut him off.

"Superstition's got nothing to do with it." Shawna's topknot waggled back and forth as she signaled her strong disapproval. "My granddaddy said that his first glance of his beautiful bride in her wedding gown coming down the aisle toward him was a moment he treasured for the rest of his life. I'm not gonna be the one to let you screw that up for yourself, Jack." She yanked open the door and pushed him out with the skill of an experienced bouncer. "Besides, it builds anticipation." She wiggled her eyebrows before slamming the door in his face.

Jack stood on the sidewalk for a moment, dumbfounded, before he grabbed the doorknob. Shawna had locked it.

A deep laugh behind him made Jack straighten up. Bobbie G. strode over from his old Hummer. At six-four and over three hundred pounds, Bobbie Gibson didn't necessarily have to show off his massive biceps, but he always rolled up the sleeves on his army-green T-shirt for maximum effect.

He looked Jack up and down, broke into a broad grin, and nodded. That was sort of a tradition with Jack and Bobbie. They didn't shake hands, no knuckle bumps. They just nodded. They'd known each other from when Jack was growing up with Aunt Haddie, his foster mother, and later Alice's. Still, Jack would always have Bobbie's back—and had done so on a few occasions, especially since they both now worked for Titus Bail Bonds.

"You always had a way with women, Jackie. I take it you did something to set Shawna off?"

Jack jerked his thumb at the door. "I forgot about the whole don't-see-the-bride-in-the-dress-before-the-wedding thing."

"It's bad luck, don't you know that?"

Jack scoffed. He didn't believe in luck—and if he did, his was getting worse. Now, on top of trying to break the news to Alice that he'd found a picture of her taped to the wall at a crime scene, he'd have to assure her that he hadn't seen her wedding dress . . . and that he was not still in love with Marisa. Jack rubbed his temples and heaved a sigh.

"I thought you were chasing down a skip in the backwoods," Bobbie G. said. "Don't tell me you caught him already. You're making me look bad."

"I ran into a problem. That's why I have to talk to Alice."

"What problem?" Bobbie G. crossed his thick arms.

Jack's attention was on the dark Cadillac slowly circling the building; the same car had been driving around the building when he first pulled in.

"Do you know Buck Mountain?" Jack asked without taking his eyes off the car.

"From a distance." Bobbie G. must have noticed Jack's concern. He turned to look as the Cadillac pulled into the lot and stopped with its headlights shining in Jack's face.

"You know this guy?" Bobbie G. asked cautiously.

"Nope."

The car door swung open and a white male who looked just old enough to buy beer stepped out.

Bobbie G. scowled. "Are you kiddin' me?"

The kid held his shaking hands out toward Bobbie. "I'm sorry, Bobbie. I totally forgot my appointment."

"It wasn't an appointment, you idiot. It was a court appearance." Bobbie stomped toward the driver. "He's Ricky Wilson," he called back to Jack.

Jack nodded, relieved. He realized he'd instinctively moved his hand to his back holster and the involuntary gesture bothered him. There was a difference between being prepared and being paranoid, and Jack worried that reaching for his gun on the sidewalk outside Alice's photoshoot was crossing that line.

"My mom told me you were looking for me," Ricky said. "I got hung up, man. Can you explain to Titus?"

"*You* can explain to Titus. But you'll have to talk to the judge first."

"Oh, come on, man." Ricky swore.

"Don't go mouthing off to me." Bobbie G. towered over the younger man. "You're the one who screwed up. The judge will probably bounce you right back out, but now I gotta take you in. You got anything on you?"

Ricky shook his head, but Bobbie G. patted him down anyway. When he was done, he cuffed Ricky and looked over at Jack. "Hey, man, can you do me a solid and explain this to Shawna?"

"Explain that you caught a skip?" Jack asked, puzzled. Shawna was Titus's office manager. Why would Bobbie G. need to explain . . .? Jack's eyes widened. *Oh.* "Are you and Shawna . . .?"

"Don't go looking at me like that, Jack." Bobbie shook a finger back and forth. "And get that smirk off your face. This is *your* fault."

"My fault? How is you hooking up with Shawna my fault?"

"I'm not *hooking up* hooking up." Bobbie G's face flushed. "We're both in your wedding party, and she said it would be cheaper if we didn't bring a date and went together. The next thing you know . . ." He cast a nervous glance at the door. "Don't get me wrong, she's a fine woman. But I was thinking we were just going together, not 'going together,' you know? And now I'm driving her around everywhere and—"

Jack started laughing. "And you thought I had bad luck."

"Shut up, Jackie. This is all your fault."

"Then I'll let you explain to Shawna why you're leaving."

"No, no, man." Bobbie G. marched Ricky over to his Hummer. "We're supposed to go over to her aunt's after this. Just tell her it's gonna take a while to get Ricky processed. Offer her a ride."

"What? No way. I have my own problems."

"You can't just leave her here." Bobbie G. put Ricky in the back of the Hummer and got in.

"I'm not leaving her here, you are," Jack responded. "Besides, she knows how long it takes to process a skip. She's gonna know if you lie to her."

Bobbie G. tilted his chin up to the ceiling of the car like a little kid having a temper tantrum. "But her aunt has all these cats. There's like fifty of them, and they smell and they climb all over you . . ." The whole Hummer rocked as he shook his head in disgust.

"Fine. Go. I'll explain."

"Thanks, man!" Bobbie G. gunned the Hummer out of the parking lot before Jack could change his mind.

Jack ran a hand over his stubble and sighed as he walked over to the entrance. Before he could knock, the door to the photography studio whipped open.

Shawna lowered an accusatory finger at Jack. "I heard the Hummer roaring out of here. What did you say to Bobbie to make him take off like that?"

"Me? Nothing. Ricky Wilson—"

"You got a lead on Ricky and you told Bobbie? Is that where he went?"

"Calm down," Jack said and immediately regretted it when Shawna placed a hand on her hip and lowered her chin. "I didn't say anything. Ricky showed up—"

"Ricky just *happened* to show up? You didn't bring him?"

"No. Ricky drove by looking for Bobbie and turned himself in."

Shawna's nostrils flared. "How'd that no-count Wilson know to find Bobbie here?"

"His mom, I think. I told Bobbie I'd give you a ride when this is over," Jack said. "How much longer is it going to be?"

"At least two hours." Shawna pulled out her phone. "And there's no need for you to give me a ride, because Bobbie will be done processing Ricky by then." Her fingernails clicked on the screen as she pecked out a number. "I'll make certain of it."

"Look, I hate to interrupt, but I have to talk to Alice."

Shawna moved to block the door. "Oh, really? Do you have any idea how long it took her to get into that wedding dress?"

Marisa appeared behind Shawna and gave Jack a sympathetic smile. "Actually, Alice wants to talk to Jack. She can keep her dress hidden."

"Fine." Shawna stepped out of the way and Jack was assaulted by the smell of roses from the set. As Jack shuffled by her and slipped inside, he heard Shawna tell Milton at the office to process Ricky right away and then send Bobbie back to pick her up. He felt bad for Bobbie, but his friend was on his own from here. Jack had enough issues of his own to handle.

"Jack!" Erica's overdramatic squeal welcomed him into the room. She clapped her hands to get everyone's attention, her neon nails reflecting the bright lights, and he couldn't decide if she reminded him more of an elementary school teacher or a trained seal. "One moment, everyone! I'd like to introduce the groom-to-be, Jack Stratton."

Jack saw only two people he didn't know among the half dozen or so friends of his and Alice's milling about the studio, so the introduction must have been for the tall man with a large camera hanging from his neck and the woman in her thirties wearing a plain but elegant blue dress. Both smiled politely as Erica pulled Jack by the hand to the middle of the room.

"Jack, this is Philip Poole." Erica's grin widened. "He's a photographic *genius*. All the big magazines—*Vogue, Cosmo*—"

"Nice to meet you." Jack reached out his hand, but Philip held on to his camera with both hands and simply nodded.

"Pleasure," he said.

Erica sailed on with her introductions, clutching the woman in a side embrace. "And this is Lenora Soriano, the daughter of Lorenzo Soriano." Erica paused expectantly, but Jack didn't have a clue who she was talking about.

Lenora jumped in to help him. "My father designed your fiancée's wedding gown." She shook Jack's outstretched hand and gave him a friendly smile.

"Nice to meet you. I'm sure it's great, but I'd marry Alice if she showed up barefoot wearing my old T-shirt." Jack couldn't help picturing Alice just that way, and he was stabbed with a pang, a hunger for her presence.

Erica straightened up like she was about to give a presentation. "Lenora's father is one of the premier wedding dress designers in the *world*. When we found out he was available, we scooped him up."

Lenora blushed. "You're very kind."

The photographer cleared his throat and pointed to his elaborate safari-style smart watch, which looked like it could take pictures all by itself. As Erica was apologizing to Philip for the delay, Jack saw his chance and took a couple of long strides, but the wedding planner quickly caught up with him and grabbed his elbow.

"I know Alice wants to speak to you," she whispered to Jack as she led him toward a hallway, "and I know there is no way to keep you lovebirds apart for long, but we're trying to adhere to a tight schedule and we're falling terribly behind. Can you please try to keep it as brief as possible?"

Brief? I don't even want to have this conversation. With all of the stress that she's already under, Alice is going to go ballistic.

"I'll make it quick."

Erica deposited him in front of a door and scurried off. Jack knocked on the door of the dressing room. "Alice?" he called softly.

The door opened a crack. Alice kept the light off to shroud his view of her. "Jack, I'm so glad to see you," she whispered from somewhere in the darkness.

"Well, I can't see you. Don't tell me you're buying into that superstitious—"

"Of course not, but I don't want to ruin the surprise! This dress is amazing." The door creaked open a little bit more. "Are you alone?"

"Yes, but listen, there's something I have to tell you. It's very important."

"Hold on, I have a question for you first. Why didn't you tell me that you invited Marisa?"

"I didn't invite her. I thought you did."

"Me?" Alice's voice rose high and then dropped back down to a whisper. "Why would I invite your gorgeous ex-girlfriend to our wedding? I went by the list you gave me. Her cover name and address were on your list."

Jack had listed Marisa as "Francis Jones" in his address book, but he never . . .

"You promised me that you went through every person on the list you gave me," Alice said.

Oh, crud. Jack didn't need to see Alice's face to tell how upset she was. She'd asked him to go over the list of names to make certain he really wanted to invite these people to the wedding, but he only skimmed it.

"My bad."

"Oh, this is a lot bigger than 'my bad,' Jack. Now what are we supposed to do?"

"Ah . . . I can try to explain it to her."

"Explain what? That neither of us actually wanted her here?"

Jack heard the rustle of fabric and imagined Alice with her hands on her hips, green eyes blazing and lips pouting—he wanted to kiss them into a smile. "I'm just trying to figure a way out of this . . ."

". . . mess you got us into?" Alice finished his sentence for him. "There's nothing we can do about it now. We'll just have to make the most of it."

Jack exhaled. "I cannot believe how understanding you're being about all of this."

"Oh, I'm going to make you pay for this, Jack Stratton. I don't know how, and I don't know when, but you *will* pay."

There's my feisty Replacement. He'd taken to calling her Alice more and more but sometimes missed the unusual, endearing nickname Chandler had given her. Jack rested his hand against the wall and leaned his face into the crack in the door.

"Hey, no peeking!"

"Sneaking a peek at you is the last thing I'm thinking about," Jack whispered. He reached inside, feeling for her hand. He touched her arm and yanked his hand back in pain. "Ow!"

A gold-headed dress pin stuck out of his finger.

"That's what you get for trying to sneak a feel." Alice giggled.

Jack winced and pulled the pin out. "I wasn't doing that either. That actually hurt."

"You've got nothing to complain about. I've been a human pincushion for an entire week! I can't tell you how many times I've been poked and prodded."

Down the hall, he heard Erica clapping her hands and calling for the photoshoot to resume. She'd be coming for Alice any minute now.

"Listen, Alice, I don't know how to tell you this, but I was up on Buck Mountain and got a radio call for an officer down. I was fifteen minutes closer than the nearest backup, so I responded. It was Donald Pugh."

"Oh my gosh! Is Donald okay?"

Alice started to open the door but Jack held it closed, knowing she'd regret revealing herself later. "He suffered a head injury, but he's in a stable condition. I'm going over to the hospital later. But there's more." Jack took a deep breath. "Inside the house, on the walls, there were pictures—sketches, actually. Of different women." He said a silent prayer and blurted out, "There was a picture of you next to one of our wedding invitations."

The dress rustled loudly and Jack braced himself against the push of the door. "Me? And an invitation? Who is the invitation addressed to?"

"No one. Remember? Erica insisted we send the same invitation to everyone and personalize *only* the envelopes."

There was a long silence on the other side of the door. Finally, he heard a sigh. "Look, it might not even be someone we invited," Alice said. "We had a box of them left over and I threw it away in the dumpster behind the apartment."

Jack ran his hands through his hair. It still didn't add up to him. "But whoever attacked Donald sketched your picture from the photograph in the paper and hung it up next to the invitation."

"Is Donald alright?"

"I don't know yet. Detective Castillo thinks it was an accident, and Sheriff Morrison agrees, but—"

"Bob thinks it was an accident, too?"

"Yes, but—"

"Jack, there's only a week left, and this wedding has snowballed into a gigantic event. Your parents are flying here in a couple of days, and I have no idea how many other people . . . Are you sure you're not just feeling the pressure and making more out of this than there needs to be? If both Ed and Bob think it was an accident, maybe that's all it was."

Jack ground his teeth and the muscles in his jaw flexed. His gut was screaming at him. *There's something about the pictures, about that place.* How could he explain that? How could he make Alice understand?

"Excuse me?" Erica knocked on the hallway wall as she strode forward. "We really need to get moving."

"I'll be right there, Erica, but I need to finish speaking to my fiancé." Alice's hand snaked out of the dressing room and gave Jack's arm a quick squeeze. "Everything's going to be fine, babe. I'll be done in a couple of hours and I'll see you at home."

"No, I'm driving you home," Jack said.

"But you can't see me now, and we won't be done for a while."

"I'll wait in the car."

Erica jumped aside as Jack stomped down the hallway.

Alice had taken the news much better than he had expected, but that brought him little consolation. He didn't want her to be upset, but he did want her to be cautious. There was something very disturbing about those pictures—whoever drew them wasn't just some random artist making sketches.

When Jack had been in that room, he had felt a presence, a strange intention behind the hand that drew those women. There had been something evil in that vacant house, and it had eyes on Alice.

CHAPTER

6

I should have brought some popcorn. Sitting here in my car, wrapped in the shadows, watching them through the window . . . it's the best show I've seen in a long time. Jack is still pacing around the living room while Alice is doing all she can to reassure him that "everything is going to be fine." Or so I imagine. I can't hear her words, but I can see her expression.

She's wrong, of course. Everything isn't going to be okay. This is just the beginning of little cracks in the dam that should be taken very seriously. And the only person who sees the signs is Jack. This was expected, of course.

The police and the sheriff didn't find anything suspicious. To them, the incident is as good as forgotten. Just a bit of paperwork as a reminder it ever occurred. That and an injured officer.

The homeowner sent me an email, asking to speak on the phone. I ignored it. The identity I gave him when I rented the place was an alias, of course. And he only has himself to blame. He's the one who rented out his home via the internet without performing a thorough background check. Bet he won't make that mistake again.

I have nothing to worry about. I'll slip away again before the dam breaks. No one will ever know it was me.

Alice is getting upset now. Even though Jack towers over her, Alice's back is stiff, defiant. Like a Chihuahua against a Doberman.

Jack intimidates most people, but she's spunky. She's had a hard life and it made her tough. But that's not why she can stand up to Jack.

It's because she loves him.

Unconditionally. There is no fear there. She knows Jack would never hurt her.

What she doesn't understand is that Jack can't protect her. He's human. Limited. He'll try. He'll fail. And when he does . . .

A shiver courses through my body. Thrill or disgust, I can't tell. Part of me doesn't want Jack to fail. The other part can't wait to push him over the edge. After all that he's been through, he'll never survive losing Alice. His rage is too strong. He'll rip himself apart.

There's a beast inside of him. But he tries to cage it and lock it away. That's the wrong approach. The beast needs to be treated right and learn to trust its handler. The beast always gets free; that's why I let it out from time to time. It's not a pet—it's wild and dangerously feral, I know that. But I can control it if I let it free when it needs to feed.

And now, its hunger is growing. In Jack, too.

Because I'm so close.

I look down at my hand. I didn't even realize it, but I'm caressing the sketches on the seat next to me. I close my eyes and see their faces. Before I take Alice, I'll need to get the others. They need to pay for what they've done. How many chances have I given them to repent?

Too many. Too long.

It's finally time.

Jack's alone in the living room, staring at her bedroom door, a vacant look plastered on his face. It's so cute that they haven't made love yet. Ever. They sleep in separate bedrooms like in some old black-and-white fifties' TV show.

I've parked where I can see a small slice through Alice's window, too. She's brushing her hair. Staring at the mirror. The smile's returned to her face. She's thinking about her wedding—I'm sure of it. Imagining the perfect day.

Or is she letting her mind go there? Is she thinking about that first night?

She's walking across the room now. Reaching for the door handle. But she's hesitating. Why? Why not go to him?

She flicks off the light. She's going to wait. She's saving herself for him.

How sweet.

But that will never happen.

I won't let it. I can't.

Jack walks to her door. He knocks. He's apologizing. Tipping his chin down. Rounded shoulders. He presses his palms against the door. He's telling her that he loves her. I can almost hear the longing in his voice.

A smile spreads across his face. She forgave him, as always. He'll be able to sleep now, at least for one more night. But there will soon be a day when he won't be able to remember what a good night's sleep was—my dream will play in an endless loop in his mind and my art will be on display eternally.

I clap silently at the thought of the never-ending exhibition of my art. My dream finally fulfilled.

But Jack's twenty-four-hour nightmare is just beginning.

CHAPTER

7

Jack had downloaded the video from his body camera and the still pictures from his phone, and it took him most of the day to review it all. He'd taken hundreds of photographs, and most of them were pretty blurry and unusable since he'd been shooting them covertly, but he had enough to put together a 360-degree panorama of the room.

There were thirteen sketches of women still left on the wall, plus the bloodied one on the floor that Lady had pinned with her paw. Most of the subjects appeared to be in their twenties; only two looked to be in their thirties. And they all appeared posed, smiling, as if sitting for a professional photographer or portrait artist.

In addition to the fourteen sketches, there were twenty-three pieces of tape on the wall where Jack could only assume more sketches had once hung. And there were also empty spaces where, assuming the pictures had hung in rows, several more were missing. Jack estimated that there could have been close to four dozen sketches.

Forty-eight women. But only one wedding invitation. His.

Erica had sent him the list he'd requested of everyone invited to the wedding. He really should have checked his list over more carefully before he gave it to Alice. There were lots of people he hadn't seen in years on the list. But with Alice throwing away a box of invitations, anyone could have found them . . .

His phone rang. It was Morrison.

"Sheriff, have you located the homeowner?"

"We have, but . . ."

Jack stood and braced himself.

"They rented it out, and it was all done online," Sheriff Morrison explained. "We're working on tracking the renter now."

"What have you got?"

"Not much yet. He's from out of state, so I've reached out to their jurisdiction, but the owner was short on due diligence and didn't do some of the background verification the rental website suggested. The homeowner has scans of all the docs—license, credit cards, everything—but they could all be fakes."

Jack started pacing, a habit as natural to him as breathing. "You're keeping the details pretty vague here, Bob. You haven't told me the homeowner's or the renter's name."

"You noticed that, huh?" There was no mirth in the sheriff's voice. "That's on purpose. I don't need you to start hunting these people down on your own. Castillo is handling this. If you want to protect Alice, your best place is by her side."

"Fine. That's fine." Jack stopped pacing; his pulse pounded in his ears. "The last thing I would do is get in the middle of an ongoing investigation." His tone betrayed his words.

"Yeah, right."

"No. I'm serious, sir. I'm not going to get involved . . . proactively. But—and I'm sure you would agree—I feel that for her own safety, Alice should know the name of the person who had her sketch and wedding invitation taped to his wall."

"Not going to happen, Jack."

"This is about Alice's safety!"

"Right now, as far as the sheriff's department is concerned, this is about an injured officer, and—"

"I've already checked with the hospital twice, sir. Donald is awake and they're running tests. They expect him to make a full recovery."

"And you're itching for the moment when they allow him to have visitors, aren't you?" Morrison knew Jack all too well. "You're dying to get a statement from Donald. That's exactly why I'm not giving you the name, Stratton. You'll make a beeline straight for the homeowner, and then the renter, and who knows what'll happen when you start asking why there's a picture of Alice on his wall."

"It's a legitimate question, sir. If he has my wedding invitation, he should be a friend. I have the list of everyone that we sent an invitation to in front of me right now. You know you should run the name by me."

There was a long pause on the other end. Jack forced himself to keep his mouth shut.

"Do I have your word that you won't contact him?" the sheriff said at last.

"I won't reach out to him," Jack said.

Morrison muttered something unintelligible, and there was another delay before he said, "Renter's name is Carson Murray. He lives in Dublin, New Hampshire. Thirty-two. Single. Do you know him?"

Jack flipped through the wedding invitation list. He had no listing for a Murray and no recollection of a friend named Carson.

"No. We didn't send an invitation to anyone of that name. Alice threw a box of unused invitations away in the dumpster behind my apartment. She thinks it's possible someone went dumpster-diving and grabbed some, but I doubt it."

"Maybe he's a date of someone coming?"

Or maybe he's some psycho who hung sketches of women up on his wall and attacked Donald.

"Either way," Morrison continued, "the Dublin police are heading to the guy's house now. I'll keep you up to date, and you remember your promise."

"Thank you, Bob. I will."

But as he hung up, Jack was thinking of a different promise, one he was about to make to Alice. She'd wanted them to write their own vows, and they had. Well, mostly she had. Jack had agreed to what Alice had come up with. But he'd changed one part. On their wedding day, he would promise to love, cherish, and protect her "till death do us part." *That's one promise I'll never break, Alice.*

Jack sat down at the computer and pulled up everything he could find on Carson Murray. Alice was way better at finding information on the internet, but she'd been slowly teaching him some of her tricks, and within an hour and a half he had a full background report on Murray, including three previous addresses and four past employers.

Never been married. No arrests, no bankruptcies. He had a profile on several dating sites—the exact same wording on all of them—and it seemed honest enough. No mention of being an artist, just the usual babble about walks on the beach, good food and wine, old movies. Murray also had social media accounts. They had been active at one time, but everything stopped six months ago.

Jack's phone buzzed with a text from Alice.

HUGE FAV. FORGOT PURSE. CAN U PLS BRING 2 PHOTO STUDIO?

Jack rapped his knuckles against the desk in frustration. The last thing he wanted was to stop what he was doing.

Groaning as he stood, he stretched and looked at the clock. It was after six o'clock. He'd been going all day and hadn't eaten anything besides a handful of pistachios. He found Alice's purse, then grabbed a protein bar and the keys to the Charger. Maybe a break would help him see things a little more clearly—that and a cup of coffee. Besides, he was happy to help Alice. So far, she was doing pretty much everything to make their wedding perfect. The way things were going, all he had to do was show up.

* * *

The lights were off inside the photography studio, but Alice's blue Bug was parked out back—the only car in the lot. *Why is she here? The place looks closed.*

Before he got out of the car, his phone buzzed again.

"Dublin PD located Carson Murray." Bob Morrison's voice was low and even, which wasn't a good sign.

"But . . ."

"Carson Murray didn't rent that house. His identity was stolen."

"That's convenient."

"It's the truth."

"Are you certain?" Jack's edge of frustration stemmed from the letdown; he was banking on this Carson guy having answers.

"Carson Murray has been in a state mental-health facility for the last six months."

Jack's fingers tightened around Alice's purse in his hand. "I told you this didn't feel right, sir."

"Hold on, Jack. We still don't know if this is more than a panicked artist who injured a cop."

Jack pulled down the visor and stared at the picture of Alice as he talked. "Actually, we now know that whoever rented that house stole a man's identity. So, it's not just some innocent artist who accidentally hurt Donald. We need to determine who the other women in those sketches are."

"And how am I supposed to do that, Jack?"

"Go to the news stations. Have them run the pictures, see if people recognize any of the women."

"Are you listening to yourself? Do you have any idea of the panic that would start? And for what? We're still not sure Donald was attacked."

"Is Castillo ever going to get a statement from Donald? What's he waiting for?"

"Ed talked to Donald." Morrison exhaled. "Donald's not making too much sense right now. The doctors think it's his medication."

"What did he say?"

"Ed didn't get into specifics, just that he was loopy on meds. He's going to try again in the morning."

"So, you're not going to do anything more until tomorrow morning?"

"Honestly, Jack, I'm giving a lot more man-hours to this just because it's Alice and your gut. But *my* gut is saying that it could still be that someone hooked up the weight over the door, Donald got hurt, they panicked and fled, and the pictures are all copied from the paper, like Alice's. Another coincidence."

"Whoever it was *also* stole Carson Murray's identity."

"And that alone could explain the redneck alarm and the running. Do me a favor—just give it a day. We found some fingerprints and we're processing them. Tomorrow, when Ed gets a coherent statement from Donald, we'll take another look at it. Okay?"

Jack's phone buzzed with another text from Alice.

R U ON UR WAY?

Jack texted back, HERE.

"I appreciate all you're doing, Bob, it's just . . ." He stared at the photograph, into the smiling eyes of his beautiful bride-to-be. "It's Alice I'm worried about."

"Me, too. Believe me, we won't let anything happen to her. I just don't want you worrying over nothing."

Maybe. Or some crazed patient stole Carson Murray's identity, escaped the mental health facility, and is stalking Alice. Nothing to worry about at all. He rubbed the fatigue from his eyes.

Jack knew that further debate would just tick Morrison off. Bob was assigning a lot of manpower to the situation. Jack had no choice but to wait.

And worry.

"Thank you, sir. Please continue to keep me posted."

"I will."

Jack flipped up the visor, grabbed Alice's purse, and shoved his door open, his mood as dark as the evening sky. He needed to talk to Donald. How long would it take for the meds to wear off? Maybe he could stop by the hospital later this evening.

A little bell above the door chimed as he entered the photography studio, but otherwise the place looked closed. The interior was dark and quiet. "Alice?" *Why are the lights off? Whoever heard of a photoshoot in the dark?*

Something shifted in the darkness. Metal crashed to the floor.

Bang!

What sounded like a gunshot echoed in his ears. Jack dropped Alice's purse, and when the lights snapped on, his gun was in his hand and pointing at the source of the noise—Bobbie G.

His friend had his huge arms raised high over his head, and a light stand was knocked over on the floor in front of him, surrounded by fragments of glass from the shattered bulb. A half dozen people, including Alice, stood in the room with streamers and confetti in their hands, ready to toss them.

"Surprise?" Shawna tossed her confetti despite the awkward quiet.

Bobbie G. kept his hands up. "Hey, Jack? That was all like Han Solo cool, but you can stop pointing that gun at me?"

"Sorry . . ." Jack quickly holstered his weapon.

Alice ran up to his side. He expected her to give him an earful for how he'd just reacted, but she looked beside herself with worry. "Jack, I'm so sorry! I didn't even think . . . with you being a veteran and . . . I'm so sorry."

"Don't worry about it." Jack gave her a small reassuring hug and tried to smile.

Shawna danced up. "Take a look at this." She held up her phone and pressed play. Her video of the moment had captured Jack drawing his gun, and then zoomed in on Bobbie G's terrified face. "I bet it goes viral!"

"Give me that phone," Bobbie demanded.

"Not on your life!" Shawna skipped away like a schoolgirl getting chased around the playground. "I'm uploading it now!"

Jack turned back to Alice. "What's this all about?"

"Tonight's our bachelor and bachelorette parties. Surprise?" Alice leaned into Jack and whispered, "I didn't really want to do this, but Erica insisted that it would mean a lot to our friends. The guilt got me and I caved. I'm so sorry."

Jack draped an arm around her shoulders. "Me, too."

Now was not the time to let their guard down.

CHAPTER

8

Alice sat with the bachelorettes at the big round table in the private room in the back of the Great Wall Chinese restaurant looking forlornly at the exit sign while trying to keep the smile plastered on her face. Surrounding her on the walls were colorful murals of China folklore and mythology. Above her head hung a large glass dragon chandelier suspended from the ceiling by silver cables. No matter where she moved, one of the little lights was always shining down on her through the dragon's scales like a spotlight, making her even more uncomfortable.

She wanted to be sure not to give anyone the idea that she was unappreciative. All of this—it was beyond her wildest dreams, far beyond what she had ever imagined for her wedding. She had never even considered having a wedding planner, a professional cake decorator, or any of the other ever-growing duties, expenses, and staff.

Truth be told, none of it mattered to her. Jack mattered.

The dragon light sparked off her engagement ring. She missed Jack; her stomach fluttered at the thought of him. She felt like she'd only seen him a couple of times in the last few weeks.

Things still weren't right since their last fight. Jack kept insisting it wasn't a fight, and maybe it wasn't exactly, but it certainly felt like one. She knew Jack wasn't upset with her, but he was upset. Things were tense and it had nothing to do with either of them.

What was she supposed to do? Run and hide because some kooky artist drew a picture of her?

"Who's a kooky artist?" Marisa asked from across the table.

Alice swallowed. "Did I say that out loud?" She chuckled nervously. "Sorry. Not you!" she added quickly. "I was just thinking about the sketch Jack found."

"That's nothing to worry about." Shawna nudged Alice's shoulder. "You should be flattered. I heard artists do that all the time. They see some model in a magazine and draw their picture. Isn't that right, Marisa?"

"All the time." Marisa smiled, but not with her eyes.

"You're just saying that to make me feel better," Alice said.

"You're right. I am." Marisa nodded. "The truth is, it's an odd situation. Especially because of the wedding invitation. I think you should listen to Jack."

"Marisa's just kidding," Shawna said quickly with a wave of her long acrylic nails, decorated with tiny stars and constellations. "What you want to do is *not* listen to Jack for one more night and relax and have some *fun*. Now, as soon as Nyah and Annie get here, we can get the party started." She waved her hands over her head and did a little dance in her chair for emphasis.

Marisa raised an eyebrow. "Who?"

"Nyah is Boomer's girlfriend, and Annie is the guest of one of Jack's friends from the army," Shawna explained.

An awkward silence descended on the table. Shawna drummed her long nails on her water glass before pulling out her phone.

"Tell you what, I'm going to call Nyah and get her ETA. Be right back." She got up and disappeared through the beaded curtain that separated their private room from the rest of the restaurant.

Alice sat staring at the beads until they stopped moving. Then she turned and forced herself to smile at Marisa.

Marisa raised her water glass and sipped. "From the look on your face, this is the last place you want to be."

"Is it that obvious? It's not you, of course, it's just . . ."

"You want to be with Jack?"

Alice nodded.

"Understandable. But it's just for a night. You can make it through this."

Alice twisted her cloth napkin so tightly it looked like a rope. "So, you think there's something more to the pictures in that house?"

"I do." Marisa calmly took another sip of water. "But Jack would never let anything happen to you."

Alice relaxed a bit. That was the plain truth. "Thanks. I really needed to hear that." She smiled across the table at Marisa, and then gave just a slight shake of her head.

"What are you thinking?" Marisa asked.

"Pierce. I still can't believe he didn't visit Hope Falls. It's so beautiful there. And you could have shown him the town."

"It was probably for the best. I'm focusing on myself. And my art."

"Kristine told me that you like the loft in the inn."

"Like is far too pale a word. I adore it. I've been devoting myself to painting, landscapes mostly, and every moment of every day God creates a new wonder for me to vainly try to capture. I've been spending a lot of time with Jack's grandmother."

"Really?" Alice struggled to keep her smile on her face as a pang of jealousy rippled through her. She would have loved to spend more time with Jack's grandmother—his biological father's mother, whom they'd found while solving the long-ago murder of Jack's father. "I can't wait to see her."

"Kristine is bringing her down here. She's also gotten permission to bring Patty."

Alice pressed her lips together. She didn't know how to take the news that Jack's birth mother would be at the wedding. Of course they'd invited her, but neither she nor Jack had expected her to make it. Her many years of drug abuse had taken such a heavy toll on her mind and body, she had been institutionalized.

"How has Patty been doing these days?" she asked, genuinely curious.

"Much better. Still, Kristine's going to have her hands full. I offered to help, but she said she could handle it."

"You've met Patty?" Alice asked, taken aback.

Marisa shrugged. "Sure. I keep Kristine company when she goes to visit. It's not too far."

Alice shifted uncomfortably in her seat. It appeared Jack's old girlfriend was spending far more time with Jack's family than Alice was; the thought made her wince. Her smile grew tighter.

"Jack's parents are coming in at the beginning of the week," Alice said. "We just spent a couple of weeks with them in Florida."

Why did I say that? This isn't a competition. But Alice couldn't help but feel like she had to prove that she knew Jack's family, too.

"Oh yes, they're very nice."

"You've met the Strattons, too?" Alice failed to mask her surprise this time.

Marisa smiled. "Only once, but we hit it off. They came up to check on Jack. I happened to be over."

Alice took a long gulp of water, trying not to think about what was happening when Marisa *happened* to be over.

"I want to thank you again for inviting me to the wedding," Marisa said. "It's very big of you. I know I wouldn't be so . . ." She paused.

Secure? Brave? Alice wanted to offer to finish her sentence in spite of the fact that she'd had nothing to do with inviting Marisa in the first place.

"Reckless," Marisa finished.

Alice's glass dinged off the table as she set it down a bit too aggressively. "Reckless?"

Marisa's eyelids, shaded in smoky silver, closed for a moment, and then her enormous brown eyes locked on Alice again. "If I can offer you one piece of advice: keep Jack close. Not because he would wander, but because other women will be looking for an opportunity to pounce."

The beads hanging over the doorway burst aside and Shawna bounded through with two women in tow. Alice recognized Nyah, an attractive black woman with her ebony hair pulled back in a tight bun, but she'd never met the other woman—a blonde with stunning blue eyes.

Shawna hesitated for a moment, her eyes traveling back and forth between Alice and Marisa, then her smile reappeared. "Marisa, this is Nyah."

Nyah gave Marisa a wave with a slender hand, then hurried over to Alice and gave her a hug before pressing a gift bag into her hand. "Congratulations, Alice. I'm so happy for you. I hope you—and Jack—like the gift." Nyah smiled impishly, her eyes sparkling.

"And this is Annie Summers," Shawna announced, gesturing to the blonde.

A huge smile broke across Annie's heart-shaped face, and she shook Alice's hand. "It's nice to meet you." She handed Alice a wrapped present.

"Thank you so much. Why don't you sit down and order yourself a drink?" Alice asked as she placed Nyah's and Annie's presents safely underneath the table. When she straightened back up, Annie stood smiling like she hadn't heard the question.

Standing slightly behind Annie, Shawna tried to covertly wave in front of her chest then tapped her ear. Alice had no idea what Shawna was trying to convey. But when Annie turned and saw what Shawna was doing, she turned back to Alice.

"I'm sorry. Did you ask me something? I'm deaf. I should have explained earlier that I need to be looking at a person to be able to read their lips. Speech-to-text apps don't always work well in noisy environments like restaurants." She gestured to the other guests.

Alice looked directly into Annie's gorgeous blue eyes as she spoke. "Please, sit down and have a drink. How did you meet Finn?"

Annie's bright smile returned. "We work together."

Marisa's hands moved in sign language as she spoke. "Nice to meet you, Annie."

Annie's entire face lit up as she sat on Marisa's other side. "You sign? That's great. I'm a little nervous—group settings can be tough."

Alice forced herself to smile. She felt like a dope that she hadn't picked up on the fact that Annie was deaf, but mostly she was frustrated with Marisa. Was there anything the woman couldn't do?

"My cousin was deaf," Marisa explained. "We spent a lot of time together."

As everyone sat down, three waiters started bringing in trays of food.

Shawna lit up. "Alice wanted to keep this a low-key, 'civilized' affair, but I say drink 'em if you got 'em, and since the booze is on the house, I'll have a double frozen margarita with salt!"

The headwaiter nodded.

"Iced tea, please," Annie said.

"I'll have a water with lemon," said Nyah.

"I'm good with the hot tea, thank you." Marisa poured herself a cup.

"I'll also have water," Alice said.

Shawna crossed her arms and frowned. "You've got to be kidding me. It's an open tab!"

Nyah shook her head. "I don't drink."

"I'm driving," Annie said.

"You drive?" Shawna blurted out, then waved her hands in front of herself. "Sorry! I didn't mean anything by that. I just didn't realize that you can be deaf and drive. I guess that makes sense but . . . wow."

"My father had me take a TEVOC class," Annie said.

"That's awesome!" Alice sat up straighter. "Jack signed me up for one. It took me a while but I finally got him to let me help him on some cases and I've been able to put those skills to use a time or two."

"What's TEVOC?" Nyah asked.

"Tactical Emergency Vehicle Operation Class," Alice explained. "Police and FBI use it. Now that I'm helping Jack with bounty hunting, he signed me up for martial arts, tactical weapons training, and driving classes. He's big on education."

"So is Finn. He's an insurance investigator and is teaching me a great deal. I'm his photographer," said Annie.

"Wow, that makes three of us who work together as couples," Shawna said. "Though technically, I'm almost Bobbie's boss, since I'm the office manager at Titus Bail Bonds."

Nyah's eyes widened. "You all have such exciting professions."

"Your job is plenty exciting, Nyah." Shawna reached for a plate of chicken fingers. "I couldn't even think about nursing. Hospitals and sick people gross me out."

Annie turned to Marisa. "And what do you do?" She signed the words as she spoke them aloud.

Marisa smiled. "I'm an artist."

"What medium do you prefer?" Annie asked.

"Pencil."

The beads rattled and flew open, and to Alice's surprise, a clown backed into the room, complete with red wig, giant blue shoes, and a white onesie adorned with gold stars. The red nose on his face bounced up and down as he bowed low, and when he came up, he held a balloon rose that he presented to Alice.

All the ladies' mouths fell open, except for Shawna's. She was dancing in her seat again. "You're early, but who cares! Let's get this party started!" She drained her margarita and pointed at the waiter to bring her another.

Alice had no idea what to expect at a bachelorette party, but a clown was definitely not on her list of possibilities. She cast a curious glance at Marisa, who gave her a sympathetic look. Puzzled, Alice turned to Shawna, who wiggled her eyebrows suggestively.

The clown pulled out a toy radio that started to play a merry tune. It sounded like the opening of a kids' TV show. The clown started tapping his oversized shoes, then spun around and turned his back to the women. He was huffing and puffing and hunched over a little bit as his hands started moving.

"Here comes the good part!" Shawna raised her hands over her head and clapped along with the music.

The clown spun back around and triumphantly lifted his arms. In his hands was a crown of balloons. He gave another bow while motioning with his free hand for the ladies to applaud, which they did. Smiling, he placed the crown on Alice's head.

Shawna's smile came crashing down. "Okay, okay, get on with it."

The clown nodded rapidly and produced a blue balloon from his pocket, which he quickly fashioned into the shape of a dog.

Shawna shook her head. "Enough with the balloon animals. Start dancing." She stood up and swayed her hips.

The clown nodded and broke into a funny jig.

"No. No." Shawna grabbed his elbow and gyrated her hips. The clown started imitating her, causing Marisa and Nyah to start chuckling. Shawna pulled at her blouse a bit, and the clown mirrored her actions.

"No." Shawna tugged the clown's arm until the man leaned down. She whispered something in his ear.

The clown looked like he'd been hit by lightning. He stood up straight and his whole body shook. "What kind of clown do you think I am?" He yanked the blue dog out of Shawna's hand and stormed out of the room, his puffy red wig catching momentarily on the beads as he went.

"You mean he wasn't a stripper?" Nyah doubled over laughing. "He was really a clown?"

Alice, Nyah, and Marisa roared with laughter. Annie looked curiously at Marisa, who somehow, between giggles, managed to sign what was going on. Annie turned beet-red and started laughing, too.

Shawna squeezed the balloon so hard it popped. Everybody jumped, but even Shawna started laughing. "Hey, I've still got endless margaritas!" She smiled as the waiter came in with her drink.

As the laughter died down, Alice glanced at her watch and sighed. The party was scheduled to go on for another two hours. She hoped Jack was having a better time at his bachelor party than she was at hers.

CHAPTER

9

Jack and Bobbie G. walked through the door of Hannigan's, and Jack smiled. Before joining the army, he'd spent many nights here shooting pool. The smell of stale beer and cigarettes was a familiar welcome.

"I got us a table in the back," Bobbie said as he waved to the bartender and held up a hand with two fingers out. "This is on me. They've still got the best drafts. Alice said you were cool if it's only a couple of guys coming, right? And knowing you, going to La Jolla strip club or hiring a stripper to come to us is out?"

"Small is good. And no strippers." Apart from an occasional raid or a disturbance call, Jack had never been in a strip club, even in the army, and he never looked at porn, either. His mother being a prostitute, he'd always had a fear that he'd open the magazine and she'd be in it; his stomach curdled at the thought, even years later. As he got older, knowing that all those girls were someone's mother, sister, or daughter was enough to keep his eyes off any of that crap.

The waitress hurried over with their beers, and Jack took his first cool sip after a long, confusing day, letting the liquid coat his throat. He was about to ask Bobbie who was coming when the front door swung wide and a short black man jumped in shouting, "Boomer is in the house!"

"Keep it down," the bartender shouted back. But judging by the smile on his face, Jack guessed this was an ongoing thing between them.

Bobbie waved. "Over here, big man!"

Boomer was only five foot two, but you wouldn't know it from the way he strutted around. He'd gotten his nickname when they were kids, because he loved explosions and large crashes—bottles, cans, bikes, fireworks—he loved making things go *boom*.

"Jack, my man!" Boomer launched into a complicated set of fist-bumping and hand-clapping that ended when Jack grabbed Boomer's wrist and dragged him forward for a shoulder bump. "How you doin', man?" yelled Boomer. "I heard you're getting hitched!"

Jack rubbed his stubbled chin and pretended to look shocked. "That's the rumor I heard, too."

As Bobbie G. and Boomer performed their greeting ritual, Jack saw two of his army buddies walk through the front door. "Finn! Mac! Over here!" he called out.

They waved and made their way to the table. Mac's freckled face broke into a grin. "Someone went and told me that you were about to do something crazy, but I didn't believe 'em until I saw it with my own eyes in the paper. I still don't believe it." He clasped Jack's wrist and pulled him forward until their chests bumped.

"Believe it, Mac. I'm glad you could make it. Now you're here, the party can start." Mac's rough-and-tumble humor and legendary capacity for drink had entertained the lonely, scared troops many times in Iraq, and Jack was truly glad to see him, as well as Finnian Church, his brave friend from the same tour of duty.

Mac moved aside and Finn reached out his hand.

As Jack shook it, he made sure he kept eye contact and didn't lower his gaze to Finn's prosthetic leg. "Good to see you again, Finn."

"Thanks for inviting me. And thanks for the reference, by the way."

"How's the new job?" Jack asked.

"Going really well. I didn't know what I thought insurance investigation would be, but—"

"Are you kidding me? You should check out his new girlfriend. She's smoking hot!" Mac grabbed Finn around the shoulders and laughed. For the first time, Jack smelled the whiskey on Mac's breath.

"She's my partner, Mac. Leave it at that," Finn said.

"I'm just bustin' on ya." Mac pulled Finn even closer. "Lighten up."

From the tightness around Finn's eyes, Jack knew Mac had crossed a line and was wondering whether he needed to cool things off when Bobbie G. flashed a look around the group and held up his big hand. "More drafts over here!"

Boomer picked up a pool cue. "I'm Boomer." He pointed at Bobbie. "That's Bobbie G. We all know Jack. So, now that the introductions are out of the way, twenty bucks a game, I break first." He grinned broadly.

"You're not hustling tonight," Bobbie said.

"He's just keeping it interesting." Mac strutted forward and grabbed a cue off the wall. "What say we make it fifty and make this a real challenge?"

"How about we make it five and keep it friendly?" Jack said. "And the beers are on me."

"Agreed," Bobbie said. "But I got this round."

The waitress came over, everybody grabbed a beer, and Boomer moved to the head of the pool table. Mac racked and Boomer broke. The five of them took turns talking and playing. Despite Boomer's and Mac's bragging, they were all fairly evenly matched, but Finn was winning more games than anyone.

But as the night rolled on, Mac was putting back three beers to everyone else's one. They had only been there for a couple of hours and were having a good time, although Mac was getting louder and more obnoxious, sloshing the beer on the floor and himself, morphing into a belligerent toddler before their eyes. The bartender signaled to Bobbie and had a short chat with him. When Bobbie walked back to the table, he was frowning. He whispered to Jack, "The bartender wants us to cut Mac off."

Jack nodded. "I don't want to single him out. Let's just wrap up. Last game!" he called out.

Mac banged his pool cue off the edge of the table. "You gotta be kiddin' me. I was just warming up."

"I figured we'd head back over to my place, order some wings and pizza. Can you still get any movie, Boomer?"

"Even if it's still in theaters!" Boomer boasted.

Mac turned to Boomer and shut one eye like he was trying to remember something. After a minute he shrugged and said, "Hey, little guy, swing by the packy and grab us a couple of cases of beer."

"Who you—" Boomer started, but Bobbie grabbed his arm.

"I didn't mean nothin'." Mac waved his hand as he racked the balls. "I forgot your name. Sorry." He gave a mock bow.

"Whatever." Boomer pulled his arm free.

Mac pointed at Finn. "You gonna break or what?"

Finn moved to the head of the table. The only mistakes he'd made so far tonight were on his breaks. When Finn leaned forward, he seemed to have an issue with his balance, and Jack knew it was not because of the three beers he'd drunk; Finn had lost his left leg just below the knee in the war.

As Finn pushed forward to break, his weight shifted awkwardly to his left leg and he pitched forward into the edge of the pool table. His cue shot upward and bashed into the light hanging over the table. It didn't break, but it bounced around like a ship at sea and made a loud clatter as it rocked.

"I'm sorry!" Finn blurted out, shame spreading across his face.

"Don't apologize," Mac scoffed. "You sound like a wimp."

Jack reached up and stilled the wildly swinging lamp. "It's fine. Nothing broken," he said.

"I'm really sorry," Finn said again.

"Stop apologizing," Mac muttered, and swore. "I mean, you don't have a leg to stand on! Get it?" He roared with laughter.

Jack stepped forward. "That's crossing a line, Mac. Back off."

Mac puffed up. "You're good at givin' advice, aren't you, Stratton?"

"What are you talking about?"

"You're drunk, Mac. Just shut up," Boomer said.

Mac ignored him and focused on Jack. "He hit a light. Big deal. He's a soldier. He shouldn't be going around groveling." Mac deliberately banged the light with his pool cue. The light shot sideways and almost struck the ceiling.

"Hey!" Bobbie G. stood up.

"Dial it down, Mac." Finn held up a hand as he put his pool cue in the rack on the wall. "Let's just head over to Jack's."

Mac swore again and leveled the pool cue at Jack, the tip dipping up and down like a fishing pole with a catch on the line. "Alison listened to you, and that's why she left me. Now, *that's* crossing a line, old buddy!"

Mac rested the cue on his shoulder and walked around the table to face Jack. Bobbie G. moved closer to Jack.

"Alison called me," Jack said, motioning for Bobbie G. to back off. "And I talked to you right after that. I drove all the way to Maine to talk to you both. Isn't Alison at the bachelorette party? You told me she was coming to the wedding."

"Maybe. That's why I'm here. I want to talk to her." Mac smiled, his eyes glassy and bloodshot.

Boomer moved behind Mac. He held up his hand and pointed at his head, the index finger circling his ear. *He's crazy*, he mouthed.

"You're not making any sense, Mac," Jack said.

"She left me 'cause of you. Won't even talk to me. I haven't even heard from her since then. It's been over four months! Right after you came up, she started on about my drinking and kicked me out! That's your marriage advice?"

"I'm sorry—" Jack started, but Mac's face twisted into a snarl and his fingers tightened around the cue. He lifted the cue off his shoulder and started to swing it at Jack.

Bobbie, Boomer, and Finn all jumped and tackled Mac to the floor.

Mac screamed, kicked, swore, and spat as he struggled against the three men. Jack thought of what he could say to calm his friend down, but one look at the drunken rage on Mac's red face told him it was pointless to try.

"Get him outta here or I'm calling the cops!" the bartender yelled.

Bobbie grabbed Mac in a bear hug and lifted him up. Boomer grabbed his legs.

"Don't hurt him!" Jack said.

Finn put a hand on Jack's arm. "I'll get him to calm down outside."

"He shouldn't be alone."

"He won't be," Finn said. "I'll take him with me to my hotel room. I'll watch out for him."

"Are you sure you can handle that?"

The muscles in Finn's jaw flexed as he glared at Jack. "What's that supposed to mean?" His voice was tight.

Jack glanced down at Finn's leg and shook his head. "No, Finn, all I meant was that it can take more than one person to deal with someone *that* drunk. You want me to go with you?"

Finn's hands balled into fists, then relaxed; he squared his posture and his lips made a straight line. Jack knew that look all too well—the expression a guy put on when he wanted to accept help but he had to say no.

"I'm good. Sorry about the party. See you in a few days at the wedding." Finn tipped his head toward the front, where they could faintly hear Mac's drunken roars outside, and could see Boomer and Bobbie holding him between them. "I'd better go calm him down."

Jack watched Finn walk to the door, his limp more noticeable now. Jack knew he'd lost more than a leg in the war. They'd all lost something—Mac included.

Some wounds were just harder to see.

CHAPTER

10

Alice parked her little blue Bug outside their apartment and shut off the engine. As she sat in the parked car, she chuckled softly at the memory of the clown storming off and getting his red wig stuck in the beads. But her smile slowly faded and wedding anxiety returned, a constant ebb and flow of excitement and stress. Ever since Jack had asked her to marry him, she'd been doubting if she was good enough for him.

If she was being honest with herself, that feeling of inadequacy had always been there.

Ever since her parents died, she'd felt cast aside, guilty about surviving, and angry at being left behind. And now that she'd found out they were killed in a car crash, and her grandfather was possibly alive, that feeling of being abandoned had only grown. Why would Jack want someone like her? Especially compared to Marisa?

Alice pulled down the visor mirror and stared at her reflection. She tried not to compare herself to the now-blonde bombshell, but she couldn't help it. Tall, beautiful, talented . . . Marisa was perfect.

Alice let her head sag forward until her forehead touched the steering wheel. She'd never wanted a big, fancy wedding, and this monster was out of control. She knew Pierce meant well, but it was too much. Too much to do. Too much stress. Too much pressure.

Worst of all, everyone was coming. Even Jack's biological mother.

Maybe we could elope?

It wasn't the first time she'd had the thought, but she slumped again as she pictured Aunt Haddie's disappointed face. No, there was no getting out of the mess she was in. She let herself decompress for a few more moments in the car, letting the solitude bring her a measure of comfort.

Less than a week. Six more days, and it would all be done. All the fittings, flowers, and running around would soon be in the past, and she and Jack would be headed to a cozy hotel in the Bahamas. Pierce had tried to give them a trip to Paris, but Jack had put his foot down on that one.

She got out of the car and started for the steps. A dark sedan was parked near the stairs, and the dome light flicked on as both the passenger and driver opened the doors and got out. The driver was a bear of a man—a short bear, only about five foot five, but he had broad shoulders and a thick neck, and his chest was as wide as a barrel.

The passenger was a middle-aged woman, slim and petite. She moved with the grace of a ballerina as she stepped around the car, stopped next to the man, and held his hand. There was something familiar about her. Was it her hair? Maybe it was the sharpness of her features? Alice found herself staring as she continued toward the stairs.

"Alice?" the woman asked hesitantly.

Alice's breath caught in her throat and her feet stopped moving. Her legs shook. Suddenly there wasn't just one thing familiar about this woman—it was everything. Her voice, her deep-brown hair, her light-bronze skin, and especially her high cheekbones. Her mind filled with images from her childhood, images of her mother.

"How do you know my name?" Alice asked, unable to take her eyes away.

The old man's face broke into a huge grin. "Kaya Kukla!" His deep voice rumbled like a summer thunderstorm.

Kaya Kukla. Little doll. Her little brothers used to call her that. Andrew would shout "Kaya!" and Alex would respond, "Kukla!"

Her knees buckled. The man rushed forward and clamped two huge hands on her shoulders to keep her from falling.

"Uncle Alex?" Alice asked, bewildered.

"She remembers!" Alex beamed at the woman and ran a hand through his thick, close-cropped gray hair. "I told you she would remember! Technically, I am your great-uncle," he added, patting her cheek.

"I am Yana." The woman placed a slender hand on Alice's back. "Your cousin."

Alice opened her mouth to speak, but no words came out. How was this possible? Why were they here now?

Uncle Alex wrapped his large arms around her and hugged her to his massive chest. He smelled of pine. His jacket felt damp and she realized she was crying.

"Don't crush her!" Yana chided as she, too, hugged Alice.

"How did you find me?" Alice finally asked, struggling to wrap her head around the idea of family outside of Jack and Aunt Haddie.

Alex glanced around the parking lot. "It's a long story. Perhaps we could speak inside?"

"Yes, of course, please come up." She gestured toward the front door. "If Jack's home, you'll get to meet him."

"Who?" Alex asked with a deep chuckle. He looked at Yana. "I think she's a little shook up."

"Jack. My fiancé."

"Don't tell me that my little Kukla is getting married? When?"

Alice stopped and looked back at them on the steps, her head spinning. "If Jack didn't bring you here, then how did you find me? Is my grandfather with you? When did you get here? Do you know about my mother?" The questions tumbled out of her mouth.

"Inside. I'll tell you everything once we're inside," Uncle Alex promised, still wiping tears from his round face.

Yana rubbed Alice's back. "I can't believe we've found you." She kissed Alice's cheek. "You look so much like your mother."

"You look just like her," Alice said softly as she fumbled for the apartment key, hands still shaking. She opened the door and had taken only half a step into the apartment when Lady trotted out of the bedroom. The dog took one look at the strangers with their hands on Alice and her ears flattened back on her head. Lady roared.

Alex swore and pulled both Alice and Yana back into the hallway, slamming the door shut.

"It's okay," Alice said, trying to reassure them, but the door shook as Lady jumped against it and began scratching. "She's my dog."

"That's no dog!" Alex shook his head. "It's a wolf the size of a horse."

"She's really nice when you get to know her. She's just overprotective." Alice reached for the doorknob, and both Yana and Alex stepped away.

"Give me a minute to get her settled." Alice cracked open the door, and Lady almost bowled her over. Alice had to hang on to Lady's collar, but with lots of petting and pulling, she managed to get Lady back inside the apartment. With an overabundance of caution, she put Lady in her bedroom. "Sorry, Lady."

The big dog whined, her pleas vibrating the wooden door.

Alice brought Alex and Yana inside. "Please sit down. Can I get you something to drink?" She headed into the kitchen.

"I think I need something strong," Alex said, plopping down onto the leather sofa. "This is a great day. I still cannot believe it! I'll take the strongest you have."

"Sorry, I think the strongest we have is milk." Right now, she'd prefer something stronger herself. This was all so surreal.

"Water will be fine for me," Yana said.

Alice filled three glasses with water and carried them into the living room.

"Is this your Jack?" Yana asked, pointing to a picture on the wall.

"Yes. He's at his bachelor party right now. I don't think he'll be too long."

Alex chuckled. "My bachelor party lasted three days. Good. We have time to talk." He reached into his jacket pocket, and held out a photograph to her.

She set her glass down and took the photo with trembling fingers. It was an old family picture. She was young, probably only three, and her brothers were just babies. She was standing right between her mother and father, nestled against their legs. Her mother and father, Alice and Chris, both looking proud, were holding the smiling baby boys. Alice choked back a sob at the sight of her dad's sparkling emerald eyes, just like hers. Beside them were her grandfather and his brother, Uncle Alex. The two big bears had their arms wrapped around each other, and both were grinning proudly.

"That is me and Andrew," Alex said.

"Yes. Alex and Andrew. My brothers were named for you and my grandfather. I forgot." Alice hung her head as she fought back tears. The lump in her throat acting like a dam against the tears was threatening to burst. She sat down in the chair beside the couch. "How did you find me?"

"A woman came asking questions. She was from the United States government. That was a little over a month ago."

"Jack has a friend in the State Department," Alice said. "He asked her to look into finding my grandfather."

"Well, she didn't find Andrew, but she did find us." Alex reached out and squeezed Alice's hand. "Have you heard from your grandfather?"

"No." Alice shook her head. "I didn't even know he was alive until a few months ago, when I found out . . ."

Alex and Yana exchanged puzzled glances and waited for Alice to continue.

"Do you know . . ." Alice cleared her throat, unsure what to say. "Are you aware of what happened to my parents?"

They both nodded. "Your grandfather and I were not only brothers; we were best friends. After Andrew's wife was murdered, he fled Ukraine with his daughter, your mother, to America. He thought you all would be safe here. I did, too. We were both wrong." Alex's creased brow became even more lined. "That night I received a call that your entire family had died. Your parents, your brothers. They said you died too, my emerald-eyed Kukla. My heart was broken. And my loss grew when Andrew disappeared."

"Disappeared?" Alice repeated, unsure of how to respond.

"Vanished. No trace. No calls. Nothing." Alex rubbed his eyes. "All these years, I wondered if they had gotten to him."

"They? Who was behind this?"

Yana held her father's hand. "The Soviet Union. It was a very bad time . . . they wanted your grandfather to put his support behind the army, but . . . he wanted a free Ukraine."

"And he never reached out to you?"

Alex shook his head. "Maybe he wanted to protect us. It's the only thing I can think of. But if Andrew found out *you* were alive"— Alex's face lit up—"then he would come to you! I'm sure of it!"

"But how can we tell him if we don't know where he is?" Alice asked.

Yana squeezed Alex's hand. They both stared at each other for a moment, and then Yana spoke. "We were hoping to persuade you to come back to Poltava with us."

"Poltava?" Alice repeated. "When?"

"As soon as you are able," Alex said. "I'm not a young man, and I don't even know if my brother is still alive. But I'm sure that if he is, and he hears that you live, he will contact you."

"I'm getting married in a week and I'm going on my honeymoon afterward."

"Poltava is very romantic. It is on the beautiful Vorskla River," Alex said with a broad smile.

"Bah!" Yana waved her hand dismissively. "Who wants to go to Poltava for their honeymoon? It's all monuments to battles and museums."

"I went to Poltava for my honeymoon!" Alex said.

"You had no choice." Yana turned to Alice and shook her head. "Ignore him. How long is your honeymoon? Would it be possible for you to visit us afterward?"

"We're going for two weeks . . ." Alice's voice trailed off when Alex winced at the length of time. "But I think if I talk to Jack, we might be able to figure something out."

Alex grabbed both her hands, engulfing them in his own. "Please. Please think about it. I'm so happy to have found you, but it's like a piece of me is still missing until I tell my brother that you are still alive. Do you understand?"

Alice nodded. She'd always felt like a part of her was gone since her family's death. "I'll talk to Jack. I promise."

Yana stood. "It's very late. We're staying at the Garden Hotel on the other side of town. I know it's a lot to take in, but—"

"What's there to take in?" Alex stood as well and leaned down to give Alice a hug. "My Kaya Kukla is alive. You have family, my little princess. A family who loves you."

Alice had waited years to hear those words. She had a family. It didn't seem real.

"Can we see you tomorrow?" her uncle asked.

"No." Yana grabbed his arm and started tugging him toward the door. "Give her time. She will reach out when she is ready to talk. The Garden Hotel. Room 407." She slid Alice a card with their numbers on it.

Alice nodded. Part of her didn't want them to leave, but she was still in shock and her legs wouldn't obey her command to stand.

"Goodnight, Alice." Alex blew her a kiss and Yana yanked him out of the apartment, closing the door behind them.

Lady scratched at the bedroom door, and Alice stood, her legs finally obeying. When she let Lady out, the huge dog almost bowled her over as she rushed out and raced around the apartment, making sure it was empty.

Alice wondered for a moment if what had just happened was real. Did she dream it?

Yana's and Alex's water glasses sat on the table right where they had left them.

It wasn't a dream.

Alice pressed her hands against her eyes and slowly slipped down to her knees on the floor. "I have a family," she whispered as fresh tears rolled down her cheeks. Lady rushed over and licked them off her face. Alice prayed for Jack to come home so she could share the good news with him.

CHAPTER

11

Jack woke up to a silent apartment and a note on the kitchen counter.

I thought I should let you sleep in. Meeting with the cake decorator, arranging hotels for your mom and dad, your grandmother, Patty, and Kristine, then meeting with the caterer.

I have something really, really big to tell you!!! I didn't think right after your bachelor party was the best time, but it's good news!

Love always,

Alice

Jack stumbled toward the coffeepot, wondering what "really, really big" news could mean. He hated waiting to hear news because he always expected the worst. He preferred to get information right away. Rip the Band-Aid off!

His phone buzzed with a text from Tina, a friend who was a nurse at the hospital. Donald was awake and could receive visitors.

Pounding down a shot of hot coffee, Jack hurried into the bedroom, got dressed, and less than five minutes later was on his way to the hospital.

* * *

The duty nurse poked her head into Donald's room and spoke briefly to someone.

"Officer Pugh has a visitor," she told Jack, "but they should be finished shortly. You can wait right there." She pointed to a waiting area near the bank of elevators.

"Thank you."

The truth was, Jack would wait all day to speak with Donald if he had to. But after ten minutes of pacing, he was climbing the walls.

I bet Donald's talking to Castillo. Morrison said Castillo was going to speak with him this morning. Would it really be a big deal if I was in there, too?

Impatience got the best of him, and Jack strode across the waiting area and down the short hallway to Donald's door. He knocked softly and peeked inside. Ed Castillo wasn't interviewing Donald. In fact, the person sitting in the chair beside Donald's bed, chatting away, was the last person Jack expected to see.

Marisa looked up at him and smiled. A gem in this dank place.

"Hey, Jack," Donald said with a loopy, lopsided grin. "Marisa here says I've got you to thank for watching out for me."

"It was nothing, buddy." Jack quietly shut the door and crossed over to Donald's bed. "How are you feeling?" He cast a quick, puzzled glance at Marisa.

"Better. Okay. Still a little out of it, I guess. My noggin is full of staples in the back." Donald let his head rest back on the pillow. "For a while I'm going to look like Frankenstein's monster."

"He had quite a bad bump on the head," Marisa said in a motherly voice that somehow still managed to sound provocative.

Donald grinned. Clearly, he was eating up her attention.

"I wasn't aware you two knew each other," Jack said.

"Donald was the neighborhood police liaison," Marisa explained. "He used to stop into my tattoo parlor during his afternoon patrol. He always checked up on me, so when I heard he was hurt, I figured it was my turn."

"It was strictly official business." Donald gave Jack a quick wink.

"Well, I'm glad to see you're doing better, that's for sure." Jack grabbed a chair and sat down. "I need to ask you a few questions about what happened."

Donald's face scrunched up. "Was Ed Castillo here yesterday? I've been having the weirdest dreams. I thought Ed was here and he couldn't stop laughing."

"I think it might have been you who was doing the laughing, Donald," Jack said. "I heard you were a little out of it. What do you remember about the call?"

Donald sank back into the pillow, still pale, and stared up at the ceiling. "Not too much. I was on patrol and I saw a front door open when I drove by. I thought it odd that it was still open on my return pass. You know there's been a lot of break-ins up there."

Jack nodded. "So, you stopped to do a welfare check?"

"Yeah. I knocked, and nobody answered. The living room was empty but . . ." Donald closed his eyes. "A door in the back corner was open."

"What happened then?"

"It's all fuzzy." Donald shook his head and opened his eyes. "I'm sorry."

Jack frowned. "Try to remember something. Anything."

Donald stared at the ceiling. He looked like a kid trying to figure out if he had Superman's X-ray vision. "It's no use," he groaned, rubbing his eyes. "I don't remember. I'm sorry."

"Don't be sorry." Marisa sat forward and took Donald's hand. "Do me a favor?"

Donald bobbed his bandaged head.

"Close your eyes," she said softly. "Take a few deep breaths and try to relax. Inhale. Exhale. Inhale. Exhale. Good. Now try to picture the room." She stroked his hand to the rhythm of his breathing and looked up at Jack for a prompt.

Jack mouthed, *What does he see?*

"Tell me what you see," Marisa said.

"The door. It's open," Donald said.

Jack held up his hand and moved his index and ring fingers back and forth in a walking motion.

"You're walking toward the door," Marisa said.

"I can't see inside the room," Donald said. "It's dark."

Jack pantomimed a flashlight.

Marisa said softly, "You turn on your flashlight . . ."

"Pictures on the wall. Lots of them."

Jack nodded.

"It's a bathroom," Donald said.

Jack shook his head. Marisa held her finger to her lips. "Describe it for me."

"There's a woman in the tub. She's lying down and taking a shower."

Jack rubbed his hands down his face. Donald had to be remembering some crazy dream at this point.

"What does the woman look like?" Marisa asked.

"I can't see her clearly because of the shower curtain." Donald squeezed her hand and opened his eyes. "I'm sorry, I just . . . I can't really remember."

"You did great, Donald. Really, really great." Marisa smiled at him, then looked at Jack and waited. "Didn't he do a good job, Jack?" Marisa's eyes narrowed.

"Yeah. Thanks, Donald." As Jack patted his arm the door opened.

Detective Castillo stopped in the doorway, and Sheriff Morrison bumped into him. Both men glared at Jack.

Jack gave them a small wave and looked down at Donald. "I hope you feel better. I'll be praying for you."

"Thanks for coming."

Marisa got up, too. "I'll stop by again, Donald," she assured him. Castillo and Morrison stepped into the room to let her out.

Jack slipped behind Marisa and out the door. "Bob, Ed."

"Hold on a second, Stratton," Morrison said as both men followed him out into the hallway.

"I was just checking on a friend, Bob. I told you I would."

Castillo frowned. "Was he making any sense today?"

"Not really. What did he tell you?" Jack asked.

"I'm not playing games, Stratton. You tell me," Castillo demanded.

"I'm not playing games either, Ed. You know that when corroborating witness testimony, the person with the most recent revelation of events should go last to keep factual preservation."

Castillo's scowl eased. "Fine. Yesterday Donald wasn't making any sense. He kept talking about seeing a lady in the shower. The shower is on the second floor and he insisted he didn't go upstairs."

Jack nodded. "He gave me the same story. And he said she was lying down to take a shower."

Castillo looked to Morrison, whose stoic expression softened. "The doctors said all his scans came back okay," Morrison said. "He has a slight concussion, but that's it."

"I think 'that's it' sums this whole case up," Castillo said, looking pointedly at Jack, waiting for a reaction.

"Did you find the real guy who rented the house?"

"No, but I will," Castillo boasted.

Jack was about to express his thoughts on the chances of that when Marisa stepped between the two men. "My apologies, but Jack and I really need to get going."

"Of course." Morrison looked like he wanted to ask her a few questions, like *What in the world are you doing back in Darrington*, but he simply smiled and nodded.

Jack followed Marisa to the elevators. He was seething inside. There was more to this. He was certain. But now even Donald's testimony was a dead end.

"Jack?" Marisa gently placed a hand on the small of his back. "You look like you're going to kill someone."

"Sorry," Jack muttered as the elevator doors dinged open.

They walked inside, leaving the musty smell of the floor behind them; the scent of Marisa's perfume filled the small box. Marisa chuckled as she pressed the button for the lobby.

"What?"

"That line you gave Ed about the person with the most recent revelation of events should go last." She laughed again.

Jack tried not to, but he grinned. "Of course I lied. If I talked first, Castillo wouldn't tell me what Donald said yesterday."

"So, you made that all up?"

Jack nodded.

"You are so bad." She crossed her arms and looked up at him through her long lashes. The elevator suddenly got much warmer, and Jack was relieved when the doors dinged and they made their way to the exit and the fresh air.

Marisa asked, "What are you going to do now? I hate to say it, but I think Ed might be right. It could be nothing."

Jack exhaled and nodded. "I hate hearing you say it. But . . . it seems everyone else agrees with you."

Marisa gave his shoulder a sympathetic squeeze. "Even the great Jack Stratton can be wrong. Don't take it so hard. Are you going to the dress fitting today? The itinerary wasn't all that clear."

"No, I get a reprieve. It's just for the ladies. Alice said it's to make absolutely sure that everyone has the right shoes, earrings, and all that jazz to avoid any surprises and fire drills on the big day. I can just see Erica inspecting the troops. I'm so glad I don't have to go."

"See?" Marisa smiled and gave his shoulder another squeeze, her fingers drifting all the way down his arm and across the back of his hand. "Your luck is getting better." With a wink, she strolled toward the west parking lot, an extra sway in her hips.

Jack turned toward the east lot, where the Charger was parked with Lady waiting inside. His jaw was set in a determined line. So what if everyone else thought he was wrong? He didn't care. Something was strange about that house, and he was going to find out what it was. Right now.

CHAPTER

12

Jack parked the Charger in front of the rental house just as he had on the night of Donald's attack. Lady had gotten quieter after they turned onto the driveway, and now she wasn't making a sound.

The sky above the mountain was bright blue, but that same dark feeling crossed over Jack as he got out of the car and looked up at the faded red house. His gaze traveled up to the two jet-black windows on the second floor. On one of those fixer-upper shows Alice had recently taken to watching, the host said the front windows of a house were "portals to its soul."

If that's the case, this house is possessed. Those blacked-out windows look like the portals to Hell.

Jack pressed the button on the dash to release Lady's harness and open her door. The locks clicked and the rear door swung open, but Lady didn't get out.

"To me!" Jack called. Lady stayed in the car. "What's the matter, girl?"

Jack walked around to her door.

Lady turned her head to the side and gave him a look that he could only interpret as, *What do you think, stupid? I'm not going in there.*

"I don't want to either, but we have to. Come."

Lady stayed put.

"What is up with you?" Jack grumbled. He reached into his pocket and pulled out one of his landlady's homemade dog biscuits.

Without a doubt, the peanut butter bacon bomb biscuits were Lady's favorite snack. But he hadn't had to resort to this trick for a while.

Lady's eyes lit up, and she shot out of the car. Jack dropped the cookie for fear of losing his fingers, although he knew Lady would never intentionally bite him. The dog caught the biscuit before it hit the ground.

After noisily munching it down, Lady turned back toward the car.

"That's not how it works." Jack attached the leash to her collar. "Come on."

Lady planted her feet. Jack grabbed her harness and half carried the enormous dog to the steps. But when Lady let out an earsplitting roar, he set her down.

"Look, dog." Jack squared off with her as she glared back at him. "Alice needs us. Alice." Lady whined.

Jack was almost certain Lady could understand him, but there was no way he was going to keep arguing with a dog. "Fine. Stay out here, you baby. I have to go in. I don't want to go in alone, but I will." He turned and stomped up the steps. Lady stayed where she was.

Jack punched in the code to the lock box. Morrison would be furious if he found out what Jack was doing, but right now, Jack didn't care. He pushed the front door open. What he was about to do was perfectly legal. Morrison had declared the house was no longer a crime scene, so Jack had offered the homeowner double the usual fee and rented the house for the week.

He flicked on the living room lights. Everything had been straightened up, and there was a guest basket with candy and popcorn on the coffee table. Jack walked across the room and opened the door to the room where he had found Donald.

A larger area rug had been placed over the floor. It wasn't new, it was worn and dusty, probably taken from another room in the house, but of course they'd had to remove the smaller one that Donald had bled all over. And that wasn't the only change.

The twisted art gallery is gone.

The sketches were no longer there; the tape had been removed from the walls. Jack suspected the pictures were in police custody, but he was sure Castillo wasn't doing anything with them. Ed was pinning all his hopes on the computer forensics department catching the real guy who rented the house. But trying to trace an IP address was a long shot. There was lots of software available to mask your true location. The fraud department had already come up empty on the credit card used to rent the house. Whoever was doing this knew how to cover their tracks.

Which made it all the more likely that they were up to something more than drawing pictures. And yet it seemed the entire police department had bought in to Castillo's theory—nothing more than a paranoid artist with a redneck alarm that accidentally injured a cop—but Jack wasn't buying it.

He walked over and opened the closet door. The art supplies and easel were gone, leaving only dust. *A woman in a bathtub lying down to take a shower.* It made no sense . . .

Jack walked around the ground floor. The kitchen was cramped and dated, with tacky green wallpaper, and no dishwasher. Instead there was a sign over the sink that declared that no man had ever been shot by his wife while doing the dishes. *I'll have to tell Alice that one.*

In addition to the living room, there were two small rooms on the first floor and a half bath with just a sink and toilet. No shower, no tub. *No way for Donald to see what he says he saw.* Jack headed upstairs. *Maybe that knock to Donald's head made him forget he went up? But even if he did go up, he got beaned downstairs, so that would mean he went upstairs first.* It still didn't make sense, but Jack continued up the old wood staircase, the stairs creaking and groaning underfoot. There were three little bedrooms upstairs, sparsely furnished and all featuring tacky 1950s' wallpaper like the kitchen. The smell of mothballs assaulted his nose.

Jack's footsteps echoed off the wood as he walked down the hall to the bathroom. He grabbed the doorknob but it didn't turn. He jiggled the knob and applied force, and the door opened with a loud click.

The bathroom looked as dated as the rest of the house, but it was clean. Fresh towels lay folded on a small wooden stool. The scent of lemon wafted from tiny wrapped soaps inside a gift basket with toiletries and a note to enjoy the stay and a plea for good rental reviews. A few tiles were cracked and chipped, but overall, not the worst room in the house.

A shower curtain was drawn across the length of the old clawfoot tub. As Jack reached for the curtain, the room dipped into darkness. A thick cloud had passed by outside, blotting out the sun and its light through the small window.

That was unnerving.

Yanking the curtain back with a rattle of metal clips, Jack stared into the empty cast-iron tub.

Nothing. *What did I expect? A body? A bloody knife?*

Half relieved and half unconvinced, he pulled the curtain closed.

Somewhere downstairs, the floorboards creaked. Jack drew his gun. Another sound came from downstairs, but he couldn't make it out. Sticking close to the wall to minimize the creaking of floorboards, he crept down the hallway. He pressed his back against the wall as he descended the stairs to the living room. Lady stood there, trembling slightly and staring into the room where they'd found Donald.

"Hey, girl," Jack whispered as he holstered his gun.

Lady kept staring at the open door, her ears lying flat on her head. She sniffed the air, her nose twitching wildly. A deep, low growl rumbled in her massive chest, her hackles rising with each moment. Jack walked up beside her and the dog slowly walked forward.

At the room, Lady stopped in the doorway and peered around. Her head hung lower and her front paws were spread like she was ready to pounce. She sniffed the air and walked to the middle of the rug. She scratched twice and barked—the signal Alice had taught her to show she'd found something.

She probably still smells the blood. Jack bent over and grabbed the edge of the rug. Lady moved over as Jack folded it in half and dragged it aside, a flurry of dust particles falling like snow with the movement.

Lady walked again to the middle of the floor, scratched twice, and barked.

Jack looked at her, puzzled. As far as he could figure, the spot she was scratching was two feet away from where Donald had fallen. He knelt next to Lady and examined the floor. Everything looked fine . . . except for a little chip missing at the end of one board.

Taking out his knife, Jack slipped the blade between the boards and pried up. A six-inch section of the board tipped back, revealing a metal ring. Lady's claws ticked off the floor as she whined and backed up.

Jack grabbed the metal ring and pulled.

A three-foot-square section of the floor lifted on hinges. He expected to find a hideaway for money or moonshine. Instead he stared into the ashen face of a recently deceased woman. Her bloated body was wrapped in clear plastic.

Lady let out a mournful howl.

Jack had seen death many times before, and it never got any easier. But the terrified expression frozen on the dead woman's face made his hand shake. Her mouth was twisted into a long-silenced scream, and her gray eyes were forever staring to her left . . . at a second woman's body, also wrapped in clear plastic.

CHAPTER

13

Aunt Haddie clapped her hands with delight. "You're going to be a lovely bride!"

Even with Alzheimer's marching slowly through Aunt Haddie's brain, she still had a way of bringing out the best in Alice, just like she had when Alice was a small, frightened foster child in her care.

"Would you like more water?" Erica asked Aunt Haddie.

The elderly black woman shook her head. "I'm fine, thank you." She was sitting in a comfy chair at the side of the room, watching the seamstress make the final adjustments to Alice's wedding gown.

Bright lights flashed in her face as Philip captured the moment with his camera.

Blinking and rubbing her eyes, Aunt Haddie said politely, "Perhaps you should focus on the bride, young man."

Alice felt like an angel. The fit-and-flare dress was dove-white satin with a lace overlay and a sweetheart neckline. The beaded bodice hugged her curves and accentuated her tiny waist. Lorenzo Soriano had made Alice submit a detailed questionnaire to get to know her a bit before he even started sketching a design, and it showed in the dress. It was perfect in every way, but more specifically, it was perfect for her. It was feminine but not too revealing and didn't overpower her petite frame. The skirt had a fluidity as she moved that only a designer gown could deliver. Alice held out the lace overlay of the skirt, marveling at the craftsmanship.

The lace was handmade and encrusted with tiny pearls and Swarovski crystals. It was spectacular. The same lace had been used for her chapel-length veil.

The photographer snapped a picture of her as she sighed with pleasure at her reflection in the mirror. "Please do me a favor, Lenora?" Alice asked. "Tell your father what an amazing job he did designing my bridal gown. It's so beautiful. And it makes me feel beautiful."

Lenora smiled. "My father will be pleased to hear that."

"Alice, you are stunning." Erica clapped her hands together. "Absolutely breathtaking."

Aunt Haddie sat forward in her chair. "Your father designs the dresses and you sew them, is that right?"

Lenora shook her head. "I only make the alterations. This fitting is a good example. Alice lost a few pounds since the last fitting. Brides get nervous, it happens. I need to take it in a bit. But my father is the master. He not only does the creative design work, he does his own cutting, fabrication, and sewing, though he gives all the credit to the lacemakers, beadworkers, and embroiderers. Without them, he says, he only has pretty dresses that remain just a dream. My mother helped him, too, until a few years ago."

Alice imagined the skilled hands needed to create such intricate artistry.

"I have a wonderful idea," Erica announced. "We should get a shot of Alice in her gown with Lorenzo at his studio. The master with his masterpiece!"

Lenora smiled and nodded, a gleam in her eye. "That would be very nice. He would like that."

Philip exhaled loudly and lowered his camera. When he spoke, he had the air of a curmudgeonly teacher who'd grown weary of having to explain things to people he considered beneath him. "For lighting, it would be preferable if Lorenzo came to my studio and not the other way around."

Lenora shook her head. "I'm afraid that's not possible. My father would love to meet you, but he is a very private man. A bit of an introvert, I'm afraid. You will get much better photographs if he's comfortable, and he would be much more at ease in his own surroundings."

"I'm certain it would be no bother going to his studio," Erica said firmly, resuming her staring contest with Philip. "You charge an extra fee for location shooting, after all."

"Because of the added challenges it presents," Philip fired back.

"Then it's settled. I just have to find the time." Erica smiled.

Alice tried not to make a face. Not only had Erica gotten her way, but she had managed to boost her paycheck in the process. The bigger the invoice for the wedding, the bigger her commission.

Before Philip could reply, Aunt Haddie cut through the professional bickering with an airy wave. "Lenora, I'm curious, how long does it take to make a dress?" she asked.

Philip crouched down and started to take shots of Lenora working.

"It depends on the design," Lenora said. She carefully lifted the delicate fabric as she pinned it. "My father designs many dresses, and when a bride sees the one she likes, he'll customize it for her."

Philip lay on the floor, but as he angled his camera to take an upward-facing photo, Aunt Haddie's foot shot out and kicked him in the backside. Philip rolled in Haddie's direction and glowered.

"Oops!" Aunt Haddie shrugged innocently. "I wouldn't take a photograph from that angle. It might show a little too much of Alice, if you know what I'm saying. And then her fiancé, Jack, might get a little agitated. Did you know he carries a firearm at all times?"

Philip, red in the face, stood up and checked his camera for damage. "I was getting a shot that included Lenora's face," he stammered. "She looks down at the fabric as she works, so I needed to get beneath her." He knelt down and focused in on Lenora's face. "It's an action photo."

"I'm certain that one will be lovely." Aunt Haddie gave Alice a little wink, and Alice smiled at her gratefully.

Then Erica took out her tablet and started to stab at it with the stylus, and Alice's smile faded. She felt as poked and prodded as Erica's tablet. Her wedding planner had become her handler. Every day, Alice boarded a roller-coaster, and she couldn't get off until Erica released her, tired and slightly nauseated. Each item on her to-do list was synchronized, color-coded, and linked to software that pushed out automatic updates to social media and beeps to her phone. Any deviation from the schedule brought things to a grinding halt and put Erica into warp speed.

When they were first working out the details of the schedule, Alice had made certain there was plenty of time for her and Jack. But then the complexity of the wedding grew and grew, and Erica kept slashing those precious minutes away, until Alice hardly saw Jack at all.

And right now, she needed him, she needed to feel the reassurance his presence brought her. He could encourage her like no one else. She was exhausted, frazzled, and about to lose it. She and Jack had an hour set aside for dinner tonight, and if Erica thought she was going to sacrifice it—

Alice's phone rang from a silver tray on the table. The Batman ringtone. A call from Jack!

"I've got it!" Erica announced, but it wasn't that she was answering the phone for Alice. "I found a time slot for a quick photoshoot at Lorenzo's. You'll just have to push back your dinner with—"

"Not a chance." Alice shook her head. "I hear ya, but it's not happening, Erica. I get one hour with Jack and I'm *not* giving it up. One hour, no discussion." She could feel her heartbeat in her ears, and she was surprised by her own tone of authority.

The phone stopped ringing. Erica folded her hands in front of herself and leveled her gaze at Alice. "You heard Lenora say how much this would mean to her father. Think about how much work has gone into that dress."

Alice's emerald eyes flashed with anger and frustration. She was standing in a designer dress she'd never dreamt of, to be worn at a lavish wedding she couldn't even fathom was to be hers. It was as if she were on an island and Jack and the wedding they had envisioned for themselves were drifting farther and farther away from her.

All eyes were on Alice. Her ponytail bobbed from side to side as she shook her head. *I am not packing my bags and going on Erica's guilt trip. Nope, nope, nope.*

Lenora shifted uncomfortably. "My father would understand if it doesn't work out," she explained, careful to avoid eye contact. The shy young woman clearly didn't like being used by Erica as leverage.

"We can go another day," Alice said, her voice rising. "Any day. I'll go after the meal. I'll go at midnight. I don't care. But I need to spend some time with Jack."

Erica looked to Aunt Haddie.

"Don't go looking at me," Aunt Haddie said. "I know that look in Alice's green eyes. That's her 'I've made up my mind' look, and you should believe me when I tell you that no one is going to get that girl to do something once she's decided on the path she's going to take. Even the angels would have to go to the good Lord for help."

Erica huffed and tapped on her tablet a little too aggressively.

Alice's phone let out a notification ding that Jack's call had gone to voice mail.

Aunt Haddie turned to look at Alice. "But . . . if I remember your schedule correctly, tomorrow you're supposed to go over to the florist's and see if you like the substitute ribbon for the boutonnieres. Can you bring the ribbon choices to Lorenzo's studio and kill two birds with one stone?"

Erica thought for a moment and nodded. "That works. Thank you."

As Alice gave Aunt Haddie a smile and a thumbs-up, her phone vibrated with a text. "Philip, would you please hand me my phone?" With a scowl, he picked it up and handed it to her.

Alice's breath caught in her throat as she read Jack's message.

911! YOU'RE IN DANGER!! CALL ME!!!

CHAPTER

14

Jack stood next to the Charger, waiting for Morrison and Castillo to arrive. He kicked at the dirt in frustration and checked his phone for the hundredth time. Castillo treated this like the scene of an accident and not a crime. *He should have found these bodies.* The police had already cordoned off the house. Two rookies stood on the front porch, glancing around the property, eyes darting back and forth from Jack to the house, unsure what to do next. One of them had thrown up when Jack showed him the bodies. Jack gave him his last bottle of water, and he wasn't about to ask for it back now.

He'd called Alice even before calling 911, expecting her to freak out when he told her about the dead women, but she barely reacted at all, apparently incapable of processing any more stress. She recognized the threat, but emotionally, she seemed more concerned about Aunt Haddie being physically up for such a long visit than she was worried about a serial killer having her picture taped to his wall in the room where he'd hidden two bodies.

Jack had sent Bobbie G. and Boomer out to be with Alice, so he knew she was safe. But still, he wanted to be the one protecting her.

Morrison's cruiser came barreling toward him, lights flashing, and skidded to a stop. Castillo got out of the passenger seat and walked toward him with a scowl.

"What? How can you possibly be ticked off that I was right?" Jack said.

"You broke into a crime scene!" Castillo's eye twitched.

Morrison stopped a good distance away, but he looked like a bull readying to charge. "Jack, what do you think you're doing?" His voice sounded like gravel was stuck in his throat.

"I didn't break in." Jack reached into his pocket and took out the rental receipt. "You declared the house no longer a crime scene, so I rented it."

"You—what?" Castillo marched forward and took the receipt from Jack's hand.

Morrison crossed his arms, but a slight grin had formed on his lips. He nodded, and Jack returned the gesture.

"You're not approving this, are you?" Castillo waved the paper toward Morrison. "His meddling could jeopardize our case."

"Calm down, Ed," Morrison shot back. "We wouldn't even have a case if Jack hadn't kept digging. Good job, Stratton."

Castillo turned his back to both men, muttering a string of obscenities.

"When you're done running your mouth," Morrison said, starting toward the house, "why don't you join me and Jack inside?"

Castillo turned back around and quickly fell into step beside Morrison and Jack. "You're not going to let him into an active murder scene, are you, sir?"

"Yes, and it's not up for debate," Morrison said. At the door, all three men slipped crime scene shoe covers over their shoes. "Did you come out here with anyone, Jack?" Morrison asked.

"No, sir. Lady, myself, and the responding officers have been inside. The homeowner must have come out at some point prior to today. They cleaned up and left some gift baskets."

Morrison turned to the senior officer. "Go over to 1226 Jefferson and bring George Grady over here ASAP. He's the homeowner. Bag his shoes. And if anyone else in the family was out here, round them up, too."

The officer nodded and headed for his car while the other stood guard at the door.

Jack led the way to the back room and pointed out the trapdoor and the rug that had replaced the bloody one.

"Looks like Donald wasn't hallucinating," Morrison said as he stared down at the two bodies wrapped in plastic.

"He must have come into the room when the trapdoor was open," Jack said.

Castillo nodded. "He must have seen the body before the killer hit him over the head."

Jack was about to point out that Castillo had abandoned his theory about the redneck alarm pretty quickly, but he kept his mouth shut. He didn't often agree with Ed's theories as a detective, but there was no reason to rub his nose in his mistake, as tempting as it was.

"What's the ETA on the ME?" Jack asked Morrison.

"Neil should be here within half an hour." Morrison looked at Jack. "You've reached out to Alice?"

Jack nodded. "She's with friends. I'll be heading there with Lady as soon as we're done."

"We might be a while." Castillo crouched down and took out a flashlight. "Is it just the two bodies?"

"It is," Jack replied. "Neither look like they've been dead long. The woman on the right is definitely in one of the sketches. I'm pretty sure the one on the left is, too."

"What did you do, memorize their faces?" Castillo asked.

Jack held up his phone.

"You took pictures of my crime scene?" Castillo stood, his arms stiff at his sides, his face flushed.

"I had the phone in my chest pocket and the camera just kept going off," Jack lied.

Castillo thrust a finger at Morrison. "Sir, that's a crime."

"Get your hand out of my face, Ed." Morrison stepped up beside Jack. "Show me."

Jack scrolled through the pictures until he found the sketch of the woman on the right. "See that mole on her lip? It's small but visible."

Morrison looked at the body of the woman in the hole and nodded. "It's her. But she looks younger in that sketch. Like it was drawn years ago."

"She's definitely older now." Jack flipped through the other sketches until he came to one of a young woman with her hair pulled up in a bun, wisps of hair framing her face. "I think this may be the one on the left."

Castillo squinted, looking back and forth between the sketch and the body. "The nose is all wrong."

"It's different." Jack zoomed in. "But her cheekbones and facial structure are the same. Maybe she got a nose job?"

"It could be her," Castillo admitted. "But only if that sketch was drawn thirty years ago."

"Or the artist sketched it from an old photograph," Morrison offered.

"There were four dozen pictures on that wall," Jack said. "There's a definite possibility that there are more bodies someplace else. You need to call in a profiler, sir."

Castillo took in a deep breath. Jack clenched his fist, ready to erupt if Castillo protested, but the detective nodded. "I agree with Stratton. This could be really big."

"Agreed." Morrison nodded. "Ed, take Jack's official statement right now, then cut him loose." Morrison's eyes met Jack's.

Jack's throat tightened. He'd worked a lot of crime scenes with the sheriff, but he'd never seen the fear that was now etched on Morrison's face. His brows were furrowed and his eyes wide. The tension was thick in the air, a new electricity buzzing around the men.

The sheriff wasn't trying to get rid of Jack to keep him away from the investigation. Morrison knew that Jack was Alice's best possible protection.

CHAPTER

15

This isn't right. It isn't fair! Even more police cars are arriving at the house now. I should have ended it before it came to this. I should have stopped Jack when he came back with that mutant mutt of his.

I knew he'd come back. It's my fault, really. I should have moved the bodies right after the police left. Did I subconsciously leave them there on purpose? Because I knew Jack would come back?

My hand tightens into a fist as anger burns through me. I feel my face flush with my next thought. Now I need two more.

For balance. Symmetry. Art.

I should have stopped Jack. He's stronger than I am, but I could have shot him. But then I'd have had to shoot Lady, too. I should have killed them both when I had the chance.

But I know why I didn't. Because Jack needs to live. He needs to see, even if it's only for a moment, even if he doesn't really understand it. I'll let him see my art, and then I can kill him. If I want. But there will be no need.

Seeing it will kill him. Slowly. He's seen so much already, but he won't be able to get my art out of his mind. Waking. Sleeping. Eyes open or closed. He'll always see.

More cars are coming now. Vans.

And there's Jack. He's not a policeman anymore, but cops are hanging on his every word. King Jack, out on the porch talking, holding court. Even the sheriff listens to him.

My chuckle slowly builds to a laugh. It's my work they're admiring, not Jack's. Now they're listening. Now that they've found the bodies, they're scared.

Standing on the porch, Jack turns and looks straight toward the spot in the woods where I'm standing. Can he see me? No. The shadows are too dark. I'm too well hidden.

Does he sense me?

He does. I know it. My chest is warm. I lick my lips. He knows I'm watching. I savor the moment, let it wash over me. But now is not the time.

I slip silently back, further into the woods and the shadows. Soon the darkness grows deeper. The trees are closer together, the ground spongy underfoot. It's not a beautiful place now, but it once was. A hundred years ago, a handful of houses popped up here, on the outskirts of Darrington. Two large farming families came together, joining their acreage. They even built a little church.

It's hard to tell where the forest used to end and the church property began. The trees grow right up to the dilapidated building, shielding parts from the sun attempting to poke through the canopy. Many of the once-beautiful glass panes have cracked, and the wooden tiles and the tall steeple have darkened from decades of growing exposure to water and mold. I pass by the family cemetery. No one besides me has been here for years, the old, carved stones now blocks of green foliage and the occasional monument in view tangled with vines. It's so sad. The graves are really special.

Crypts, technically. Little stone buildings with brass doors. Each held several coffins.

That made things easier for me. I didn't have to dig.

There's still enough light to see easily as I slip in the back door of the church. I prefer to go in that way. I feel like I'm peeking in on my masterpiece in all its glory. And it's such a beautiful spectacle.

I glide over to the vestibule door and peer into the sanctuary. Everyone's there, waiting. The pews are filled with all the guests. I had to invite the original church members, of course, which is why it was so nice that I didn't have to dig. I did my best to keep couples together, and I ignored the whole "groom side, bride side" nonsense. It's a wedding, after all. A celebration. I was so glad that the crypts held so many men, since most of my special guests are women.

The two spots that are still vacant spoil my mood. They're ruining my art. Like blank areas on a canvas, they beg to be filled in with color.

Stupid Jack Stratton.

But he won't stop me. I'll just have to find two more.

I slip inside the sanctuary. The service hasn't started yet, so I'll go unnoticed, as always. I can't remember how many weddings I've been to, but no one would ever recall my being there. Unbelievable, really. It's like I'm invisible.

"Oh, no, Mrs. Oliver."

Mrs. Oliver is slumping forward in the pew. Her flowered hat is now resting on the back of Mrs. Fletcher's head. That will never do.

It takes me a little while to rearrange Mrs. Oliver. I only got her two weeks ago, and it was so difficult to make her sit still. Rigor mortis always presents such a challenge—perhaps the biggest. My compositions would not remain exactly as I designed them to be if it weren't for the countless hours I've put into honing my craft. But working with death is like working in any other medium in art—it takes a lifetime to master. *I should call them my decompositions.*

I smile at my own wit and continue to shape Mrs. Oliver's stiff body until I'm pleased with the pose.

There.

I slip back into the shadows. Everything is almost ready. I still have some empty spots, but those should be easy to fill. I've never had too much trouble inviting people.

But . . . am I being too selfish? After all, most of the guests are mine. I had to invite them so they could see the wedding. But what about the bride? Should I invite some of her family?

Or Jack's? He was adopted, but now that he's found his real mother and grandmother, there are so many to pick from. His adoptive parents should be here soon, too. Another couple would be nice.

Or . . . maybe I need some diversity. That's it! And she could be included in both the bride's and the groom's family!

I silently clap my hands together.

It's perfect. I'll just have to invite Aunt Haddie to the wedding.

CHAPTER

16

Jack paced back and forth across his living room, rubbing the tension out of his neck. Alice watched him from the center of the room with her arms crossed. Bobbie, Boomer, and Shawna sat on the couch, following the conversation with rapt attention.

Jack stopped pacing and faced Alice. He took a deep breath, knowing there was nowhere to run from the bomb he was about to detonate, and said, "We have to cancel the wedding."

Alice looked like she'd stepped on a live wire. Bobbie slapped his forehead. Boomer rolled his eyes.

"Oh, you didn't just go there," Shawna said.

"We have no choice," Jack said.

"Are you kidding?" Alice's arms shot down stiffly at her sides. "There is no way I am canceling our wedding!"

Jack took a step back. "Maybe 'cancel' was too strong a word."

"Ya think?" Shawna said.

"Reschedule," Jack said.

Alice marched forward, her eyes shooting green sparks. "I am not canceling, not postponing, not changing one single thing about our wedding. It will go on as planned. I don't care what crazy psycho may or may not come after me. Believe me, at this point, they should be a lot more scared of me than I am of them!"

"I believe it!" Boomer said, raising his hand.

"Me, too!" said Bobbie.

Lady began to bark.

"Hush, Lady. Alice, you need to listen to reason," Jack said. "This guy has killed at least two women. He had forty-eight pictures up on his wall, and you are in one of them. Sheriff Morrison is bringing in an FBI profiler—"

Boomer raised his hand again. "I saw this episode of *The Real World of Serial Killers*, and it took the cops like twenty years to catch this one dude."

"Shut up," said Shawna, pulling his hand back down.

"No. Boomer's right," Alice said. "You don't expect us to delay our wedding twenty years, do you?"

"I'm not saying that," Jack said. "But there's a killer out there."

"I know, Jack! What do you want me to do about it?"

Jack cracked his neck. There was no way she was going to like this plan, but he couldn't think of an alternative. "I think you should go away to a safe place while I hunt the guy down."

Alice walked into the kitchen, picked up a plate, and shattered it in the sink.

"I think that's a no," Boomer said.

"Of course it's a no!" Alice shouted, coming back into the room. "We're a team, Jack! Do you think I'm going to run and hide while you risk your life?"

Jack swallowed. "I was kind of hoping you would."

"Would you do that? If the situation were reversed and someone was threatening you—would you hide while I looked for the guy without you?"

Boomer laughed. "Not Jack. No way."

"You can't stay here," Jack said.

"You can't make me leave."

"Alice . . ." He ran his hand through his hair again.

Her lip started to tremble. "Is there some other reason you want to cancel the wedding?"

The question rocked Jack onto his heels. "What? No."

"Are you sure?"

"Sure about what? Marrying you? Of course I am. I mean, I'm nervous, but—"

Alice burst into tears, raced into her bedroom, and slammed the door.

Boomer shook his head. "Never hesitate."

"Shut up." Shawna stood up. "You're not helping."

Jack rubbed his forehead. "How is this possibly turning around on me?" he asked no one in particular. "There's a serial killer on the loose."

Shawna put a hand on her hip and leveled her gaze at Jack. "If you had any idea of the stress that girl is under, you'd cut her some slack."

Jack's voice rose. "I'm just trying to keep her safe!" He let out an exasperated sigh.

Bobbie G. shook his head. "Well, good luck with that. There's no way Replacement's running."

Even in his current mood, Jack couldn't help but crack a small smile at hearing Alice's nickname. He walked to the kitchen and started picking the pieces of broken plate out of the sink. "Then what am I supposed to do?"

"Catch the guy," Boomer said.

"You just said it yourself, sometimes it takes decades to catch a serial killer."

"I was right about that?"

Shawna slapped Boomer in the back of the head.

"You can still guard her," Bobbie suggested. "Just stay by her side."

"Then how do I catch the guy? I can't do both."

"I got it! I got it!" Boomer waved his hand in the air.

"This isn't school," Bobbie said. "You don't have to raise your hand."

"Alice could come back to the hood with us!" Boomer grinned like he'd just made a game-winning shot.

"You actually think Alice would be safer in the hood with you?" Jack asked in disbelief.

Boomer nodded rapidly. "If that show was right, serial killers are always white guys."

"Not the Atlanta child-killer. He was black," Shawna pointed out.

"Yeah, that's still like one out of a thousand," Boomer said. "So, if we take Alice back to the hood and some white guy shows up, well, he's gonna stick out, isn't he?"

Jack nodded slowly. "That actually makes some sense."

"We can stay at my house," Shawna said. She smiled at Bobbie, who swallowed nervously.

"There you go, Jack," said Boomer. "Between me, Bobbie, and Shawna, we got this. Shawna's like Dirty Harriet. She's packing legal."

"Me, too," Bobbie reminded Jack.

As Jack was thinking it over, Alice's bedroom door opened, and she stuck her head out. "I'll agree to it as long as you keep Lady with you, Jack," she said. "But first I need to speak with you."

"Then come on out," Boomer said.

Shawna smacked him in the back of the head again.

Jack went into Alice's bedroom and she shut the door behind them. He opened his mouth to speak, but she held a finger up to his lips. "Please don't say anything. I'm sorry about the plate. My nerves are shot. It's not an excuse, but . . . I understand you're worried about me. Trust me, I get it. I'm always worried about you. But we're a team, Jack. We work together. And this wedding is going forward. I promise I'll stay safe. No unnecessary risks. But know this—" Alice looked at Jack, and her gorgeous green eyes with the golden flecks began to well with tears. "You made me dare to believe that a love like ours could exist, that someone like me could be loved by someone as wonderful as you. You are my world, Jack." She put her slender hand on his chest. "In five days, I am going to vow to love you for a lifetime. Are you in?" Her lip trembled.

Jack nodded. "I'm in. No one, and I mean no one, is going to keep me from marrying you, Alice."

She smiled, revealing the dimple that made Jack melt every time.

"Do me a favor?" Jack reached down, his fingertips brushing her cheek as he wiped a tear away. "Write down what you said to me a minute ago? I think you just created our vows."

"Can you do me a favor?" She smiled up at him. "Catch this guy."

Jack pulled her close. "I will. I promise."

CHAPTER

17

Some people love going to bookstores, not just to get something to read but because of the feeling they get when they enter. Others prefer train stations or airports. Jack had even heard of people who went barefoot because it "grounded" them, made them feel an energy. Jack felt that way about the county sheriff's office.

After a fitful night's sleep, he drove there first thing in the morning. The parking lot was already filling up, banter and greetings ricocheting around as his former colleagues got out of their cars. As he walked through the front doors, a wave of emotion rocked him. It was this very station where police had brought seven-year-old Jack after his birth mother abandoned him at the bus station. At that time, Jack could never have imagined that this place would become his grounding point.

The whirlwind of action ground to a halt as office workers and officers stopped and stared. Brian Murphy, once Jack's biggest rival on the force, strode over and shook Jack's hand. He didn't say anything, and even though Jack had saved the man's life, he doubted he and Murphy would ever be friends. But their relationship had improved. Murphy respected Jack. That was enough.

"Glad you could make it, Stratton." Morrison's tone was stern and his voice was loud enough for everyone to hear.

Jack understood. The sheriff was making a point. Jack had been forced off the job by the previous sheriff. He had disobeyed a direct order to save Marisa's life. It had cost him his career and everything he dreamed of since being a child, but he'd do it again without hesitation.

Jack chose to serve and protect over obeying the law, and some people here were no doubt upset that Morrison was not only allowing Jack into the station but had invited him as a consultant. The sheriff was letting everyone know that he had the power to do so and that it was his decision. Jack just hoped Morrison wouldn't pay a political cost later. The sheriff was still an elected official, after all.

Morrison led the way to the big conference room. Half a dozen officers were seated at the desks, with Ed Castillo in the front row. A thin man in gray suit pants, white shirt, and an elaborate shoulder holster stood at the front of the room. He pushed his round glasses up his nose as he shuffled a stack of papers.

Unsure where he should sit, Jack remembered one of Aunt Haddie's many scriptural lessons and took a seat in the back row. She always said to never take the best seat just in case someone more distinguished than you has been invited. Having to move would be pretty humbling. If your host asks you to move up to a better place, then you'll look like a rock star.

Murphy entered as well and took the seat in the front next to Castillo.

"Good morning, everyone," Morrison said loudly as he walked into the room. "Before I introduce Special Agent Frank Thomas, I would like to acknowledge a private consultant that I've decided to bring in on this case. Most of you already know Jack Stratton. Jack?" Morrison motioned for Murphy to get up, then he held his hand out to the now-vacant seat in the front. Murphy's displeasure showed on his face. He scowled at Jack.

Everyone who exalts himself will be humbled, and the one who humbles himself will be exalted. Thank you, Aunt Haddie.

"It goes without saying," Morrison continued, "that you will show him due respect. But Detective Castillo and I remain your first and main points of contact. Am I clear?"

"Yes, sir." The response, though universal, was slightly disjointed, and a brief murmur rippled through the room afterward.

"I've invited Special Agent Frank Thomas here to develop a profile of our killer. He's just arrived, and will be spending the morning at the crime scene. He'll interview witnesses this afternoon. I'll turn the briefing over to him now."

"Good morning." Thomas placed his hands behind his back and puffed up his chest, scanning the room. "Good morning," he said again, a fraction of a decibel louder.

"Good morning," most people repeated back, including Jack. Forcing people to repeat your greeting was a power play, but Jack would do nothing to upset the delicate position of his current role of consultant.

"As you are all aware, we have a serious situation here." Thomas lifted up the stack of papers and handed them to Morrison. "Everything in your briefing is online. These are the instructions for accessing your accounts and communication protocol." He walked over to the wall and shut off the lights. An overhead projector turned on, with Thomas's name and contact information on the first screen. "Rule number one: Do not speak with the press. If you are asked for any information regarding the case, direct them to Sheriff Morrison or myself."

Castillo shifted in his seat. He looked like he was about to say something but instead chose to write something down in his notebook, his hand furiously scribbling across the small page.

"Thanks to the work Detective Castillo has already put in, we've been able to identify one of the victims." The slide changed, and the screen showed a picture of a middle-aged woman. "Delores Gill. Forty-three. Married. Three adult children. Reported missing nine days ago from Coventry, New Hampshire."

An officer in the third row raised his hand. "Isn't Carson Murray from New Hampshire?"

"Very good." Thomas nodded approvingly. "Carson Murray is the person whose identity was stolen and used to rent the house where the bodies were located and Officer Pugh was attacked. Mr. Murray is hospitalized in a state mental facility in New Hampshire. We're currently looking into that."

Thomas advanced to the next slide. "Thanks to Sheriff Morrison's team and Detective Castillo, we've also managed to identify five of the women in the sketches found in the home. All five of them have been reported missing within the last two years." He gestured to the screen, which showed five red dots on a map of the United States. "These markers indicate the locations where the victims were last seen. As you can see, the abductions span four states.

"Our top priority is to identify the remaining women in the sketches. Each of you has been assigned a territory. Your log-in pages contain links to a digital package of scans of the sketches. You are to contact the police departments in your territories and work on identifying these women, using their missing person reports.

"As for the two known victims, the ME's office is working overtime on processing the bodies. We should have some results by EOD."

Castillo handed Jack one of the papers. It was a list of log-in names. Jack's was noticeably absent.

"Are there any questions?"

Despite himself, Jack felt his own hand rising. He suddenly felt like he was in primary school again.

"Stratton?" Thomas resumed his power pose with his hands clasped behind his back and his chest thrust out, prominently displaying the shiny gun in its new holster.

"I completely agree with the importance of identifying the women in the sketches," Jack said. "But if we concentrate solely on missing person reports, we'll fail to identify the ones who are currently not missing. They could be potential targets."

Thomas crossed his arms. "Actually, we're narrowing the field, plain and simple. Once we rule out the missing women, we can concentrate on looking for potential targets, as you said. Besides, there's no more efficient way of locating these unknown women from sketches alone. Facial recognition software isn't quite there yet. Unfortunately, real police work isn't like on TV."

Jack let the jab pass. "There's another route we can take, similar to the one you're already proposing." He worked up what he hoped was an encouraging smile.

Thomas raised a skeptical eyebrow, highlighting the deep creases in his forehead.

"Right now, it's very smart using our limited manpower to run the sketches through the missing person files. But we could also expand that reach and run the sketches by thousands of eyes. We should reach out to a news station—"

Murmurs of disbelief passed through the room.

"Need I remind you of rule number one?" Thomas said. "The last thing we want to do is contact the media. No one—I repeat, no one"—he fixed Jack with a stare—"is allowed to say more than these two words to them: No comment."

"Respectfully, sir, what I'm suggesting is your plan, just a little more robustly implemented," Jack said.

"I'm not going to start a panic, Stratton. And if you want to discuss this any further, we can do it offline. Am I clear?"

Jack didn't have a problem with authority. He did have an issue with people who didn't consider any options that they themselves hadn't personally come up with. But if he was going to stop this killer, he needed the police's resources. There was no way around this. He needed to play along. Alice was counting on him. He swallowed down his anger and nodded, willing his foot tapping to cease.

"Good." Thomas shut off the projector and flicked the lights on. "Sheriff, Castillo, Stratton, meet me at the morgue in half an hour. Let's go talk with the ME."

CHAPTER

18

Jack hated the morgue even worse than the hospital. The tiled room felt like a tomb. He stood awkwardly with the sheriff, Ed Castillo, and Frank Thomas as they talked to Mei Lai, the assistant ME, who was always very helpful. Neil Fredrick, the ME, was at the capital.

"Is his trip related to this case?" Morrison asked.

"Yes. He needed to confirm some test results and run a chemical analysis on this." Mei walked over to a fifty-inch computer monitor. After a few clicks of the mouse, a picture of a piece of dark-blue cloth appeared. "We found it wrapped up in the plastic with Delores Gill's body."

"A handkerchief?" Thomas asked.

Mei adjusted her rectangular blue-and-pink glasses. "More specifically, it's a silk pocket square."

"What's the difference?" Thomas asked.

"One's for show, one's for blow." Morrison chuckled. "My wife loves saying that every time she gives me a handkerchief. She always gives me two."

"A pocket square is specifically designed to go into your jacket breast pocket," Castillo said. "It's a fashion statement."

Jack noted the pocket square in Castillo's own jacket pocket. It matched his red tie.

Thomas took out a tablet. "So, it belongs to a man?"

Mei nodded. "We believe so. Especially because there was still an aroma on the cloth—men's cologne or aftershave. Strong too. They have machines in the capital that can tell us the brand. Neil also needed to confirm his findings regarding the other woman's cause of death."

"Which was?" Thomas asked.

Mei shifted nervously as she flipped through her notes. Jack understood her hesitation. If the ME had felt he needed to go to the capital to double-check his findings, it made sense that she was reluctant to share those findings until Neil had answers to his questions.

"Poisoning," she said. "There was also bruising evidence that indicated forced injection."

"How could you determine if it was forced?" Jack asked.

"This second woman was restrained. There was a pattern of bruising across her upper arms and chest consistent with being bound by ropes or twine. Her wrists and ankles were tied individually. There were three small surface punctures directly around the injection wound, indicating that it took a few tries to get the needle in."

"Were you able to get any fingerprints from the victim's body?" Thomas asked. "We still haven't been able to identify her."

"We were able to retrieve a great set of prints, but there was no match in the database."

"Do you have a cause of death for Delores Gill?" Jack asked.

"Carbon monoxide poisoning."

"Was that from being wrapped in plastic?" Castillo asked.

"No. The plastic would result in asphyxiation. Her body shows signs of carbon monoxide poisoning before being wrapped, mostly likely combustion fumes from a fuel-burning appliance or an engine. We still need to confirm that."

"Any defensive wounds? Signs of a struggle?" Morrison asked.

Mei shook her head. "No defensive wounds on either of the victims. Of course, we still took DNA scrapings from underneath their fingernails."

"Did they have anything on their persons?" Castillo asked. "Any smartphones or devices? A fitness monitor?" Smart devices were a great way of tracking people's movements.

"Only jewelry. Both women wore earrings, a necklace, and a watch." She clicked the mouse a few times, and a photograph of various pieces of jewelry appeared on the monitor. "These belonged to the unidentified victim." The photograph showed three rings, a gold necklace, a gold watch, and pearl earrings. "We're analyzing the watchband for fingerprints and DNA. We found a print on the watch face that doesn't match the victim's."

"Full print?" Thomas asked hopefully.

"Partial thumb, but it should be usable." Mei clicked the mouse and another photograph appeared, featuring more jewelry—a slender gold watchband, a small gold cross, a ring, and two gold earrings that looked like leaves. "Delores Gill," Mei said simply.

Jack leaned forward and peered at the monitor. "Her wedding band is missing. Was that all the jewelry recovered?"

Mei nodded.

Thomas pointed at the diamond-encrusted gold band on the monitor. "Isn't that her wedding band?"

"No, that's her engagement ring," Jack corrected him. "It's part of a combination set. Trust me, I just looked at hundreds of them. And there was no wedding ring in the other woman's jewelry, either."

"Perhaps she wasn't married," Thomas suggested.

"Can we see the corpse of the unidentified woman, Mei?" Morrison asked.

"Of course, sir." Mei walked over to a table and pulled back a sheet. The woman's body lay underneath.

"She doesn't have a mark around her left ring finger," Castillo said, "If she wore a wedding band, you'd expect a mark or a change in coloration where the ring was."

"There is a mark on her right ring finger," Thomas pointed out.

"There was no ring on her right ring finger when we recovered the body," Mei said. "We noticed the depression in the skin as well."

"It could have been a wedding ring," Jack said. "In some traditions women wear it on the right hand. And some just prefer it on their right hand."

"Jack's getting married next week," Morrison said to Mei, to explain why Jack was so knowledgeable about wedding rings.

"I'm happy for you." Mei pressed her lips together as she pulled the sheet back over the corpse. The smell of ammonia wafted over them.

Jack thought he heard some disappointment in her response. She was never flirtatious, but Mei had always seemed a little smitten with him.

"Looks like we've found a possible commonality," Thomas announced. "Between the wedding invitation and the missing rings . . ." He looked at Jack. "You picked an unlucky time to get married."

"When is the wedding?" Mei asked.

"In four days."

"On the fourth?"

"Yes, April fourth. Why?"

Mei's face went pale. "In China, the number eight is lucky, because it sounds like the word for fortune or wealth. So, a lot of people get married August eighth. Eighth day of the eighth month."

"I guess I'll only be half as wealthy," Jack joked. "Beats being broke, though."

Mei shook her head. "It's very bad luck to marry on the fourth. Especially April, because it's the fourth month. Four-four."

"What does that mean in Chinese?" Castillo asked.

Mei's eyes met Jack's, and he saw true fear. "The word for four sounds like the word for death. Your wedding date means two deaths."

CHAPTER

19

Jack was halfway to his car when he saw Mac stepping out of a white rental. Gray streaks cooled the flames of Mac's unkempt fiery red hair. His shirt was untucked, and there were dark circles under his eyes. He didn't meet Jack's gaze, and his hands were balled into fists as he stomped forward.

Jack didn't want to fight his friend, but he had a rule about never letting himself become someone else's punching bag. When Mac was still ten feet away, Jack called out, "Morning, Mac." It was a greeting, but it was also a warning to stop.

Mac swayed as he slowed.

"One second." Jack took out his phone, typed a quick text, and hit send.

Mac's whole body was so tense he was shaking, a vein threatening to burst from his neck. "You don't give me orders, Stratton!" he bellowed.

Jack looked over at the Charger, now rocking back and forth. Lady was pacing in the back seat.

"You shouldn't have called her, Jack."

"I told you, Alison called *me*. She was worried about you. We all are now. You fooled me for a while there. You said everything was fine."

Mac's head snapped up and Jack saw the pain and rage in his eyes. "What do you want me to say? You want me to break down and cry? Fall apart? No way. I'm a soldier doing what we're taught. I just keep fighting."

"Sure," Jack said, "but you got wounded. You've got to heal before you get back in the action."

"Wounded? Not me. I'm the only one who made it out without a scratch."

Jack touched his own chest. "Some of the worst wounds you don't see."

"Alison said that, too." Mac's mouth twisted into a sneer. "Did she get that from you?"

"Her words. Not mine."

"You're doing fine."

Jack scoffed. "Fine? I have nightmares every time I close my eyes. I was just where you are not long ago. I thought I could drown the pain. The only problem is you drown yourself, and anyone who cares enough about you has to try to swim out and save you."

"Are you talking about Alison? I'd never hurt her!"

Lady pushed her snout out through the four-inch gap at the top of the window and growled.

"No, I'm talking about Alice," Jack said. "My drinking was dragging her down with me. It was hurting her. Just like your drinking hurts Alison."

Mac swore and gazed out into the parking lot, unable to look Jack in the eye.

Jack crossed his arms. "Truth hurts. My mistake. I thought you could take it."

Mac pressed the knuckles of his right hand against his head. He swore at Jack again. "Mind your own business! If she calls you again, don't talk to her."

"Too late." Jack uncrossed his arms and readied himself in case Mac chose to attack. "She called me last night."

Mac's eyes blazed. "You told her about the bachelor party?"

"I did. And she told me that you'd been trying to get sober."

"I have been!" Mac screamed, the veins in his neck prominent against his red skin. Jack wondered if he'd have much of an interior left in the Charger the way Lady was thrashing about. She wanted out. She wanted to do her job—protecting Jack.

"I'm doing everything I can to save my marriage," Mac said. "I'm working. I'm paying the bills."

"I know that. And Alison knows it; she sees how hard you're working. She's also really worried about your drinking."

"Because of you! You told her to go to that group. All they do is sit around and bad-mouth me. Do you know that? They sit in a circle and complain and tell her what a loser I am!"

"That's not what happens, and you know it, Mac. Alison doesn't know how to help you, but it's gotten to the point where she needs to help herself."

"We help each other. We should be together."

"You're hurting her, and you don't even see it."

"I'm trying! You have no idea how hard I'm trying." Mac stumbled sideways. "I even went to the doctor to get some happy pills."

"Which is another reason you shouldn't be drinking."

Mac shrugged. "The pills weren't working. I figured they needed some help."

"You're going to kill yourself, Mac. Those pills need time to kick in. You need time and you need help. You're fighting on your own, but there are people who want to help you."

"I'm a soldier! I don't need anyone else."

"You didn't say that in Iraq."

"None of those guys would sit in some room and cry like a bunch of babies."

"That's not how it works." Jack reached into his pocket and took out a business card. "Remember Boomer?" Mac nodded. "His girlfriend lives in Marshfield. It's one town over from your house. There's a support group there."

"I'm not going to AA."

"It's not AA, although I think you need that too. It's a survivors' support group."

"Why is Boomer's girlfriend there? Was she in the military?"

"She saw her brother die in a drive-by. It's a support group for survivors of violence."

"That ain't me. What violence did I survive?"

"You don't get more violent than war. There are a lot of us veterans there." Jack held out the card.

Mac spat on the ground. "No thanks." He turned back to his car, then spun around to face Jack once more, swaying like a reed in the wind. "Stay away from Alison. I'm warning you."

"I can't let you drive."

Mac's chuckle turned into a forced laugh and his glassy eyes tried to locate Jack. "Really?"

"C'mon, Mac, give me the keys. I'll give you a ride wherever you want to go."

"The closest bar?"

Jack held out his hand.

Mac cracked his knuckles. "I've always wanted to see if you're really as badass as everyone says."

Jack took out his Taser. It was a kinder option than using the remote to open the Charger's door and letting Lady set Mac straight.

Mac stopped, confused. "I thought you wanted to fight me."

"That's the last thing I want. Not to sound like one of those sappy guys sitting around in a circle, but I love you, man. You saved my life. I'm trying to repay the favor."

Mac's face twitched and he pointed at the Taser. "That ain't fair. Fight me!"

"No. Keys."

"This is illegal." Mac shook his head. "You can't just Tase me."

"If you want to file a complaint, the sheriff's office is right behind me. Keep in mind, I'll lie and say you attacked me. You're drunk. They'll believe me."

"You're a Boy Scout. You can't lie."

"Chandler was the Boy Scout. You picked the alternative. I can't let you drive and risk killing yourself or someone else. I can call the cops, but they'll arrest you. Or I can shoot out a couple of your tires with my gun. That would actually be my preferred option, if we weren't in the back parking lot of the sheriff's department. So . . . I have to Tase you." Jack aimed the Taser at Mac's chest. "Were you drinking beer?"

Mac shook his head. "Vodka. Why?"

"Proof?"

"One fifty-one."

"That's unfortunate. I hope you didn't spill any."

"Why?" Mac's eyes rolled around like pinballs as his puzzlement grew.

"The Taser barbs give off an electrical spark. Vodka with that much alcohol content is flammable. If you spilled some on your shirt . . . I could turn you into a s'more."

"You're crazy, Stratton."

"I like to think of it as 'determined.'"

A car sped into the parking lot and skidded to a stop, followed by the scent of burning rubber. Finn got out and hesitantly approached. "I got your text."

Jack smiled. "Thanks for coming. Would you mind giving Mac a ride?"

"Sure. Where?" Finn stopped next to Mac.

"Anyplace but here." Mac tossed his keys to Finn. "The company sucks." He turned and stormed over to Finn's car.

"I'm sorry about this," Jack said as he holstered his Taser.

The back door of the sheriff's department burst open and Murphy came out. "What's going on, Stratton?"

Jack gave him a friendly wave. "I was just showing off my new Taser. No issues. Thanks for checking on me, buddy!" He smiled broadly.

Murphy's face twisted in confusion, but he waved and went back inside.

Finn chuckled. "You never change."

Jack shook his head. "You're wrong about that." He handed Finn the card. "That's the contact information for the leader of a survivors' support group. The guy is a friend of Nyah's, Boomer's girlfriend. I hate to ask this of you, but Mac needs help, and he can't be alone right now. I'd do it, but . . ."

"No problem. It won't be the first time I've had to be a sober companion. I've got this."

"Are you sure? What about your date?"

"Annie? She'll understand." A smile spread across Finn's face. "She's fantastic."

"Really?"

Finn cleared his throat and nodded. "But we're not dating. We're business associates."

"Alice said she was very nice. I appreciate this, Finn."

"That's what friends are for."

As Finn turned and walked over to Mac's rental to lock it up, Jack remembered a time when Finn, on a bet, jumped from a standing position onto a tank tread. The man had been a tremendous athlete. Now he had to concentrate when putting one foot in front of the other while the world continued to turn.

Jack drew a long, jagged breath, trying to cope with the pain his friend was obviously in. When Jack met Mac, back when he came into the army, Mac had a different nickname. They called him Happy, because the guy never stopped smiling. He was grinning all the time, and it was infectious. Now Mac sat in Finn's car staring daggers at Jack like he wanted to kill him. And Jack believed him.

He remembered that Nyah had given him two cards for the survivors' support group, and he felt in his right pocket. His fingers closed around the other card. He tucked it in his wallet. He knew he'd changed, too. He wasn't the same man who went to war. The Jack who shipped out . . . wasn't the Jack who came back. Neither was Finn or Mac.

Did any of us really make it?

CHAPTER

20

Bobbie parked his huge Hummer in front of La Bonne Patisserie, a cute bakery with candy-striped awnings. Alice rode in the passenger seat, and Boomer and Shawna sat in back.

"Cake tasting?" Boomer's eyes lit up. "Is that really a thing?"

Alice smiled. "I didn't believe it when I saw it on the schedule either. I thought I'd just be choosing vanilla or chocolate."

"Sweet!" Boomer said, and he and Bobbie exchanged high-fives. "And here I thought that following you around everywhere was gonna really suck."

Shawna smacked him in the back of the head.

"Ow! What? What guy wants to spend all morning looking at flowers?"

Shawna shot him a cross look.

"I really appreciate everyone coming with me," said Alice. "Especially since Jack couldn't make it. But if you three need to be somewhere else, I'll be fine."

"Nope!" Shawna popped the P. "We're happy to help. Right?"

"I am! I am!" Boomer winced, and Alice guessed Shawna was digging one of her long nails into his side. "Who doesn't love cake?"

Bobbie shut the car off. "Just remember it's a cake tasting, not a cake buffet!"

Everyone except Boomer laughed as they got out of the car. The sweet smell of fresh pastries greeted their noses.

"Man, that Pierce guy must have some serious extra cash," Boomer said. "I got my aunt a tiny little cake from this place once, and it ran me fifty bucks. I don't even wanna know what they charge for a big cake. Hey, how big is yours gonna be?"

Alice frowned. The truth was, she had no idea. And with the ever-growing guest list . . .

"As big as it needs to be!" Erica said as she stepped out of the bakery.

Alice was temporarily blinded by bright flashes as Philip appeared from down the sidewalk, snapping pictures. He must have been waiting outside for them, but she wouldn't even have noticed him if not for the flash.

"Paparazzi Phil is here," Boomer muttered. "That guy creeps me out."

Shawna poked him and Boomer glared up at Bobbie. "Can you get your girl to stop smacking me?"

"Sure. Just stop ticking her off," Bobbie said with a wink. He held the door open for everyone.

"Good answer," Shawna said with a smile.

Erica led them behind the counter, through a kitchen with a long row of ovens, and into a small room where a single long table was covered with a white tablecloth, five chairs set up on one side. "Will anyone else be joining us?" she asked.

Alice shook her head.

"What about your Aunt Haddie? She was very helpful the other day."

Alice pressed her lips together. Aunt Haddie was a very private person, and her struggle with Alzheimer's wasn't something Alice was comfortable discussing. "Once we make our choice, I'll bring a sample by for her."

"I just want to make sure that she feels included," Erica said. "I know she's been like a second mother to you. Would you like to invite her to the final dress fitting?"

Alice nodded; she appreciated Erica's attention to detail, but the truth was, that would depend on Aunt Haddie. Her good days were getting less frequent, a fact that scared Alice so much, she usually tried not to think about it.

A teenage boy came in carrying a tray with water glasses and a pitcher. He set the table, poured the waters, and left. Alice reached for a glass, eager to do something with her hands. Once everyone was seated, Erica set a piece of paper and a pen down next to each plate.

"The final selection is up to Alice, of course, but it would also be helpful to hear from her close friends. Please score each sample from one to ten."

They all looked down at the sheets. Boomer and Bobbie grinned, but Alice's stomach was already complaining.

"There are twenty-four slots on this sheet!" Boomer said. "Are there really that many choices?"

Erica nodded.

Alice's stomach grumbled. How could there possibly be two dozen different flavors of cake?

Only an hour later, Alice didn't ever want to see another piece of cake. At least she had been smart enough to take only one bite of each. Boomer and Bobbie had gotten into a contest, and judging by Boomer's greenish hue and uncharacteristic silence, he was losing.

A phone buzzed and Alice reached for hers, but it wasn't in her pocket.

"Sorry," Shawna said. "It's mine."

Alice felt a flash of panic as she patted herself down. She definitely didn't have her phone. "Has anyone seen my phone?" Her nervousness was quickly rising. What if Jack had been trying to call her? What if he needed her? She felt the cake threatening to make a reappearance.

"You were charging it in the Hummer," Bobbie said, slumped back in his chair.

Erica smiled in her cheerleader fashion. "Only two more pieces to go! I need everyone to hang in there for just a little bit longer."

Alice stood. "I'm sorry, Erica, I need to go to the bathroom."

"I'm so full, I may pop," Bobbie said, rubbing his stomach.

"Please, don't. And Alice, please hustle." Erica tapped her watch for emphasis.

"I'll be right back. The others can keep eating."

"I don't know if I can." Boomer set his fork down.

"Are you giving up?" Bobbie held up a hand in victory. "I win!"

"Not yet." Boomer picked his fork back up, wincing as he clutched his stomach. "Bring on the pain."

"Men." Alice chuckled as she hurried down the hallway. She made a quick pit stop in the ladies' room and then headed out the front door to get her phone and check if Jack had called. She opened the Hummer's passenger door and grinned. A long box sat on the front seat and a small white envelope lay on top. She unplugged her phone from the charger and picked up the envelope. It read, *For the Bride.*

She checked her voice mails. Jack had called three times and texted her four times.

Just checking on you.

Is everything okay?

You're supposed to keep your phone on.

Call me now or I'm coming over there!

The last text had come in only a minute ago. She speed-dialed Jack as she opened the envelope and pulled out the little card. On the front was a picture of a diamond wedding ring, and inside, typed text read: DIAMONDS ARE A GIRL'S BEST FRIEND. A red line was drawn through the word DIAMONDS.

Jack's phone rang only once before he picked up. "Alice? Where are you?"

"Sorry!" Alice set the card on the seat. "I forgot my phone in Bobbie's car."

"That totally goes against the safety rules. I agreed to this, but you promised me that you'd be careful."

"I am being careful. And thank you for my present." Alice grabbed the long box.

"What present? Stop!"

Jack's panicked warning startled her so badly that she dropped the lower half of the box, but her left hand held on to the lid. The box landed open on the seat.

"Alice! Alice!" Jack yelled. "Don't open anything! I didn't give you a present!"

Alice's breath was coming in short little puffs. She wanted to say something. To tell Jack she was okay. But no words were coming out.

Inside the long box was a single rose. It had been dead for a long time, but like potpourri, a faint tinge of color highlighted the bud and stem. There was another card inside the box, white, the size of a business card. Written on it in red letters were the words

FOREVER MINE.

CHAPTER

21

The Charger skidded to a stop outside the bakery and Jack jumped out. He scanned the parking lot. Alice was standing beside Bobbie's Hummer, leaning against the door and rubbing her temples, while Bobbie, Boomer, Shawna, and Erica had congregated outside the door of the bakery.

Alice rushed up to him and threw her arms around him.

"I'm glad you're alright," Jack said, pulling her closer.

"I'm fine. Where's Lady?"

"She's at home. Mrs. Stevens is watching her." Jack took Alice by the elbow and led her away from the car. "Why did you open the box?"

"I thought it was a gift from you," she said, flustered and overwhelmed, a lump in her throat making her choke out the words.

Jack took a deep breath, looked suspiciously at the Hummer, and led her an additional twenty feet away.

"What are you doing?" Alice asked.

"He could have left something else, too. Maybe something under the car. I need to contact the bomb squad."

"Jack?" Alice's hand on his elbow made him stop pacing. "I'm fine. You need to dial it back a bit." She glanced around, making sure no one had reacted to the "bomb" buzzword.

Jack ran both hands through his hair and glared up at the blue sky. She was right. Freaking out wouldn't help anything. He closed his eyes, took a deep breath, and exhaled. "Okay. Tell me what happened."

"We were at the cake tasting and I realized that I left my phone in the Hummer."

"So, you and Bobbie and Boomer came out to get it?"

"Just me."

"What do you mean, just you?" Jack's voice rose.

"I was just going outside for a minute—"

"There is no 'just going outside'!" Jack fumed. "A killer has you in his crosshairs. Don't you get that? He's killed at least two women already, probably more, and now he wants to kill you." Jack marched over to Bobbie. "You let her walk out to the car alone?"

"I screwed up. I own it," Bobbie G. admitted.

Boomer nodded. "Bobbie should have gone with her."

Shawna smacked him in the back of the head. "No, one of us should have gone out and gotten Alice's phone for her while she waited safely inside the bakery."

Jack turned to Alice.

"I didn't tell them I was going to get my phone, Jack," Alice admitted looking down at her feet.

"You know better than this, Alice, and we had a deal."

"I'm sorry. I have been so preoccupied with the wedding stuff." Her eyes welled with tears. "It's as if I checked out of our life weeks ago and into some weird bride-o-sphere where nothing else matters but dresses, flowers, and cake, with someone taking six million pictures of my every move."

"You have got to get your head in the game. You're a target! And when I arrived just now, why were you standing next to the Hummer by yourself and not with everyone else?" Not waiting for an answer, he glared at his friends. "Do you guys realize just how close this guy got to her? What would have happened if Alice came face-to-face with this nut while he was putting the box in the Hummer? Do you realize that if that had been an explosive device, she'd be dead right now?"

Two police cruisers with lights blazing pulled into the parking lot behind Jack. Morrison opened his door with a scowl, but Officer Kendra Darcey jumped out of the other cruiser and laughed. "Man, you can drive," she said to Jack. The twenty-five-year-old wore her blonde hair pulled back in a ponytail, not trying to hide the four-inch scar which ran from the corner of her chin to her eyebrow, and her blue eyes seemed to glow from some constant energy source within. "You lost us on the first turn and then you went down Jefferson like a bat outta—"

Morrison turned to her with a raised eyebrow and she cut herself off.

"I brought you onto this case as a courtesy, Jack," Morrison said. "Your speed—"

"Was reckless, and I apologize. I was wrong, and it won't happen again."

Morrison looked ready to say something more, but instead looked at Alice. "Are you okay?"

She nodded. "Just a little freaked out."

"Who wouldn't be? Is this the car?" Morrison pointed at the Hummer.

"It is," Jack said. "You know Bobbie Gibson, right? It's his."

Morrison shook Bobbie's hand. "I'm afraid we'll need to process your car as a crime scene."

"Do whatever you gotta do," Bobbie replied.

As Kendra returned to her cruiser to get the equipment, Jack and Morrison walked with Alice over to the Hummer. The passenger door was still open. The long flower box was on the seat, and the lid and a card lay on the floor mat.

"There are two cards," Alice said. "I dropped one, and the other is still in the box."

Jack looked inside the box. The card lay on top of a dried rose. FOREVER MINE was written in red on the front. He took out a pencil and used it to flip the card over.

A poem was written on the back, in charcoal pencil.

Always watching
Never seen
I was there
The day of their dreams
They remember the moment
But never me
Closer than breath
I was waiting
But they all forgot
So I came calling

"I didn't think a dead rose could get creepier," Alice said as she read the card. "But the bad poem pushed it over the edge."

"This killer is insane." Jack dropped the card back down. "What's the ETA on the crime scene?" he asked Morrison.

"On the way. So are Thomas and Castillo."

"You need to assign police protection to Alice."

"What?" Alice shook her head. "No. I have all the protection I need." She nodded to the others, who were walking over.

"I agree with Alice," Boomer said. He quickly ducked and held up a warning hand at Shawna. "Stop hitting me."

Bobbie G. stepped forward. "I'm sorry I let you down, Jack. I messed up. It won't happen again."

"It's not that, Bobbie. This guy is evil crazy. The two women in the morgue were just the tip of the iceberg. This is about as bad as it gets. I still want the three of you to watch over Alice, but even that isn't enough. For any of you. You need more eyes—and another gun."

Boomer stepped away from Shawna a couple of feet. "Are we talking 'eating people' type crazy?"

Bobbie smacked him in the head. "You watch too many movies."

"Both of you stop hitting me!" Boomer tried to push Bobbie, but he didn't budge.

"I'm not going into hiding," Alice said firmly, despite looking absolutely deflated.

"I'm not suggesting that," Jack said. "But look, the guy was brazen enough to leave a box in Bobbie's car in broad daylight."

Alice's head darted around like a bird's as she scanned the area.

Jack smiled. "The police will go to every business around here and see if they have cameras."

"You knew what I was thinking?" Alice said.

He nodded. "And I know that you won't cancel the wedding. But I'm requesting a police detail."

"You have it," Morrison said. "Consider it authorized. I'm going back to the station to coordinate the team from there."

When Morrison was out of earshot, Boomer chuckled. "No way. I never thought I'd be working with the cops."

"I don't know why you're smiling so much," Shawna said. "This crazy guy wants to kill Alice. And in order to get to her, he's gotta go through you first."

CHAPTER

22

Jack waited by Bobbie's Hummer as Castillo and Agent Thomas approached. "We finished canvassing the surrounding businesses. Not one camera," Castillo announced with frustration.

"And zero witnesses," Thomas added.

"And no fingerprints found on the car other than the owner's and known occupants'," Jack said. A crime scene team had come in and gone over everything, with Jack watching closely. "Whoever left the package in the car was wearing gloves, and the gloves removed the existing fingerprints on the door handle."

"So we have a generic card, in a generic box, with a dead rose and a poem. No witnesses and no forensic evidence," said Castillo glumly.

"We know someone is watching Alice. Or at least they know her schedule," Jack said. "They knew she was here and that she was riding in Boomer's car."

Thomas took a deep breath and stared at the bakery. "The guy has some serious guts. Either that or he just doesn't care about being seen. Look at those windows."

Jack turned to the bakery. The entire front was glass from knee height to the ceiling.

"How could no one have seen anything?" Castillo scowled.

"They were busy working," Jack said. "And the kitchen is in the back."

"But the killer didn't know that. They'd have to think there was a chance of getting seen."

"I agree." Thomas crossed his arms. "They're not afraid to take chances."

"How many women in the sketches have been identified?" Jack asked.

Thomas took out his tablet and pulled up a photo of the sketches on the wall. "There were fourteen sketches at the scene; we've now identified eleven of them. Excluding your fiancée, the identified women are all missing persons." He pressed a button, and red squares appeared around all the sketches that had been identified. "These women are known to be missing. But this is interesting." He pressed another button, and blue squares appeared around the three unidentified sketches. "These three women are not in the missing person files."

The three blue squares were all off to one side, and all in a row. Grouped together, as if in a different category.

Castillo said what Jack already knew and had been dreading. "They're targets."

"We have to identify these three women quickly," Jack said, his gut twisting. "We need to get more eyes on it. You need to go to the media."

"And start a panic? That's the last thing we need right now," Thomas said.

"The way social media blows up every news story," Castillo chimed in, "we'd have so many people claiming to be from news organizations they'd swamp the investigation."

"What's the alternative? Leave the women uninformed and unprotected? That's just wrong," Jack said.

"The media is not our friend right now, Stratton," Thomas said. "And I'm certain the sheriff will agree with me."

Castillo moved between the two men, trying to play peacemaker. "There are other ways we can identify the women. I know you said the feds' facial recognition software isn't quite there yet, but it's got to at least be worth a shot."

Jack shook his head. "Enhancements have been made to the FBI's Next Generation Identification Program to include facial recognition, but there's a case backlog on that. I already checked. Besides, it's not going to do well with sketches. The odds of making a match from a sketch are very low—probably less than ten percent. And it adds significantly to the time of the search. Weeks, if not months, or so I was told."

"You contacted the FBI?" Thomas bit his lip. "I was warned about you, Stratton. They said you fly off the handle. That you strike out on your own. Are you going to prove them right?"

"You're FBI, so I'm sure you checked me out thoroughly," Jack responded. "Which means you're aware of the case concerning my foster sister, Michelle Carter. When our foster mother filed a missing person report, Michelle had already been missing for two weeks, and do you know what the officer told her regarding this straight-A, hardworking college kid? 'Give her a week or two and she'll come home. Probably looking for money. They always do.' I'm not flying off any handle. I know what it's like to have someone you love out there, missing. The wait is indescribable." The void in Jack's chest returned in a flash. "And I know the pain of my sister getting murdered. Do I blame the police for not saving her? No, I don't. Do I feel that they didn't take it seriously enough at the beginning? Yes. And rightfully so."

"I came across your foster sister's case when reviewing your file, Stratton. And I'm sorry for your loss. But you can't let it cloud your judgment on this case." Thomas looked at Jack with an expression that seemed to say, *I have an answer—the only right answer.*

Jack stuffed down his growing frustration and chose his words very carefully. "Not trying to find these women as quickly as possible, by any means possible, is flat-out wrong. But if you don't care about that"—Jack held up a hand, cutting off Thomas's protests—"then look at it this way. You think the media is a problem now? What will the media do to you if you don't do everything in your power to warn these women . . . and then something happens to one of them?"

Castillo nodded slowly, letting the words roll around in his mouth before responding. "Agent Thomas . . . I have to say, I agree with Stratton."

"Well, it's a good thing neither of you is running this investigation," Thomas snapped.

Castillo looked taken aback. But he quickly recovered. "I'm taking this to Morrison."

"Great," said Thomas, calling Castillo's bluff. "Let's go speak with him together and see what his decision is." He started walking to his car.

"Thanks for trying," Jack said. Castillo gave him a curt nod before following Thomas.

As Jack watched them walk away, the anxiety that he had pushed down exploded to the surface. His hand twisted into a tight fist, knuckles turning white. The political part of police work was raising its ugly head, and he wanted to kill it.

Funding. Budgets. Elections. He knew those things would sit on one side of the scale, and that Morrison would balance them against the things that really mattered. Justice. Protection. Service.

If Morrison said no, Jack knew what the right thing to do would be. But what price would he pay for doing it?

CHAPTER

23

I should try to let my anger at Jack go. It's not his fault, really. He's just doing what he was made to do. He's a protector. A guardian. Would I yell at the sea if a wave knocked down my sandcastle?

I would. I'd curse and I'd throw stones at it, but the sea would keep on being the sea.

Jack will keep being Jack, but he can't stop me. Because I, too, am only doing what I was born to do.

I'm an artist.

And the two I picked out were perfect. Now I need two more.

Stupid Jack Stratton.

The dust tickles my nose. I hold my finger up and fight it back. I can't sneeze. Mrs. Hershberger would hear me. She really should clean her closet. The smell of mold is just horrid in here.

There she is. It's so strange watching someone through these slats. They're angled slightly down, so I don't think she can see me. Besides, her glasses are thick. She's old. I should be fine.

Her tea is still on the coffee table, untouched. Tendrils of steam long gone.

Pity.

I still don't know the right mix. I thought I had it right, but Mrs. Fulcher died. I diluted it a little today.

In the darkness, my fingers close around the handle of my backup plan, the Taser. I wanted one that shoots out those needles, like Alice's. Hers is pink. The two leads with barbs are attached to a beautiful thin silver wire. Confetti even pops out when you fire it, like a party. I smile but it fades.

Mine doesn't shoot. No confetti either. But it has the prettiest blue glow. A cross between cobalt and azure. And it crackles. Still, I hope I don't have to use it. I don't like it when they fight, or cry. The crying is the worst part.

It hurts my ears, but not my heart.

I couldn't care less if they beg. I don't have a choice. Art demands sacrifice.

I'll have to pick up a taser like Alice's.

Mrs. Hershberger comes back into the living room. She's humming now. Tidying up the place. Pillows over here? Pile them up at the end of the couch? No, move them so they appear to be tossed all around, but make sure to arrange them so all of the cute little sayings embroidered on them are clearly visible.

Blah.

Drink your tea. I need to get to work.

There's still so much to do to get ready for Alice's wedding. Though I really should stop calling it that. After all, it won't be the wedding she's expecting, and it will be at my church, so I really should call it my wedding.

The Wedding.

The title for my work of art finally hits me, and my knees go a little weak. I put out my hand to steady myself, and bump into something in the darkness.

Mrs. Hershberger stops her manic tidying.

"The Wedding." It's perfect!

Mrs. Hershberger is peering at the closet now.

Does she see me? Does she sense me?

It's not just any wedding. It's The Wedding, the one that all others will be compared to. Fifty brides from fifty years, plus the one about to say "I do."

My masterpiece.

Mrs. Hershberger is close to the closet now. She's leaning forward. Reaching for the door handle. I can hear her breathing.

I hold my breath. My fingers tighten on the Taser.

The phone in the living room rings.

She jumps with a start, and so do I.

Hand to her chest, eyes wide, cheeks flushed. A beautiful shade of red. I'll have to remember it in my sketches.

She hurries to the phone and I start breathing again.

"Amy, you startled me to no end," she answers, glancing down at her tea.

Drink the stupid tea. I almost whisper my thought aloud.

She's listening. Wetting her lips. She leans down and picks it up.

"What? Oh, you have to be kidding. I'm so sorry for you." She's standing stiffly now. Listening. The cup slowly rises. She takes a sip. Licks her lips and gulps down another.

Finally, something is going right for me.

"Now?" Mrs. Hershberger sets the cup down. "No, it's not too late. Fifteen minutes? Certainly. I'll be waiting."

In the darkness I'm fuming. It will take twenty minutes for the medicine to make her go to sleep. Now I have to do this the hard way.

Mrs. Hershberger comes back into the room carrying a flowerpot.

I reach out and bump whatever it was that I hit before. It pushes against the wall.

Mrs. Hershberger turns around. She's more aggravated than frightened this time as she marches forward, grabs a handle in each hand, and yanks the gull-wing doors open.

My Taser crackles and the prettiest blue light flashes like indigo lightning.

The look on Mrs. Hershberger's face is one of horror and pain. Part of me wants to be sorry, but . . . in art there must be sacrifice.

CHAPTER

24

Jack walked through the doors of the sheriff's department and headed straight to Morrison's office, hoping to beat Thomas there. The station house was oddly quiet. He'd heard that emergency calls were down thirty percent last week—a huge drop. Statisticians might speculate over the cause, but Jack had his own theory: evil had a hierarchy. It was like when a great white moves into an area to start hunting. The other predators, without even seeing the shark, flee. They sense a more ruthless killer and, like most bullies, are scared of a real fight.

Through the window, he saw Thomas in Sheriff Morrison's office. He was poised and relaxed. *Not a good sign.* Jack waited, leaning against the empty cubicle used by patrol officers to fill out their reports. He used to hate sitting in there. He detested the endless hours of paperwork that came with each and every shift. *I'd give my right arm to be in that seat now.*

Jack didn't even try to lay odds on what the sheriff would do. It could go either way. He just tried to be patient, and not look in Morrison's office again. But in spite of his best efforts, he peeked. Morrison caught Jack's eye, and Thomas turned to look at Jack, too.

Thomas smiled—and Jack had his answer. His jaw flexed and he started for the door as Thomas was leaving.

"Jack." Thomas held the door open as Jack marched by.

Jack stopped at Morrison's desk, rigid and at attention, a force of habit. "Sir."

"Sheriff Collins made you do that, son. I don't. Take a seat." Morrison shuffled the paperwork around on his desk, apparently debating how to begin the conversation. The room smelled of fresh coffee, though it looked like it had yet to take effect on the tired man. "I've weighed both sides of the situation." He looked up. "Thomas is working up a profile of our killer and running the three unidentified sketches through the FBI facial recognition program."

"That won't be fast enough. We need an answer now."

"We always want an answer right away. But this is police work. It takes time. You know that as well as anyone."

"With all due respect, sir, we need to go to the media. Put the pictures out there so we can warn these women."

"Look, Jack." Morrison sat forward, resting his elbows on his desk. "Going to the media is a double-edged sword. I feel we should give Thomas a chance first."

"I don't agree with that decision, sir. I know the reporting hasn't been exactly fair—"

Morrison slammed his hand on his desk, making Jack's heart race. Sudden and loud noises still had that effect. "It's been downright lies. They've already driven Cunningham and Dwyer out of office. Mary Dwyer was on the town board for twenty years! Those reports made her look like a fool. How are we to know how the media would spin this? They could report that a serial killer is out there and not even show the sketches. We have no control over them."

"We could make them agree to terms that—"

"That's where you're wrong, Jack. They hide behind 'journalistic freedom' now. They could promise us that they'll show the sketches and go back on their promise just as fast by claiming freedom of the press."

"But sir—"

Morrison sat up in his chair, his back rigid and his jaw set. "I'll rethink using the media—but first I'm going to give Thomas more time. End of discussion. Go home and get some sleep. That's an order."

Jack stood. There was more that he wanted to say, but he could see now that it would be pointless, like talking to a wall. Morrison had made up his mind, and no amount of arguing would change that.

Jack had already decided what he was going to do, too.

CHAPTER

25

J ack waited outside the hotel room door with his hand up and
ready to knock, but he hesitated.

I need her help. We're still friends; there's nothing wrong with asking—

The door opened, and Marisa stood there smiling at him. "I got
tired of waiting for you to bend your wrist and knock. How did Alice
ever get you to bend your knee?"

Jack felt color rush to his cheeks as he lowered his arm. "You
knew I was out here?"

She placed a delicate hand over her heart. "I felt you."

"Like sonar?" Jack joked.

"Maybe." Marisa stepped aside to let him in. "Are you allowed
to come in?"

Jack didn't know if that was a dig or a legitimate question, but it
made him think of Alice and whether she would agree to Jack seeing
Marisa in her hotel room.

*Maybe? Who am I kidding? If I asked Alice, the answer would be a flat-
out NO. That's why I didn't ask.*

He stepped into the room and was relieved to see that it was a
two-room suite, with the bedroom separate. It was some small
comfort knowing he wasn't alone in a room with Marisa and a bed.
Not that that would carry much weight with Alice or that the lack of
a bed had ever stopped Marisa.

"Thanks for meeting with me this morning. I need your help."

"Again?"

Jack smiled. Marisa had helped him several times in the past, even when they weren't on the best terms. When he'd needed her, she'd always been there for him.

"It's about those sketches."

"The ones you thought were almost as good as mine?"

"I'll apologize again if it makes you feel better."

"It might." She smiled impishly. "You can try."

"I thought you didn't like it when a man begs."

"Did I say that?" She winked.

Jack crossed his arms. "You're the best artist on the planet as far as I'm concerned. And I mean that."

"You know the way to touch my soul, Jack Stratton." She stepped toward him and stopped just a little too close. She smelled of bergamot and roses. "What can I do to help?"

Jack shook his head as if to rid it of the explicit memories her intoxicating fragrance evoked. "Clean up one of the sketches." Jack wiped the sweat that had begun to form from his brow. "It has blood on it that obscures part of the woman's face." Jack pulled out his phone and showed the photograph of the sketch to Marisa.

Her eyes narrowed. "I've never been squeamish around blood, and I'm totally desensitized after running the tattoo shop, but I do hate it when art is defiled. You're right, this sketch is good."

"Can you scan in the picture and remove the bloodstains? Is that possible?"

"I can do one better—I can re-create the sketch. But it'll take a little while." Marisa gazed up at him underneath her long lashes. "Would you like some coffee? I have brandy."

The truth was, Jack would love a good stiff drink. But he couldn't right now, not with all that was going on, and especially not in a hotel room alone with Marisa. "Coffee, please. But I'll pass on the brandy."

Marisa walked over to the bedroom door and stopped, one hand on the doorframe. "Make yourself comfortable. I'll be right back." Her sensual smile was dangerously beautiful, like that of a mythological siren. *If she starts singing, I'm running for the door.*

Jack looked around the hotel room as he waited. It was immaculate; either she hadn't spent any time here, or housekeeping had just come through. The television remote was still in its place, the welcome card was still on the coffee table. Jack looked through the door to the bathroom and saw that the toilet paper still had the fold at the end of the roll making it into a crisp triangle.

He had sat down at the desk and was lost in thought when Marisa touched his shoulder. He jumped a little.

"Sorry." She was carrying an artist sketchpad and some pencils. She set them down on the coffee table in front of the couch, then walked into the kitchenette. "I didn't mean to startle you. It's the artist in me. Always watching. Never seen." She opened a cabinet and removed two coffee cups and a bottle of brandy. A coffeemaker sat on the counter, and she poured a cup for each of them, never taking her eyes off Jack. To hers, she added a splash of liqueur.

He watched her every move. Every gesture, every motion, was filled with a fluid grace. Unhurried. Refined. He wondered if he could ever tire of watching Marisa. She had an innate elegance about her that would captivate anyone. She was like a ballet dancer; you'd have to be an idiot not to admire her beauty.

She crossed over to the couch, taking a sip as she went. She sat down and put the coffee cups on coasters before picking up the sketchpad and pencil. She lifted her eyes to Jack expectantly.

"What?"

"Well, I was hoping you would come over and join me. A woman likes to feel wanted, even if she's just a friend. Besides, I need to see the original sketch."

Jack held the phone out.

She didn't move to take it. Instead she glanced down at the spot on the couch next to her. "Would you mind holding it for me? I can't sketch and hold the phone at the same time."

"Of course." Jack sat down at the end of the couch opposite Marisa and held the phone at arm's length.

Marisa smiled slyly as she started to draw. Jack soon understood why. After only a few minutes of holding his arm straight out, he began to tire. A few minutes more and his hand was shaking.

Marisa's smile grew. "Slide in closer. Rest your elbow on the back of the couch and your hand on this pillow." She propped a pillow up next to her thigh.

Jack slid closer, and the temperature in the room felt like it rose fifteen degrees. There was no way he could touch the cup of hot coffee now. The phone screen went dark and he swiped it to activate it again. He tried to sneak a peek at Marisa's sketchpad, but she held the pad up against her chest and scowled. "No peeking."

"I want to make sure that the picture just *looks* like the original. Not too good."

Marisa chuckled. "I can fake anything. In fact, if I wanted to sway to the dark side, I think I could find a new career as a forger. I'll match it exactly. But the person who drew this sketch is very good. Exceptional, actually."

"Would you consider it professional?"

"If you mean, does this person make a living with their art, that's difficult to say. It would also be difficult to say if they went to school specifically for art. It's undeniable that they have talent, however. A gift."

"When you're done, I'd like to show you the other sketches and see if you can tell me anything from them. I took several close-ups of the paper and some of the art supplies I found in the killer's closet."

"Certainly." Marisa set her pencil down.

"We can wait until you're finished with the sketch," Jack said.

Marisa crossed her legs and smiled. "I'm finished." She turned the sketchpad around.

Jack was floored. It was a perfect duplicate of the original. He glanced back and forth between his phone and the sketch. "How did you do that so fast?"

"Do you like it? I think it's a very close likeness."

"Close? It's perfect."

Marisa handed him the sketchpad. "I'm glad you are pleased with it." She placed her left hand on his arm and took his phone. Zooming in on the picture, she studied the details of the sketch for a moment and then nodded, seemingly satisfied.

Jack went to stand up, but Marisa placed a restraining hand on his thigh. "Didn't you want to show me something else?"

"Oh—yes." Jack's voice was slightly higher than normal. His eyes darted down to her hand on his thigh, then met hers.

"Forgive me." Marisa slowly removed her hand and folded it with the other hand demurely in her lap.

Jack took his phone back and pulled up the close-ups. "Can you tell me if anything stands out to you regarding the paper, or perhaps the charcoal used?"

Marisa took another sip of coffee, placed her cup back on the table, then shifted so she was looking down at his phone.

Jack held the phone in his right hand so he could scroll with his left. Marisa leaned forward to stare intently at the screen, her right hand coming up to cup his hand in hers. A bead of sweat rolled down Jack's back.

After several minutes, Marisa leaned back and shook her head. "It looks like a charcoal pencil and ordinary sketching paper, similar to the paper in my pad." She nudged her sketchpad on the table with her foot. "The art supplies are generic. You could pick them up in any art, craft, or hobby store."

Jack nodded and scooted away a few inches. "I appreciate all your help, Marisa."

"What are you going to do?"

Jack thought for a minute before answering. "I'm going to share the sketches with the news media. Morrison wants to wait, but I don't think we can afford to."

Marisa took another sip of coffee and stared at Jack with her signature Mona Lisa smile. It was times like these where he wished he could read her mind, because he had no idea what she was thinking.

"Aren't you going to warn me about burning my bridges?"

Marisa raised an eyebrow. "Why? I might as well ask the flower why it opens when the sun comes out. You're doing what you think is right. I can't stop you—no one can. It's one of the things that I love about you."

Jack swallowed. He gave a little nod that came off more like a bow as he tried to hide his embarrassment. "Thank you again for the sketch." He glanced down at the picture in his hand and froze.

"What's the matter?" Marisa set down her drink.

"You drew three freckles on her cheek. But the original didn't have them."

Marisa reached out her hand. "May I see the original again?"

Jack took out his phone and pulled up the sketch. He pointed to the woman's cheek. No freckles, just some blood splatter.

Marisa took the phone and zoomed in. "There. Beneath the blood you can see the freckles."

Jack squinted and nodded. "I see them now. It was just the light." But the truth was, he didn't see the freckles. He stared at the photo, trying to force them to appear, but they wouldn't. Maybe they were just too faded for him to see them clearly, or his eyes were tired. Marisa saw them, so they had to be there. Right?

He forced a smile as he rose and walked to the door. "Thanks again."

"Are you going to be at the photo session tomorrow?"

"The what?"

Marisa rolled her eyes. "It's on the wedding schedule," she said. "I'm just going to lend a hand. All the bridesmaids are supposed to be there. Well, except Kiku. Alice said she won't be able to make it."

"Did Alice say if Kiku is still coming to the wedding?"

"I believe so. So—tomorrow?"

"I'll try to stop by."

Jack lied again, and again was unsure why. When he left the room and the door clicked closed behind him, he was gasping for breath. It wasn't just the freckles—the freckles that Jack couldn't see but Marisa somehow knew were underneath the blood. It was what Marisa said earlier, when she came out of the bedroom.

"'I didn't mean to startle you. It's the artist in me. *Always watching. Never seen.*"

The opening lines of the note the killer left for Alice.

CHAPTER

26

As Jack started up the Charger and drove across town to the Channel 5 TV station for his meeting with Paula Thompson, sweat was pouring down his back. The encounter with Marisa had left him wondering if he could trust anyone, and now he felt like he was betraying Morrison, but what choice did he have? Thomas had his opinion, and Morrison had backed it. And Jack was convinced they were both dead wrong. The safety of those women was at stake. If Jack didn't warn them, and something happened . . . Alice smiled down at him from the photo on his visor and he repeated his vow to protect her.

He parked across the street from the building and unlocked his doors. A minute later, Paula Thompson got into the passenger seat and shut the door.

"I was surprised to receive your call," she said.

"I was surprised to make it," Jack said drily. "Look, I know I'm asking for a huge favor here, but I need to remain anonymous."

"Of course. I would never reveal a source."

"I'm not telling you how to do your job, but the last thing we need to do is start a panic."

"I take it that this meeting is off the record and the police don't know you're here?"

Jack nodded and cleared his throat. "Sheriff Morrison is a good man. But there's a situation, and I need your help." He handed her copies of the three sketches, including the one Marisa had drawn.

"These women's lives are in danger. They're potential targets, and we haven't been able to identify them."

"Is this related to the two bodies you found on Buck Mountain?"

Jack's jaw flexed. "I'll lay it all out to you off the record, but first I need one more assurance."

"Which is?"

"You'll run this story tonight as part of the Channel 5 Investigation Team series. You'll say your investigating has revealed that these three women's lives are in danger and you need the viewers' help identifying them. Don't mention that it has anything to do with a police investigation."

"You're worried that you'll be kicked off the investigation," Paula said. It was a statement, not a question.

"Yes. Morrison has allowed me to be a consultant, for now, but that can change in a heartbeat."

"He brought you in because of your fiancée." Paula twisted the wedding ring on her left hand. She must have picked up on Jack's surprise that she knew. "I have other sources in the police department. You're risking a lot giving me these."

"I'm torn about it," Jack admitted, rubbing the spot of tension behind his head. "Sheriff Morrison is a good man. I don't want this to come back negatively on him. He's brought in a profiler—Special Agent Frank Thomas, FBI. He doesn't care for the press."

Paula shrugged. "The feds usually don't."

"He doesn't feel the gravity of the situation. These women are targets of a killer. They have a right to know that. Before there's another murder."

Paula glanced down at her wedding ring and smiled ruefully. "I know that journalists are . . . unpopular with the police these days. But I have nothing against law enforcement. And the last thing I want to do is sow unwarranted panic. You may not believe it, but there are reporters who still have journalistic integrity. And . . ." She looked down at her glistening ring again. "My husband passed away four years ago. Heart attack. But . . . he was a cop."

Jack felt his eyes widen. "I'm sorry. I didn't know."

She shrugged. "I don't mention it to many people. I was going to tell the sheriff when he was railing against my defense of the freedom of the press and my 'bias' against the police. But it felt cheap bringing it up then. It hurt. I'm not anti-police." She reached over and squeezed Jack's hand.

He didn't expect the sudden contact, the sudden empathy. It moved him. And so did her story. He had misjudged Paula. Badly. "I apologize," he said simply.

She squeezed his hand again and reached for the door handle. "No need. Just don't think I'm on the same level as an ambulance chaser or tax collector." She opened the door but didn't get out. "I understand your need to protect your fiancée, the sheriff, and yourself. And I respect what you're trying to do for these women. I'll do the best I can."

Jack watched her walk back to the news building. He had been wrong about her. Prejudiced, actually. It was a behavior he hated, yet he'd let himself slip into it.

His guilt shifted to fear, his heart skipping a beat. If he was wrong about Paula, was he making the same mistake about Marisa?

CHAPTER

27

When I see Jack, I'll have to congratulate him. Bringing Alice back to his old neighborhood so his friends could babysit her was sheer genius.

The residents know that I'm not from Darrington, and they make me feel it, too. Their distrust of outsiders is palpable. Everyone watches me as I drive down the street. All heads turn to look. I feel their eyes bore into me. I don't meet their gaze. I try to act as natural as possible.

It's a bit of a thrill, really. My stomach flutters with this unexpected twist. It's the same feeling I get when I walk too close to the edge of someplace high. I'm walking on the razor's edge now. They're looking right at me. They judge me. Am I a threat? Then I see the answer written on their faces. No. They dismiss me.

They think I'm weak. They believe they're stronger than me. They think they have nothing to fear, but they're so wrong. They have no idea what I'm capable of. After all, how many have I taken? The ones I found don't count. By the time I'm done collecting, I'll have fifty guests at The Wedding. Alice and Aunt Haddie will make fifty-two.

And the others? I can count them too, can't I? All the husbands who vainly tried to protect their wives from me. The children who, instead of running, wanted to help their mothers.

No. I can't count them.

I hide my smile in a blank expression. Let the world think less of me—they already do anyway. Artists are never really appreciated.

I roll to a stop at the traffic light, and my thoughts drift back to Jack.

I can see his face if I close my eyes. It's a handsome face. Expressive. I should sketch his many different looks, thousands of different faces. There's a confidence there that must be captured. An underlying one. It's been growing. I've underestimated him. I didn't think Jack would move Alice as quickly as he did. I never believed he'd allow her to leave his side with someone like me in pursuit.

That was a foolish mistake on his part. They're stronger together. Still, his strength worries me, I'll admit. His intelligence intimidates me. But it's the raw power of the emotions churning inside him that really scares me.

His childhood was much harsher than mine. No one could escape that without scars. But you can't see Jack's scars, except the rough one that encircles his wrist. He took all that pain and hurt and buried it. It's like spent nuclear waste. Buried. It usually leaks out and kills people. But Jack has found some way to use that hate and pain as a kind of fuel. Is that what drives him? Is that why he won't give up?

I wonder what will happen to all that pent-up hate once I kill Alice. Will he be able to hold back that rage? Or will it break free from its cage and rip Jack apart?

I drive through the green light but only make it a block before the next street light turns red. I stop. More people stare. I don't meet their gaze. I keep my eyes forward like most people in this neighborhood.

This is the fourth time I've driven around Shawna's apartment. I've seen the same man twice now. He looks at me suspiciously. I take out my phone and pretend to look at some unseen map— puzzled that my GPS has let me down. I like this game. Will he believe my acting?

He seems to buy it and goes on his way. But I can't make another loop around the building now. If he saw me again, what would he do? I'll never know.

I take a left instead, and head for the highway. It was nice being so close to Alice, if only for a moment. I picture her often, pretty and sweet, perfect proportions too, an artist's dream. Did she feel my presence? I hope so. She's as busy as I am getting ready for the wedding. There's still so much to do.

I pick up my phone, to use it for real this time. I bring up my software. The screen blinks and flashes as it makes the connection to the cameras I mounted inside. My church is quiet. The people sit silently in the pews, waiting for The Wedding to start. With a touch of my thumb I can check on my art from anywhere in the world. The Internet is truly a gift. A microphone allows me to listen in. I love listening almost as much as I love watching, and it's so quiet here. But when the time comes, there's a speaker so I can speak to my guests right from my phone.

It's that special moment right before a wedding, where everyone is waiting. The anticipation is building. The bride will soon be here.

And there's nothing Jack Stratton can do to stop me.

CHAPTER

28

Alice listened patiently as Erica went through the upcoming schedule of events. They were gathered in Shawna's apartment, which was smaller than Jack's and had a cozy feel, thanks to all the family pictures; it reminded her of Aunt Haddie's a little. It was nice, and a welcome change from cake tasting and dress fittings and photoshoots, but it did little to improve her mood. There just seemed to be no end to it all. Every minute of every day before the wedding was packed and planned.

As Erica prattled on, Alice's phone buzzed. It was Mrs. Stevens, their friend and landlady. "Sorry, Erica. I have to take this," Alice said as she got up and moved toward the kitchen.

Bobbie G., Boomer, Shawna, and Kendra Murphy, the sheriff's deputy assigned to protect Alice, all rose. Alice didn't know if they were that eager to guard her or simply eager for an excuse to get out of the room, too.

"One second, Mrs. Stevens." Alice covered the phone. "Guys, I'm just going into the kitchen—alone."

The others sat back down, except for Kendra, who pushed open the kitchen door and scanned the small room. It was just a tiny functional kitchen: fridge, oven, dishwasher crammed in side by side, and a single window above the two-chair table.

"There's only the one door," Alice said, trying to smile. "I'll be fine."

"Stay away from the window," Kendra instructed.

Alice was relieved to close the kitchen door behind her and get a moment of privacy. Kendra was a great cop, but she was acting as though she were protecting the president.

"Hi, Mrs. Stevens. Is everything okay?"

"Yes, dear. Lady and I are having a ball, but you sound sad. Are you all right?"

"I'm fine," Alice lied, trying to keep her voice steady. "Just a little frazzled with all the wedding plans and everything else going on."

Jack had told Mrs. Stevens about the sketches and the wedding invitation pinned to the killer's wall. Mrs. Stevens was keeping an eye on Lady while also watching their apartment for anyone suspicious.

"Well . . ." Mrs. Stevens cleared her throat. "The last thing I want to do is add to your stress, but this older gentleman and his daughter have stopped by a number of times. He said he's your uncle and asked me if I could give him your phone number. I refused, of course, but they asked if I would take their number and pass it on to you."

Alice's throat tightened; her eyes burned with unshed tears. Between the wedding planning and a killer stalking her, she hadn't reached out to her uncle yet. Maybe it was because she wanted to tell Jack first. Or maybe part of her just couldn't believe that she had a family. It didn't seem real. The memories that Alice had lost, they knew. Her great-uncle could tell her all the things about her parents that she wanted to know.

"One second, Mrs. Stevens." Alice scanned the cramped kitchen for a pen and spotted one on the magnetic pad hanging on the refrigerator. "Okay. What's their number?"

Mrs. Stevens read it off twice. "Are they really your relatives?" she asked, her voice thick with concern. "I don't mean to pry, but I thought all of your family . . . had passed on."

"I did, too." Alice exhaled. "But it's true. He's my great-uncle. My grandfather's brother."

"Oh, that's wonderful. I hope they didn't think it rude of me not to give them your number. But you and Jack always tell me to be careful. Especially now."

"And you should. You did great, Mrs. Stevens. I'm going to call them now."

"Give my love to Jack!"

Alice hung up and leaned wearily against the refrigerator. Right now, she'd like to give her own love to Jack. She missed everything about him. Closing her eyes, she imagined him wrapping his strong arms around her shoulders. She'd squeeze back and nuzzle up against his broad chest, inhale his warmth. . . "Soon," she whispered. Even though he wasn't there, just thinking about him had given her the boost she needed. She dialed the number Mrs. Stevens had just given her.

Her cousin answered. "This is Yana."

"Hiya, cuz." Alice decided to go the lighthearted, informal route.

"Alice!" Yana said her name in a way that made Alice feel missed and wanted all at the same time. "How are you?"

"Swamped." Alice chuckled. "In a good way. I'm planning my wedding and it's just been so crazy."

Yana laughed. "Maybe you should have eloped."

"Don't tempt me."

"I hate to impose . . ." Yana paused. "But my father really wants to see you again. There's so much he wants to tell you. He and your mother were very close . . . but I understand how busy you are."

"It's not just the wedding." Alice moved away from the kitchen door, then stepped to the side of the window, letting her eyes wander the streets. "It's really complicated."

"Is there any way you could see him? Just for a few minutes?"

"I want to see him too. But . . ." Alice closed her eyes, and she felt tears coming. She thought she'd lost her family, and now that she'd found them, she couldn't bear keeping them away. It wasn't that she didn't want to see her uncle. She really did. She was desperate to talk with him and find out more about her family. This was a chance that she'd dreamed of and yet had never expected would actually arrive.

"I'm in the city. Fairhaven Avenue." She gave Yana directions to get there and where to park.

"Excuse me one minute, Alice, let me tell Papa." She heard muffled voices on the other end. Then Yana came back on the line. "You made Papa's day. He's dancing around the living room. We'll be right over."

Alice smiled. "I can't wait."

As she hung up, she tried to brace herself for Erica's guilt trip. Her great-uncle's visit was sure to derail something "vital" that was scheduled. Taking a deep breath and squaring her shoulders, Alice walked back into the living room.

"That was my great-uncle. He's coming over with his daughter."

Erica shook her head. "Right now?"

"I don't know if you're allowed to have visitors," Kendra said, though her voice lacked conviction.

Alice crossed her arms. "I'm not under arrest."

"That's right," Boomer said. "This is America."

"Shut up, Boomer." Bobbie G. stood. "Kendra's just thinking about Alice's safety." He winked at Kendra, and she returned the gesture along with a smile.

Shawna got up, scowling. "Is Jack cool with this?"

"I haven't had the chance to talk to him. He doesn't even know they exist. I just found out myself." Alice crossed the room and flopped down onto a chair.

"Hold the phone, girlfriend." Shawna hurried over to her. "You'd better dish."

Alice explained to them all the events of meeting her great-uncle and cousin. When she was done, Erica's hand flew to her mouth.

"Are they coming to the wedding? Of course they are! Oh, no. The whole seating arrangement will have to change!" She scooped up her tablet, rushed to the bathroom, and slammed the door.

"That woman is really starting to freak out," Boomer said.

"Wait a second, Alice." Bobbie's voice was soft as he crouched down in front of her chair so his big brown eyes were level with hers. "You've never met them before now?"

"No, I did. Long ago. I don't remember my cousin, but I do remember my great-uncle. Why?"

Bobbie placed a huge hand on top of hers. "All I know is that I owe it to Chandler and Michelle to keep you safe. I've got no clue how to do that. Don't tell Jack this, but I keep thinking, what would he do? And when some great-uncle just happens to show up outta the blue while a killer is running around and drawing pictures of you— Well, I put all that through my Jack filter, and it makes me real nervous."

Alice squeezed his hand. "There's nothing to be nervous about. They're my family." She smiled, but it was short-lived. "And they'll be here any minute."

Bobbie stood, and he and Kendra exchanged looks.

"Of course there's nothing to worry about!" Shawna declared. "We'll be right here. We won't let anything happen to you."

CHAPTER

29

Jack sat at the computer desk near the window and Lady lounged by his chair while he pored over the data on the missing women. The tiny home office had been transformed into his own command center. Perfect for a task force of one.

As if reading his thoughts, Lady growled beside him. Jack looked down at the dog and chuckled. "Okay, two." For a moment he thought she was asleep and dreaming, but then she opened one eye and peered up at him. "Now you're creeping me out. If you're so smart, help me figure out the link here." Lady huffed and closed her eyes. He heard her loud and clear: they were both missing Alice.

The police had identified ten women. They'd disappeared from five different states, all in the last year. Besides their gender they had very little in common. All different ages. Seven white. Three black. Six were married. Two divorced. Two widowed.

Where does Alice fit into this? Just placing his fiancée onto the list of missing women made Jack's stomach sour. But he had to. Serial killers usually have a pattern. Typically, there would be a commonality among the victims.

Jack needed to find it.

He hoped Special Agent Thomas was having more success. Jack didn't care for the man personally, but right now, he was happy to have an experienced FBI profiler on his side. A lot of profilers concentrate on motive. But when it comes to serial killers, the motives involved are different from those in typical murder cases.

Some killers murder because they think someone is ordering them to do so. Some kill just because they enjoy it, savoring the adrenaline rush of hunting their prey. Those are the psychopaths.

The thing about psychopaths is that they seem normal. Like they have it all together. But they're far from sane. They were typically abused as children, and most were also bullied.

This killer was different in one major aspect. Most serial killers have a cooling-off period between killings—days, weeks, sometimes even years. But the pace was increasing, if anything. They were on fire. And that was consistent with the pressure serial killers sometimes have to kill, and kill again, around an event that's symbolically charged for them.

Jack thought back to the rickety house on Buck Mountain. There was one clear inconsistency in the pattern: the wedding invitation. Why was that there? Did the wedding somehow bother the killer? Was the killer trying to get to Jack through Alice?

Marisa's face flashed in his mind. He shoved the thought aside. It was ridiculous. Maybe Marisa still had feelings for him, and maybe she wasn't exactly happy about his getting married, but she would never . . .

Always watching. Never seen. She said it. There was no denying that fact. Marisa was an artist. And she didn't want Jack to get married.

Jack stood suddenly and Lady lifted her head, shaking her head and herself awake.

"Shhh." Jack reassured the dog as he picked up his phone.

Even as he dialed, Jack admonished himself, *You can't ask her over the phone.* It was going to kill Marisa that he was even considering the possibility, but he had to ask. For Alice.

Out in the hallway, a phone rang.

Jack stared at the door.

The phone in the hallway chimed once more and went silent. Jack looked down at his phone. The call had been terminated. His stomach fell like a stone. Jack walked over to the front door and opened it. Marisa stood there with her phone in her hands. Her breathing was shallow and rapid. Her cheeks were flushed, and Jack was sure it wasn't from climbing the stairs. She sauntered into the apartment, reaching back and closing the door with one hand while never taking her eyes off him.

"You sensed me." Her voice smoldered.

Jack swallowed and backed up. It took two tries but he finally found his voice. "I needed to speak with you."

"I know." Marisa stepped closer. "I knew when you were leaving there was something you needed to say to me. What is it?"

Jack bumped into the recliner and stopped. Marisa stood inches from him. Her large brown eyes searched his. Pain? Pleasure? Happy? Sad?

Bittersweet.

"I'm an artist. You suspect *me*?" The fingertips of her left hand touched the tips of his right.

"Always watching. Never seen," Jack whispered.

Marisa raised an eyebrow. "What an artist should be doing."

"You said that to me when you came out of the bedroom at the hotel."

She nodded. "Yes. And?"

"That's the opening of the poem the killer left for Alice." Jack's mouth ran dry.

Marisa's chuckle grew into a laugh. "Please forgive me." She grabbed his hand and interlaced her fingers with his. "I was coming here worried I might have to kill you."

Jack's breath caught in his throat.

Marisa laughed harder and held his hand up to her face and kissed it. "I understand now. I totally understand."

"Then can you explain it to me? Because I don't."

Lady's claws clicked off the floor as she stood up and shook out her coat.

"After I made the sketch," Marisa said, "I saw it in your face. It was a look I'd never seen before. Distrust. It hurt."

"I'm sorry. But . . . it was more than that."

"'An artist should be always watching, never seen.' It's a very well-known quote. Source unknown. It's written on the front of my sketchpad and millions of others."

Jack's eyes widened.

Marisa smiled. "You believe me now?"

"Of course I do." But his mind raced.

Marisa stepped closer, wrapped her arms around Jack's waist, and hugged him. "Thank you," she whispered.

Lady growled.

"What is it about Alice?" Marisa asked softly. "Even Lady is protective of her."

Jack nodded, lost in thought. Marisa had read that quote off the sketchpad; there was a possibility the killer had, too. Maybe they purchased it recently? How many places in Darrington sold paper like that? Was there a sketchpad in the art supplies the killer left behind in the house?

Jack's heart started to beat even faster, rousing him from his concentration. Marisa placed her hands on Jack's lower back and he forced himself to step away from the flame, his mind now laser-focused on Alice.

"That was fun while it lasted." She leaned towards him and smiled. "But from the look on your face, I've already lost you."

Jack nodded. "I love Alice and I want to marry her, Marisa. I wish you would just accept it."

The beauty released a resounding laugh. "I meant, I've already lost you to your thoughts . . . you're chasing the killer in your mind." She turned to face him. "And I am trying to accept that you have chosen Alice, but until you say 'I do,' there is still a chance. I've been honest with you, Jack."

"You have to try harder. And cool it with the touching."

Marisa cast another smoldering look at Jack.

"And absolutely no more of that! Try to help me here, will you? Please?" His brown eyes pleaded with the vixen to behave herself.

"Fine." Marisa sighed.

"Tell me, where did you get that sketchpad?"

"An art store on Fifth Avenue."

"How many art stores are there in Darrington?"

"It's the only one in town. You can buy art supplies other places, but The Drawing Place is the one for serious artists. That sketchpad was very high-end. I doubt any other place sells it."

"That's fantastic. Do—"

Jack's phone buzzed, bringing him back to reality. He pulled it out of his pocket. It was a text from the sheriff.

Come to my office ASAP. I need to speak with you about Channel 5 News.

Jack's jubilation came crashing down. Color drained from his face.

"What's wrong?" Marisa asked.

"I went behind the sheriff's back on something. Now he knows."

CHAPTER

30

Jack parked the Charger in the sheriff's department visitor parking lot and read his text from Alice.

SOMETHING BIG HAPPENED! GREAT NEWS. WHEN WILL U B HOME?

Jack texted back, TALK 2 U 2NIGHT. GOOD NEWS WELCOME.

He added a heart emoji. No use bringing Alice's good mood down, but the veins in his temple were throbbing as he got out of the car and marched toward the front doors. Had Paula betrayed his trust? If she had, Morrison would definitely remove him from the investigation. Jack could think of no other way that Morrison could know about Channel 5 already. The news story hadn't broken yet. It wasn't set to air for another hour.

Jack walked through the entrance, greeting old friends with a nod but heading straight for Morrison's office without stopping. Through the office window, Jack saw the sheriff at his desk, with two people seated on the other side, Special Agent Frank Thomas and Channel 5's Paula Thompson.

Jack clenched his jaw. He should've known better than to trust a reporter. Now he was going to get kicked off the investigation, and with Paula sitting in Morrison's office, was she even going to run the story?

The look on Morrison's face was grim as he waved Jack toward the empty seat.

Thomas was seething, and besides a curt nod he didn't so much as glance at Jack. He couldn't read Paula's poker-face mask. She gave him a tight-lipped smile before looking back at Morrison.

"We need to discuss these," Morrison said as he laid out the sketches of the three unidentified women on his desk—the originals, sealed in plastic.

Jack sat down and kept his mouth closed. Whenever he found himself in a situation where he was jammed up, he fully utilized his right to remain silent. He'd learned that as a little kid, when he was constantly in trouble. He understood that Morrison was waiting for Jack to confess; it was one of the first things they taught you at the police academy. Ask open-ended questions like, *Do you understand why I pulled you over?* And you hope the guy will say, *I was speeding because I'm nervous because I have a kilo of cocaine in the trunk.*

But Jack never volunteered the rope to hang himself.

Morrison reached forward and tapped the blood-splattered picture. "Rebecca Hershberger."

Jack crossed his arms, confused. How did Morrison find the woman without the news story airing?

Morrison's shoulders slumped. "She was reported missing this morning by her niece. I've reached out to Paula to have Channel 5 air the other two sketches and ask for help in identifying the two unknown women."

Paula turned to Jack, and now he picked up on what she was trying to convey with her poker face: *Don't say anything.*

"We're happy to assist the police for the sake of public safety at all times," Paula answered diplomatically. "We should be able to get them on the air within an hour."

"That quickly?" Morrison asked.

Paula nodded. "My team is fast. And I hope you'll see it as a peace offering. Do you have an official statement that you want to make?"

Morrison held out his hand toward Thomas. "Frank, please explain your approach to Paula."

Thomas nodded. "I've finished with the profile of the killer. There's only one common thread connecting any of them." Thomas turned to Jack. "Jack Stratton."

"Me?" Jack shook his head. "The only woman in those sketches that I know is Alice."

"That's not true. I'll explain once we've finished with Paula, but we need to get this story to air as soon as possible."

Yesterday you wouldn't even think of going to a reporter, and now the media can't move fast enough for you? Jack wanted to point out Thomas's hypocrisy, but he held his tongue, well aware he was walking a thin line in this case.

Thomas turned back to Paula. "Right now, we don't want to mention the possibility of a serial killer. We can't start a panic." Jack nodded in agreement.

"My report can simply say that we want to find these women and that they might be in danger," Paula said, echoing Jack's earlier words to her. "That way we stress the importance of finding them quickly while not causing a riot."

"Good. We also don't want to feed this sociopath's ego. So, don't mention the other missing women. The only other thing that I want to be sure you mention is that Jack Stratton has been brought in to assist in the investigation."

"Do you want me to report that Jack is helping the police?"

"Not just report it—really play it up. Say he's instrumental in this investigation."

"As a consultant?" Paula scribbled a quick note.

"No. Something more." Thomas looked to Morrison.

"A special consultant?" Morrison offered. "Private investigator?"

Thomas clicked his fingers. "No. Refer to him as Detective Jack Stratton."

"I'm not a detective," Jack pointed out.

Thomas continued looking at Morrison. "You're the sheriff. You can deputize him."

"Wouldn't that make him a deputy?" Paula asked.

"No," said Morrison. "Technically, under posse comitatus, I can deputize people for a number of different roles. I've never heard it done for detective, but it's within my power."

"Then it's settled. Detective Jack Stratton. You need to repeat that at least half a dozen times." Thomas was smiling now, clearly pleased with his plan.

Jack was pleased, too. *Detective Jack Stratton.* From the time he was a little boy, he'd dreamed of hearing those words. And now it was official. *Finally.*

After working out the call-in numbers and when the reports would run, Paula thanked everyone, gave Jack a quick look, and left.

"We've gone to the news station, Stratton," Thomas said as he shut the door. "Honestly, I'm a bit surprised you didn't beat us to it."

"Let's not start this out on the wrong foot, Frank." Morrison indicated for Thomas to sit back down. "Why don't you tell Jack what you've found out?"

Thomas turned his chair so it was angled toward Jack before sitting down. "You're the key, Stratton. I'm certain of it. I've found a link between you and four of the women."

Jack sat back in his seat. "Can you explain expound that? I don't recall ever meeting any of them, other than Alice of course."

"Alice is the first. Second is Delores Gill. You served in Iraq with her son. Martin Gill."

"Gill . . ." Jack racked his brain for any memory of a Gill, Gilly, Marty, or Martin. He couldn't recall anyone. "He was in my unit?"

"No. Your battalion."

"There were close to eight hundred men in my battalion. Was he in my company?"

"We're pulling the records on that." Thomas picked up his tablet. "Third: Olivia Hastings. You pulled her over for speeding two years ago." He turned the tablet around so Jack could see the photo.

Olivia was an older woman with a pleasant smile and a surprisingly flattering license photo. Jack didn't remember her.

"I gave her a ticket?"

"A written warning. She drove a white Audi."

"I don't recall her or the car. I gave out hundreds of tickets."

"The fourth woman was a substitute teacher in your grade school." Thomas picked out another photograph on his tablet and showed it to Jack. It was a hawk-nosed woman with close-set eyes and bushy eyebrows. "Wanda Peterson."

"Witchy Wanda," Jack said.

"What?" Morrison asked.

"Sorry. It's kinda mean," Jack admitted. "That's what the kids called her. She was a recess monitor and used to scare the kids."

"You do remember her?" Thomas started taking notes.

Jack nodded. "I do now. The sketch looks completely different from how I remember her, giving everyone the evil eye at recess. My friend Chandler and I snuck out of recess to get something at home one time. Wanda saw us in the woods and chased after us for a quarter of a mile."

"Did she catch you?" Morrison asked.

"No." Jack had to stifle a chuckle. "She got stuck in the middle of this briar patch, then fell in a big mud puddle on the way back to the school. She wasn't completely sure it was me she was chasing, but she had it in for me after that."

"So she held a grudge?" Thomas asked.

"Not for twenty years." Jack shook his head. "I just meant the rest of the school year if something happened, she would say, 'It must have been Jack. He's always been a troublemaker.'"

"She was right on that," Morrison said under his breath.

Jack shot him a look, though he had no leg to stand on when it came to his own defense.

The sheriff shrugged. "I'm just saying that considering how you are as an adult, you must have been a real handful as a child."

Jack looked at the two men in turn. "So, I gave one woman a ticket and I embarrassed another," Jack said. "Not much to go on. What did I do to the third one? You said her son served with me, but I don't even remember him."

"He didn't make it home," Thomas said simply.

The words hit Jack like a punch in the gut. Survivor's guilt seemed to always be close at hand, and now it pounced. He pressed his hand down on his knee in a vain effort to stop it from shaking.

"Well, that's all news to me, but I might have figured out part of the poem," Jack blurted out as his fingernails dug in, adding pain to pressure. "'Always watching. Never seen.' It turns out to be a well-known quote by an unknown author that's written on high-end sketchpads sold at The Drawing Place on Fifth Avenue. We should compare the paper and tear patterns to the sketches found in the house and see if we can get a list of anyone they were sold to recently."

"We will." Thomas typed a note. "Do you have one of those pads?"

"No. I was going to stop by The Drawing Place, but then I got Bob's text."

"How did you find out about the quote?" Thomas asked.

"I have a friend who's an artist."

Morrison's eyes widened and Thomas picked up on the shocked look. "Who's the friend?" Thomas asked.

"Marisa Vitagliano," Jack replied.

Thomas tilted his head to Morrison. "She was kidnapped last year, wasn't she?"

Morrison nodded.

Thomas's fingers danced across the tablet.

Jack's foot was doing a jig, and no matter how hard he pressed down or how tightly he squeezed his knee, he couldn't stop the growing tremor.

"She has nothing to do with it," he said. "But I know my saying so won't stop you from looking into it." He stood. "I need to get some air." That was all he could manage before heading out the door. Both Morrison and Thomas said something in reply, but Jack didn't hear them. His sole focus was on the front doors and getting outside. He bumped against a counter, sidestepped a young couple, and shoved the doors apart.

Sweat rolled down his back and made his shirt cling to his skin as he gulped the crisp spring air and tried to drive the images of the dead and dying out of his mind. Guilt had torn him up so many times before, but every time those old scars reopened and bled. And the question that had no answer came rushing back.

Why did I live?

He gripped the metal railing and let the cold burn his hand. Closing his eyes, he embraced the pain and let the guilt wash over him. He couldn't lose it. Not now. A killer was hunting Alice.

And only Jack could stop him.

CHAPTER

31

Alice paced back and forth as she waited for a knock at the door. When at last it came, she started toward it nervously. Kendra cut her off. "I'll answer it."

"Please don't tell me that you're going to frisk them," Alice said, only half joking, though she quickly added, "They're family."

Kendra peered through the peephole, then opened the door. Alex and Yana stood outside, clearly surprised at being greeted by a police officer. Though their smiles still beamed.

"Hi," Alice said with a wave. "Sorry about the crowd. Come on in."

Alex and Yana exchanged nervous looks, but their smiles returned when Alice gave them both a quick hug.

"Alex, Yana, this is Kendra, Shawna, Bobbie, Boomer, and Erica. Everyone, this is my great-uncle Alex and his daughter, Yana."

Alex grinned broadly. "So nice to meet you all."

After hands were shaken and pleasantries exchanged, an awkward silence filled the room.

"Why don't you sit down?" Alice said, looking around for an unoccupied seat.

"They can sit here." Shawna prodded Bobbie and Boomer to get up from the couch.

"We can stand," Alex said.

"Nonsense." Shawna shook her head. "Would you like something to drink?"

"No, thank you," both Yana and Alex replied.

"Tell you what." Shawna put her hands on her hips and looked at the crowded room. "Why don't you guys have a little visit and we'll all go into the kitchen."

Kendra raised an eyebrow, but Shawna didn't back down. "Alice needs a minute with her family."

Kendra looked Alex and Yana up and down. Alice didn't know if she was frisking them visually or perhaps even debating doing so physically, but in the end, she nodded and Shawna began herding everyone through the kitchen doors.

Boomer rolled his eyes. "Do you really expect us all to—ow!"

The door swung shut behind them, and the awkward silence returned to the living room.

Alice started to sit down on the recliner, but Alex shook his head. "Sit with us? Please?"

As soon as she settled between them on the couch, Alex dropped a thick, hairy arm around her shoulders and pulled her in for a hug. He kept apologizing as his eyes welled up. "Sorry. Sorry. Yana said I shouldn't be so clingy, but I just can't believe it! It can't be happening. 'Pinch me,' I keep saying. And I even do it!" He laughed and pinched his thigh to demonstrate. "No, I'm not dreaming. You're alive!"

"I can't believe it myself," Alice said softly, feeling like she was falling into some dream realm.

"And all grown up. You're even getting married. You're a woman now."

Alice blushed.

Alex pointed to the kitchen. "I see your Jack isn't with you. I'd very much like to meet this young man of yours."

"No. Jack's not here." Alice felt her breath catch in her throat. "He's—"

Somewhere out there, trying to protect me.

"You don't owe us an explanation of why he isn't here."

Yana lightly touched Alice's arm, and the simple gesture almost made her burst into tears. Alice hadn't wanted to upset them but she suddenly found herself telling them the whole story. Not only did she bring them up to speed on the serial killer, but she vented about everything happening with the wedding as well. When she was finally done, she felt a thousand times better. "I hope you don't think I'm a complainer."

"A crazy man is after you!" Alex thrust his hands upward. "Of course you're upset! You have every right!"

"That is so horrible." Yana wrapped her arm around Alice's shoulders. "You are strong, Alice."

"Ah . . ." Alex pointed back at the kitchen. "Is that why the police officer is here? Because you've been threatened?"

"The sheriff is a friend. He thought we should be extra careful."

Yana squeezed her closer. "You must be scared to death."

Alice chuckled. "Actually, I'm not. Jack used to be a police officer. I know he'll find the guy."

"You have a lot of confidence in your Jack."

Alice smiled. "Yeah, I do."

Alex's eyes became misty again. "I just found you and now you're getting married. And what a big event it must be to have so much going on! To think you need a wedding coordinator."

"It wasn't my idea." Alice sighed. "I wanted a really tiny wedding."

"What does Jack do for work to afford such a wedding?" Alex asked.

"We both have a private investigator business. But we're not paying for the wedding. A friend of ours is."

Yana lit up. "You are very fortunate to have such a generous friend."

"We are. I keep trying to tell him that he doesn't have to be quite so generous, but he won't listen."

"Take some advice from an old man. Be a grateful receiver." Alex laughed, but it quickly trailed off. "I can't believe my brother will miss your wedding too."

"Too?" Alice asked.

Yana shot her father a cross look. "Never mind, Papa. I'm sure Andrew would be here if he were able."

"And if he knew." Alex slumped forward, his elbows resting on his knees. Slowly, he turned his head to look at Alice. "He's never reached out to you?"

"No. I didn't even know he was still alive until a couple of months ago. Jack wanted to get me an engagement present and realized that I didn't have a picture of my family. So he tracked down an old neighbor of my parents, a friend of my mother's, and got a picture from her. But my mother's friend also told Jack that the man who was driving the car that killed my family got away."

Alex's right hand tightened into a fist. He glared straight ahead as he listened to her story, teeth grinding.

"I'd always believed he was killed in the crash. But when Jack's friend looked into it, that's when we found out my grandfather may still be alive. And we also found out that . . ." Alice paused. She had trouble forming the words.

"That the car crash was no accident," Alex said.

Alice's heart sped up. "You knew?"

All the color drained from Alex's face. He looked much older as he hung his head and nodded. "My brother was in the army. In Poltava, most men joined. I never did." He touched his chest. "Heart murmur. I'm strong as a bull, but they still wouldn't take me. But Andrew gave his life for the dream of a free Ukraine. And it cost him the thing he loved most: his wife." Wiping his eyes, Alex stood and walked over to the window, trying to compose himself.

"Your grandmother was killed by a car bomb," Yana explained to Alice.

Alex looked out the window as he continued. "The country was divided, and they wanted your father to pick a side. My brother chose democracy. He and five of the leaders of the army hid the gold deposit of the treasury of Poltava from the Soviets. They said when the people elected the president, they would return the money. They made their choice. So, the Soviets killed them."

"They killed them all?" Alice asked.

Alex turned back to face her. "Every one, as far as I know. But my brother escaped. That is why he is hiding. As long as that money is missing, he's not safe."

Yana squeezed Alice's hand; it felt natural, not what she would expect from someone she recently met. "And neither are you."

Alice's head was reeling. "What? Why me?"

Alex rushed back over to her, knelt in front of her, and took her hands. "My Kaya Kukla, we meant to bring you only joy by coming here." Yana nodded, tears in her eyes threatening to spill over. Alex squeezed Alice's hands almost painfully. "But we may have brought you more trouble. If someone finds out that the granddaughter of Andrew is alive, they will try to use you to make him tell them where the money is."

Yana locked her eyes with Alice's and gripped her hand tightly. Her voice trembled with urgency. "There might be more than one person after you now."

CHAPTER

32

"Slow down. Slow down!" Jack was practically shouting into the phone as he paced a trail into his apartment floor's carpet and tried to understand what Alice was telling him. She was close to frantic and speaking a mile a minute, so loudly that Lady could hear her voice from the phone and watched Jack expectantly from her bed. Alice had explained that her great-uncle and cousin had found her and had paid her a visit at Shawna's apartment.

Alice's voice trembled. "Jack, they said that my grandfather and five others took a lot of money and held it as a bargaining chip, trying to do the right thing for their people. The others were killed. And as long as the money is out there, they will hunt for my grandfather and may use me to get to him."

"You've got to be kidding me," Jack muttered. He stopped and stared at the ceiling. He didn't believe in superstition, but he was starting to think that getting married on April fourth wasn't the best idea.

"What should we do?"

"I'll handle it," Jack said reassuringly, though he had no clue what he was going to do. "Right now, you need to tell Kendra, Bobbie, and Boomer that no one is to get within a hundred yards of you."

"That's going to be a little difficult with this gigantic wedding."

Jack started pacing again. He pressed his left fist into his forehead and ground his teeth. "We need to cancel the wedding."

"Nope, not happening. I'll elope with you right now or we're getting married on April fourth. Anything else is out of the question."

"Alice—"

"The only thing that's changed is that now we know someone else *may* be after me. Or maybe not. Whoever's searching for my grandfather might not even know that I'm alive. Right?"

"Your great-uncle managed to find out where you were. Other people could find you, too." Jack was now fighting a two-front war, and he didn't even know who his enemies were. "Please put Kendra on the line."

"Don't get her freaked out any more then she already is. Seriously, or I won't get a minute alone, even in the bathroom."

"If I'm going to agree to this, I need to speak with Kendra."

Alice mumbled something, and Jack heard her stomping across the floor. A moment later, Kendra came on the line.

"Hi, Jack. What's happening?"

After Jack brought Kendra up to speed, he said, "I need you to request an additional sheriff detail."

He hoped she understood that his wanting more protection for Alice had nothing to do with Kendra's abilities, and everything to do with the level of the threat. He expected her to argue, and was surprised when she agreed right away.

"I'll contact the sheriff now."

The relief of avoiding another confrontation was a small measure of improvement. "Thanks, Kendra." Jack hung up and dialed his friend at the State Department. She wasn't there, so he left a frantic message asking her to call him back ASAP. He hurried into the bedroom, opened his bureau, and took out the burner phone Kiku had given him. He dialed the only number stored on it and waited.

"Are you calling because you have cold feet and need reassurances that you are making a wise decision?" Kiku said, followed by a light laugh.

"Unfortunately, no. I'm in the middle of two huge problems."

"I am beginning to believe you and I were destined to live in the midst of storms. They never seem to end for us, do they?"

Jack explained everything to Kiku. By the time he was done he was so frustrated he wanted to smash something.

"I do not need to tell you what you surely already know, but you are in a very, very dangerous situation. And I am speaking only of the situation with Ukraine."

"That's what I was hoping you could help me with. I know I've already asked so much of you and I can never repay you—"

"There is no need. There is also no limit placed on what a true friend may ask. But as I said, we live in the maelstrom. I am dealing with a situation right now that will take me at least two more days to clear up."

The wedding was in three days. Jack was on his own until then.

"I understand."

"Pardon me for asking. But why . . ." Kiku's voice trailed off.

"Why what?"

"I answered my own question. I was wondering why you and Alice did not cancel the wedding and run away."

"And then you realized that Alice would never run away."

"No. I thought, if I were marrying you, would I give up the chance to place a ring on your finger? No."

Jack opened the window and let some cool air in. "But you do agree that the smart thing to do is run?"

"You are assuming that Alice is thinking with her head. She is not. She is being led by her heart. Though I do see her side of the argument. Right now, you are both in a familiar place where you know the people around you. You are on guard, you have implemented additional security measures, and you are actively trying to neutralize the threats. If I can complete my work faster, I will come straight there. However, I would not count on that happening."

"But you are going to be here for the wedding?"

"I would not miss it for the world. Besides, my date is eager to speak with you."

"Your date?" Jack asked. "Who?"

"I do not want to ruin the surprise. Besides, it will give you something else to think about other than your problems. I will see you soon, Officer."

Kiku hung up, and Jack turned his face toward the open window. Closing his eyes, he divided up his problems. On one side, he had the new threat from Alice's past. On the other, a killer who was on the move. The killer was the immediate threat. Once that threat was resolved, then he could focus on the ghosts from Alice's past. The logical side of his brain took over, and it provided him a moment of peace, an illusion of control.

He closed the window, went over to the desk, and logged into the police database. Thomas had posted his profile of the killer in the secure section, along with all the data on the case. Jack had already seen the basics—most likely male, late thirties, abusive childhood, revenge motivation, etc.—but he was looking for specific details now. The ME hadn't posted anything yet on the pocket square or the cologne, but in his report he stated that Delores Gill was killed by carbon monoxide, while the still-unidentified victim trapped under the floorboards with her had been killed as a result of arsenic poisoning. Both women were missing their rings.

Jack drummed his fingers on the desk, his leg bouncing at his side. Thomas's profile centered on Jack as the focus of the killer's attention, but Jack thought that theory was tenuous at best. He grabbed his notebook and a pen, flipped to a blank page, and began a brainstorming exercise his father had taught him. Writing down all the words that came to mind, he ended up with a page covered with text. One word leapt out: *Wedding*.

Except for Alice, all the women had one thing in common—they'd all been married.

Jack switched back to the database and exported the wedding dates of all the victims. Most had been married in the summer, but that was consistent with general trends. Apart from that, there was no common denominator in the months or days of their weddings. But as he created his list and checked it against his initial pictures from the Buck Mountain crime scene, he found something interesting—not a commonality, but a pattern nonetheless. None of the women had been married for the same length of time. But four women whose pictures had hung next to each other on the wall were married for sequential numbers of years—seven, eight, nine, ten.

Was the killer targeting women based on how long they were married?

Jack cross-checked the dates that the women were reported missing, and his eyes widened. All the women went missing within a week of their wedding anniversary.

That was it. He was sure of it. The killer was targeting women on their anniversaries.

And if he was right, Alice was supposed to be victim zero.

CHAPTER

33

The news story worked. Shortly after it aired, the police received a call identifying one of the women as Sara McCorkle. When Thomas texted Jack with the news, Jack called him back and tried to tell him what he'd discovered regarding the wedding anniversaries. But Thomas was in no mood to listen, already on his way to McCorkle's address and busy coordinating a security detail to meet him there.

Yet now, as Jack pulled into the driveway of McCorkle's house, there wasn't a police cruiser in sight. He double-checked the address in Thomas's text against the one painted on the mailbox: 173 Deer Creek Lane. Yep, it was the right house. So why was no one here?

Opening the car door, Jack pulled his shirt over his concealed pistol. He scanned the street and surrounding homes for any sign of anything out of place, but the neighborhood was quiet—a picture postcard of suburban peace and prosperity.

He walked up the brick walkway toward the front door. It opened before he got to it, and a woman in her fifties stood holding open the door, a look of angst creasing her already wrinkled brow.

"Detective Stratton?" She swallowed nervously.

Jack stopped on the lower steps and tried to peer inside the house. "Yes, ma'am. Are you okay?" He held his fist tightly against his chest then made a thumbs-up and thumbs-down, trying to signal to the woman to do the same. It was a trick he'd learned in Iraq. Insurgents would sometimes have civilians answer the door and lure soldiers inside, then try to kill them. Jack didn't know if he was being paranoid or not, but the woman was obviously distressed, and he wasn't taking any chances.

"Ah . . . Frank would like to speak with you inside."

"Can you please let him know I'll talk to him out here?" Jack shifted his right foot slightly behind him as he moved into a shooter's stance.

The woman looked back into the house, and Special Agent Frank Thomas appeared, scowling at Jack. "Get in here, Stratton," he muttered through clenched teeth.

Jack followed them both into the living room. The woman walked over to an older man, who wrapped his arms around her. He recognized the look on their faces—he'd seen it a thousand times as a police officer. They were scared out of their minds and desperate for help.

A sheriff's deputy stood in one corner. All the shades were drawn, the small room illuminated with a pale-yellow light overhead.

"You did great, Sara," Thomas said, smiling. His smile vanished as he faced Jack. "Let's talk in private, Jack." He gestured for Jack to follow, then walked back into the hall and led Jack to a study.

"Is this your first rodeo, Stratton?" Thomas growled as he shut the door hard. "You made me reveal myself."

"What do you think this is, *Mission Impossible*?" Now it was Jack's turn to get angry. "You could have texted me a heads-up. I'm not trained to blindly walk into a building."

"I assumed you'd be familiar with protocol in this situation."

"What protection protocol are you following?" Jack's lip curled into a snarl, and he leveled an accusatory finger at Thomas. "You're not operating under one, are you? You're setting a trap and you're using me and that innocent woman as bait."

"Lower your voice." Thomas crossed his arms. "The best way to protect her is to catch the killer."

Jack shook his head. "Not at any cost."

"Mrs. McCorkle already had a target on her back."

"But you brought me here to wave the red flag in front of the bull." Jack looked away, and his gaze fell on some pictures on a shelf. Sara and her husband. He was sure he'd never met the woman before. "You haven't found a link between me and Sara, have you?"

"Not yet, but I will. You're the connection."

"No, Frank, I'm not. I tried to tell you over the phone, there's another connection. One that applies to all the missing women, without exception. Wedding anniversaries. Every woman that we've identified went missing during the week prior to her wedding anniversary."

"Which is not inconsistent with my own theory," Thomas said. He uncrossed his arms and pointed at a wedding picture on the shelf. "Good news, though—Sara's anniversary is in two days. They were planning on going upstate for a weekend getaway, but I convinced them to stay. If you're right about this, we won't have to wait long."

"Are you nuts? We should protect this woman. Park some cruisers out front. Let the killer know that this woman is off-limits. Instead, you're encouraging the killer to make a move!"

"Don't tell me how to run my investigation," Thomas said, his eyes flashing.

"If anything happens to her, it's on you." Jack headed to the door, unable to look at his face any longer.

"Your theory is wrong, by the way."

Jack turned. "What are you talking about?"

"A caller identified the woman in the last sketch. She's another local, Alyssa Snyder, 14 Cedar Lane." He held up his tablet, showing a report. "I heard you on the phone. I checked out your theory. Alyssa Snyder's wedding anniversary is in December. Over eight months away. So, unless our psychopath is really planning ahead . . . well, looks like your theory isn't holding up."

"I'm not helping put a bigger target on these women's heads." Jack walked out the door. There was no point in arguing further with Thomas. The person he needed to speak to was in the living room.

Sara and her husband looked up as he entered. When he saw the desperate pleas in their eyes, he knew what he had to say.

"Special Agent Thomas thinks you're safest here," Jack began. "He believes that the killer will come after you. I think he's correct about that, but wrong that you should pretend you don't know. I think you should demand that he place two marked police cars out in front. Make a statement that the police are watching over you."

Sara's husband turned to look at Thomas, who stood in the doorway shaking his head.

"That's his opinion," Thomas said. "But believe me, you're safest my way. One officer will remain here. We'll be monitoring carefully and when they make their move, we move in." He nodded confidently.

Sara looked at Jack. "You're the man who caught the Giant Killer, aren't you?"

Jack nodded.

Sara turned to her husband. Jack could see she was scared and unsure, eyes darting across the room at any little movement.

Her husband took her hand in his. "I think we should listen to the professionals, honey," Mr. McCorkle said. "He may have captured the Giant Killer, but he's just a bounty hunter." He nodded toward Thomas. "I'm inclined to go with the advice of the FBI."

Jack pulled a card out of his pocket with his number on it and laid it on the table. He walked out the front door without saying another word. What could he say? Sara was going to follow Thomas's advice.

And Sara was going to die.

CHAPTER

34

Lady whined in the back seat as Jack drove the Charger hard, barreling down the back roads of Darrington. From the very beginning of this investigation, Thomas had taken too many risks. The man wanted to catch the killer—Jack understood that. But that was only part of the job. The other part was protecting the innocent. And Thomas was going to get innocent people killed.

Jack's phone buzzed with a text message. It was from the ME's assistant, Mei. Test results had come back on the pocket square found with Delores Gill. It was a mass-produced pocket square sold in many big box retail stores during the 1990s. The cologne on the square was an inexpensive men's cologne called Proper Modern Gentleman sold online and in men's barbershops.

In other words, these things could have come from anywhere. Jack tossed the phone down on the seat and lowered the window, letting the wind buffet his face. What had he expected? That the pocket square would have the killer's initials embroidered on it?

Lady whimpered. Jack opened the glove compartment and took out a dog treat. He started to pass the treat back to her, then suddenly yanked his hand away.

"Wait a second!"

Lady, clearly frustrated, barked loudly in protest and sat, anticipating his next command in hopes he'd relinquish the treat.

"Oh, don't be a baby." Jack broke the treat in half and gave her some. "You'll get a lot more once you do me this favor, girl."

Jack turned the Charger around and headed back toward town. As his speed increased, his senses sharpened and his heart pumped hard. A determined smile spread across his face. The hunt was on.

CHAPTER

35

After stopping by his barbershop and picking up a jade-green bottle of Proper Modern Gentleman cologne, Jack headed straight for the mountain. As the Charger wound its way up the curving roads, Lady sniffed the air excitedly.

"That's right, girl. You're going to get the chance to show off now. And I really, really need you to be a superstar on this one."

Jack parked in front of the rental house. Technically he was still the renter, although police tape hung across the door. He reached into the glove compartment and took out his secret weapon: one of Mrs. Stevens's super-deluxe peanut butter treats.

Lady was already drooling in anticipation. Jack pressed the button that unleashed Lady's harness and opened the back door. She bounded out of the car, landing with her feet set wide apart. Recognizing the house that held death, she let loose three enormous roars, daring anyone within earshot to challenge her.

Jack walked up onto the porch and Lady followed hesitantly, growling her displeasure the whole way. "Don't worry, we're not going inside." Jack held up his secret weapon and chuckled as Lady started dancing and prancing on the porch. She barked.

"You have to earn it. Ready?" Jack opened the bottle of cologne and held the cap down so Lady could sniff it. She sneezed, shook her head, and then shook her entire body. She backed up two steps and glared at Jack.

"Find it! Find it!" he said in a high voice, trying to sound like Alice, excited.

Lady stayed where she was and looked up at him, puzzled.

"Go find it! Look for it? Get it? Please?"

Alice had been training Lady to follow scents. The problem was, when Alice taught Lady tricks, she used command words that Jack would never think of.

What command would she have chosen for this?

A thin smile played across Jack's face as he remembered. "Hunt!"

Lady's ears flattened against the back of her head and she sniffed the mountain air. Jack held the cap down once more. Lady sniffed it and began pacing back and forth on the porch before heading down the front steps. She slowly moved out in an ever-widening circle before running back up onto the porch. Then she scratched at the front door and whined.

"No. Not inside. Outside. Hunt!"

Lady barked and scratched the front door, pulling off a piece of police tape with her paw.

"Okay. One second." Jack punched in the code on the lock box and opened the front door.

Lady rushed into the house and began sniffing around. She started in the living room and hurriedly went from room to room, pausing at the spot where they had found the bodies. Then she went into the kitchen and right up to the back door.

Jack opened the door, and Lady leapt off the back steps and began sniffing her way along the path that led to the driveway. Jack prayed the trail didn't end there. Given the number of women missing, Jack had a theory that there were more bodies buried on the property. Thomas's team had searched the house and surrounding yard, but maybe they missed something.

Lady's head snapped up and with one quick bark she took off. Jack had forgotten how fast she could run, and he didn't want to stop her or even slow her down if she was onto something, so he just sprinted after her through a field of tall grass and ferns behind the house. Had Lady been smaller, Jack would have lost sight of her, but the giant dog was easy to track as she raced in a straight line toward the trees in the distance, bowling over all the grass in the process.

"Lady!" Jack was forced to call out as she reached the trees. He was fifty yards behind her and the woods were dark. He couldn't keep up with her in a field, let alone a forest.

She took an interest in one particular tree, and paused to sniff around its base, allowing Jack to catch up to her, out of breath. The dog concentrated on one side of the tree, even rising up on her hind legs and sniffing the bark higher up, whimpering.

Jack took a quarter from his pocket and placed it at the base of the tree to mark it. He got out his phone and took several pictures of the tree, then videoed the path of trampled grass leading back toward the house so he could find the spot later and search more thoroughly.

As Lady started smelling the ground again, Jack whipped off the leash around his shoulders and clipped it onto Lady's harness. The huge dog jerked him forward as she moved deeper into the woods.

"Good girl! Hunt!" Jack encouraged.

He came across a path where the ferns were matted down by a single, deep tire track. Jack considered what that could mean. Whatever had made the track, it had to have been heavy to make such a rut. And it wasn't a motorcycle or a bicycle, or there would be two tracks. Every several yards, there were two outer depressions; one on either side of the tire track. Tire track only, then two more divots, tire track only, then two more divots.

Jack realized what it was. These were the stop-and-go tracks of someone pushing a heavy wheelbarrow.

The ferns eventually gave way to a worn path through the woods. Flat, old, and well-traveled. But the ground had been wet recently; tracks and shoe impressions were still visible. Jack stepped around these carefully so the police could take molds later, but not before snapping a few photos of them himself.

The darkness grew deeper as the tree canopy thickened. After a while, Lady slowed down. Jack wondered if she had lost the trail, but when the dog turned her head to look back at him, he could see it in her face. She was scared.

An old black wrought-iron fence appeared up ahead. It surrounded a dozen high mounds covered with grass and small, bent trees. The metal gate was open. Lady stepped through it, growling as she went.

Jack realized the mounds were crypts—he'd just entered a cemetery. He drew his gun.

Stupid zombie movies.

Sitting among the first four crypts, at odd angles, were a number of tombstones. The names of the people buried there were illegible, worn down by time.

Lady skirted toward the next section of crypts. Jack noticed the metal door on one of them was slightly ajar.

Please, don't have the trail lead there.

Jack exhaled as Lady passed it. The cemetery came to an end, and a stone building appeared through the trees. A church. And from its dilapidated condition, it had clearly long since been abandoned and forgotten. It was covered in moss and vines, as if the forest itself was trying to reclaim the land, the church—all of it.

Lady stopped before the front steps. Jack walked up next to her and put his hand on her back. The poor dog was panting and shaking violently. She whimpered and pressed against his leg.

Jack patted her neck. "Shh . . . Good girl. You did your part. Thank you." Jack gave her a treat and Lady gobbled it down. "Now it's my turn. Stay here."

The cracked stained-glass windows in the front of the church prevented him from seeing inside. He debated sneaking around to the back but quickly dismissed the idea. He didn't expect the killer to be here anyway, and if he was here, walking through all the dead leaves alongside the church would only alert him to Jack's presence. He'd make less noise going straight in.

Jack squared his shoulders and started up the steps. The worn front doors of the church were slightly ajar. Sweat ran down his back, and he tightened the grip on his Glock, grateful for the contoured handle. He searched the doorway for tripwires. It was a habit he'd developed in Iraq.

The inside of the church was swallowed in shadow, but some light broke through the dingy glass. Jack could see the backs of most of the pews inside. He stepped forward and froze.

The thick smell of death hung in the air, a combination of rotting flesh and dank mustiness. Some of the odor was more pungent, some was older decomposition. The effect was so strong that Jack could taste its rankness. It permeated his body, death surrounding him and filling his lungs.

Dozens of bodies sat silently in the wooden pews, their backs to him. Dead faces posed to stare eternally at the altar. Only one corpse faced Jack and the macabre congregation. It was standing at the altar at the front, dressed in a black suit with the white collar of a clergyman. The face was nearly mummified.

Jack's breath returned in strained gasps. The silence was so intense that his ears hurt. He fought the shock that threatened to immobilize him as he surveyed the grisly scene. This church had once been a place of worship and love, where families gathered to celebrate marriages and dedicate their babies to the Lord. Now it was host to the evil display of a madman.

Jack wiped the sweat from his forehead with the back of his hand. Behind the altar to the right sat the remains of the church organ, piled high with bits of the collapsed ceiling above, its pipes twisted and torn from the wall like a gnarled brass hand reaching out. At the center, tattered and torn maroon velvet drapes were pulled back, revealing an empty baptismal chamber. To the left was an empty choir box, and behind it a partially open door.

If a living threat was here, the only place they could be hiding would be behind that door, in the choir room.

Jack tried to swallow, but his mouth was too dry. He started forward down the aisle. The bodies in the pews had clearly been carefully posed. Some sat cross-legged, while others had their hands folded in their laps. A few were clearly couples. One pair of corpses held hands, while another was posed with the man's arm wrapped across the woman's shoulders.

Most of the women appeared to have died more recently. Some were bloated, their skin threatening to burst, their faces puffy and alien. The men, meanwhile, looked as though they had been dead for decades; husks of people, dried and old, decay having already run its course. Even the men's clothes looked like they were from a different era.

Jack thought back to the open crypt and shuddered.

At the choir box, he crept quietly to the open door. The little room in the back was empty, but another door led outside. It, too, was ajar.

Jack turned back to look at the macabre scene once more, and this time he noticed something new: the corpse of a tiny child. The child was propped up, with a ring pillow lashed to its hands.

The hairs on the back of Jack's neck rose.

It's a wedding.

A gleam of red light in the upper corner at the back of the church caught his eye. Jack pivoted around, aiming at the source. At first, he thought it might be a gun's laser sight. But no—it was a camera.

It moved and pointed directly at him.

"Hello, Jack."

CHAPTER

36

No. No. No!

I glare down at the computer monitor in sheer horror. He's found The Wedding.

How? That doesn't matter. The point is he found it.

He's aiming a gun at the camera. His other hand is in his pocket. He's looking right at me.

"Hello?"

He's calling to me now. I turn up my speaker. I shouldn't have said anything, but I couldn't let him go. With my voice modifier there's no way he could tell who I am, but still, I shouldn't have said anything. I shouldn't say any more now.

What can I do? He'll ruin everything.

"You know my name," Jack shouts. "What's yours?"

I can't tell him, of course. What should I say? I'm fifteen minutes away. He'd be gone by the time I got to the church to stop him.

"Can you hear me, or is this connection only one-way?"

I got the voice modifier for the ceremony. I couldn't play all the parts without it. But I have to use it now. Jack can't find out who I am. Not now. Later, of course—I want full credit for my work. But not now. It's too soon.

Jack turns toward the front door. Is he leaving?

"Wait!" I shout. The word is wrenched from my chest; he is sure to sense my panic now.

Jack slowly turns back to face the camera. He appears calm, but he can't be. It's an act. I'm sure of it. He crosses his arms and stares up at the camera. It's like he's staring into my eyes.

"Why don't you come on down to the church?" Jack asks. "You and I can have a little talk about . . ." he glances around the pews, taking it all in, "the wedding."

He knows. He recognizes what it is. The Wedding. My art.

Jack might actually understand. He might if I explained it. I could tell him all about it, explain all the whys. And then kill him.

No. I want him to suffer first. I want him to hurt.

"Okay," I whisper. "I'll come to you. But first, empty your gun."

Jack doesn't hesitate. He drops the magazine from the weapon and catches it deftly in his other hand.

"Throw it through the hole in the ceiling on the left side."

He winds back his arm and heaves the magazine out of view of the camera.

"Throw your gun down, too."

Jack stares at the camera for a moment. He's debating. I know he's left a bullet in the chamber. They always do that. That was the ace up his sleeve. But he tosses the gun. He makes a good show of it, but I can tell that he doesn't throw it hard, and I hear it land somewhere inside the church.

"Walk closer to the camera," I order him.

Jack walks down the aisle slowly. He's cocky. So sure of himself.

"I have to tell you," Jack says, smiling up at me, "I've never been to a wedding like this one. Personally, I'm hoping mine's a little livelier."

Is he mocking my art? Taunting me?

I adjust the tone on the voice changer to lower my voice even more. I want it to sound like a demon from the pit of hell. "Your wedding will never happen, *Jack*." I spit out his name.

"Why don't you come down here and we can talk about it?" He glances at the floor as he approaches, no doubt looking for traps. The soldier in him, always present in the action.

"Take out your phone. Hold it up so I can see it."

Jack hesitates. He's still smiling, but there's a tightness around his eyes. Why?

"Take out your phone!" I'm almost shouting now. He's up to something. I'm sure of it.

Jack reaches into his pocket and holds up his phone. The screen is blank except for a red bar across the top.

"What have you done?!" My fists come down and smash the table in front of me.

"Sorry." Jack shrugs. "When you started talking to me, I kinda panicked and decided to call for backup. Do you know what happens if you press the side button on your phone five times?"

"You called 911!"

Jack smiles. "Yeah. And since I didn't say anything, they're on their way here now. But if you still want to talk, I can call and tell them to hold off."

The police are on their way. There's no way I can save my wedding now. It's gone. Ruined.

"I didn't mean to spoil your plan," Jack says as if he can tell what I'm thinking. "But you did have some things here that are just wrong."

Wrong? Nothing is wrong about my wedding—until now. It was perfect. He's the only thing wrong with it.

"Take the minister, for instance." Jack walks up the three steps to stand on the dais next to the minister. "He needs to move over a little."

I carefully strapped the minister's body to a metal display stand to hold him in place. Now Jack Stratton is roughly manhandling the body and sliding him over two feet.

"He should be slightly off-center to give the bride center stage. You know that, right? Unless this is supposed to be a bad minister. A good minister knows that today is really about the bride and the focus should be on her. I'm surprised you didn't know that."

I'm screaming now. Obscenities pour from my mouth like smoke from a coal fire.

"Calm down." Jack's smile grows. "I'm sorry. I didn't mean to get you upset. But since you clearly don't know much about weddings . . ." He smirks. "Why don't you come down here and I can give you some pointers?"

I grab my gun. I want to run to my car and beat the police up Buck Mountain and unload the entire clip in Jack's smug face. I aim at the camera, my finger on the trigger, and it hits me.

I understand now.

"You're trying to make me hate you."

"What? Hate me? I'm just trying to help you out. You need to fix this mess up before anyone else sees all of your mistakes. Look, take this couple in the front row. They clearly don't belong together." Jack grabs Mr. Mitchell and drags him over on the pew. His hat falls off, along with his head.

"Stop! Stop ruining it!"

Jack slowly turns back to smile at the camera. "I could really use your help. I'm so clumsy." He flicks Mrs. Cipriano's hat off her head. "I'm afraid I'll trash the whole wedding without you."

I laugh. I wonder how it sounds in the church. From the look on Jack's face, I imagine it's terrifying.

"You don't want to help me. You're trying to goad me into coming after you!"

I laugh harder. A guttural and genuine laugh.

Jack's face twists into a dismissive scoff, but his hands tighten into fists.

"I'm right. I know it. You're the white knight. But now answer me this: What happens when Prince Jack fails to save the princess? Does he fall on his sword or throw himself off the castle tower?"

"You've got me all wrong, you twisted freak. If I wanted to tick you off, I'd probably start by talking about what a wuss you are for going after old women. But I just want to talk to you. I took those sketches to a real artist to see what she could tell me, and she said I should look for someone who failed out of art school. I think she actually said that a first-year art student could draw a better sketch by throwing ink behind their back and farting on a canvas."

"I'm going to cut your heart out." My hand is shaking uncontrollably as I grab the microphone stand. "You haven't stopped anything. I'll still have my wedding. And you'll reap the pain."

"Come after me, then, you no-talent hack."

"I will. But first, I'm going to kill Alice and everything you love."

CHAPTER

37

As Alice got out of Bobbie's Hummer outside the photography studio, she was quickly surrounded by Bobbie, Kendra, Boomer, and Shawna. But even they couldn't protect her from Erica, who emerged from her car and tried to shoo them all inside. They were meeting because Philip Poole had demanded another photoshoot; there was some problem with Alice's photographs.

"Chop-chop, let's get a jump on this, people! We've got a schedule to keep to."

"Can't he just take more pictures at the wedding?" Boomer grumbled.

"This is for the celebration dinner slideshow," Erica said as she opened the front door of the studio. "Knock, knock!" she called out as she barged in.

The foyer was empty, but the lights were on in the main room.

"Philip?" Erica called out as everyone followed her in. She frowned at her watch, then turned to Alice. "Why don't you go ahead and get dressed while I call him." She took out her phone.

Alice trudged down the hallway. The last thing she wanted to do was dress up and take pictures. She was hoping that Philip would figure out a way to use the photographs he already had. But there was no use arguing with her wedding planner. So far, all that had ever accomplished was prolonging the inevitable. In the end, Erica always got her way. She was going to make sure Alice had the perfect wedding even if it killed her.

That woman is a master manipulator. Queen of the guilt trip. She'd probably tell me a story about poor Philip jumping off the nearest bridge if I don't go along with retaking the photos. Alice got undressed and slipped into her bridal gown. It was exquisite, and she smiled. She had dreamed of her wedding day so often; she couldn't believe it was almost here.

She reached around and tried to get her zipper in the back, but it was stuck. She didn't want to pull too hard; the fabric of the dress was so sheer, she might rip it. Cracking the dressing room door open, Alice peered out at Shawna and Boomer waiting in the hallway.

"Where's Kendra?"

"Erica needed to talk to her," Shawna said.

"Where's Bobbie?"

"In the bathroom."

"Can you give me a hand with my zipper?"

"I can," Boomer said, stepping forward.

"Jack will kill you," Shawna said in a singsong voice.

"Never mind." Boomer leaned back against the wall. "And you know I was just kidding, right?"

"I do," Alice said, stepping aside as Shawna came in.

The dressing room was small and with the two of them inside with the bulk of the wedding dress, it was a tight fit. Shawna struggled for a few moments but managed to free the zipper.

"Perfect." Alice exhaled. "Thanks."

"No problem. It just had a bit of fabric caught—" Shawna tripped on Alice's shoe and crashed into the wall. The thin wall shook, and an old smoke detector mounted up high dropped down two inches and now hung suspended by colored wires. "Oh, crap. I'm so clumsy." Shawna stepped up onto the bench by the wall and inspected the smoke detector. "I don't think it's broken."

"Stop," Alice said. "Let me look at that."

"It's fine," Shawna said. "I'll just click it back in place."

"Please don't. I want to check it out."

Shawna let go of the smoke detector and got off the bench while Alice stepped up. "Do you see the plastic tabs?" Shawna said. "It just clicks back on those. It's not a big deal."

But Alice wasn't listening. All of her attention was centered on the blue cable coming out of the device. It was a data cable—Alice had seen thousands of them while installing computer networks.

Why would an old smoke detector have a data cable?

Alice carefully lifted the device away from the wall. The blue data cable was connected to a black box wedged inside the smoke detector. Plastic had been cut away to make it fit. Alice turned the device over in her hand and stared at the small opening next to the test button. The overhead light gleamed off a little lens.

Alice laid the smoke detector back against the wall and got down off the bench.

"You didn't even try to fix it." Shawna started to climb back up, but Alice grabbed her arm. "What?"

"I need you to remain calm, but we have to get Kendra."

"Why?" Shawna's eyes grew large.

"There's a camera in that smoke detector."

"What? No!" Shawna looked right at the lens. "Oh . . ." She let fly with a flurry of swears and ripped open the door.

"Shawna, stop!" Alice tried to hold on to her, but Shawna pulled free, a woman on a mission.

"I got naked in that room! That little pervert probably already plastered my body all over the internet!"

Boomer perked up. "What's this we're talking about?"

"Go get Bobbie and Kendra now!" Alice ordered. "Shawna, stop!"

But it was too late. Shawna was already marching down the hallway, a determined look on her face, her plum lips pursed into a thin line.

"Bobbie!" Boomer yelled as he ran in the opposite direction.

Alice darted back into the dressing room, grabbed her purse, and pulled out her Taser. Then she hurried after Shawna, her wedding gown flowing behind her.

She rounded a corner and saw Shawna pounding on a door. The door flew open, and Philip Poole stepped out with his eyes blazing and his hands balled into fists. "I said one second!"

Shawna punched Philip in the mouth, knocking him backward through the doorway. "You perverted son of a—"

Philip kicked the door closed. Shawna grabbed the doorknob, but Philip had locked himself in.

Kendra, Bobbie, and Boomer all came running as Shawna swore and pounded on the door.

"What's going on? Stop!" Kendra shouted.

"I found a hidden camera in the dressing room," Alice said.

"Get out of the way, Shawna!" Bobbie ordered.

Shawna stepped aside just before Bobbie lowered his shoulder and smashed the door open. They were just in time to see Philip climbing out the window.

Alice raised her Taser, but Bobbie was in front of her. He just missed grabbing Philip, who disappeared down the back alley.

"Stay here!" Kendra ordered as she climbed out the window and gave chase.

Alice was about to dive through the window after her when Bobbie G. grabbed her.

"Let go!" Alice glared at him.

"Your dress is too big to fit," Bobbie said apologetically.

"You're little enough, Boomer," Shawna said. She grabbed him and started pulling him toward the window.

"Hey! Hey!" Boomer protested. "That dude could have a gun!"

With a look from Shawna, Bobbie G. set his shoulder against Boomer's backside and rammed him through the window and into the alley.

Alice turned and bolted through the studio and out the front door. Philip had once said that he lived in the Meadows Apartment

Complex, which was two blocks south. Everyone on the street stopped and stared at the little bride dashing down the road in her bare feet, brandishing a pink Taser. She didn't see Kendra or Philip, but that didn't stop her. Jack had taught her that if a crook runs and you know where they might be going, get there first.

As she raced across the next street, she saw Philip running into the apartment complex.

"Call 911! Call 911!" she shouted to a passersby and pushed herself to run even faster. She was almost to the entrance to the complex when a blue sports car skidded out of the complex and onto the road. She saw the driver. Philip.

His eyes narrowed. He screamed something she couldn't make out and spit flew against the passenger window. He jammed down on the gas and the car rocketed out of the driveway and past her, leaving the sound of screeching tires ringing in the air. Alice bent down, grabbed a rock, and heaved it as hard as she could. It barely clipped the lower edge of the rear window, but the whole window shattered. Then the car disappeared from sight.

Alice was gulping in air, but a satisfied grin spread across her face. If Philip was the man after her, now Jack knew who he was hunting.

CHAPTER

38

Jack stood impatiently in front of the church as he waited for Morrison to arrive. Lady was pacing along the edge of the woods. She didn't want to come any closer, and Jack couldn't blame her.

Two deputies stood guard outside the front doors, and another was stationed around back. They had all peeked inside the church, but none had entered. They all turned their heads as Morrison, flanked by two officers, came into view down the overgrown access road.

The sheriff was bathed in sweat as he greeted Jack.

"Where are Thomas and Castillo?" Jack asked.

Morrison's face was a neutral mask. He held up his hand like he was calming a dog, but it had the opposite effect on Jack. His adrenaline kicked in.

"What else is wrong, sir?"

"Alice is okay." Morrison placed a hand on Jack's shoulder. "She just called 911."

Jack would have run all the way back to the Charger if it weren't for Morrison tightening his hold on him.

"Kendra is with her and I've assigned another officer to protect her, too. Alice is surrounded by shields. It's the photographer, Philip Poole. He had a hidden camera in the dressing room at his studio and Alice found it. Poole took off after being confronted. Kendra gave chase, but he managed to evade capture."

Jack ran his hands through his hair and glared up at the sky. "This guy is as crazy as they come. We have to get him now, and I mean right now."

"Everyone's looking for him. That's what I have Thomas and Castillo doing."

"Have you notified the state police?"

Morrison nodded. "All local channels are running Poole's photo every other commercial break, and we enacted the emergency broadcast system so his face will be all over social media, with descriptions given via radio as well. We'll catch the guy."

"We have to. What I just found confirms how insane he is. Wait until you see this." Jack jerked his thumb toward the church.

Morrison fell into step beside Jack, a new confidence about him. "From the description you gave, I'm not looking forward to it. How did you find this place?"

"Lady followed a scent trail from the rental house to here. There are some good footprint impressions in the woods. Crime scene should get a mold and match them to Poole's shoes for prosecution later."

"You need to come back on the force, Jack. You've got law enforcement in your DNA," Morrison said. "Seriously, I could make your detective status permanent and . . ." His voice trailed off as they stepped through the front door of the church.

"I appreciate that, Bob, but right now we need to deal with this." Jack held his hand out towards the sanctuary.

The air was thick with the stench of rotting flesh. Both men fought to keep the contents of their stomachs in place.

The sheriff's eyes were wide. "This is a nightmare."

"I assume these are our missing women," Jack said. "There are also men, though I suspect most of them were taken from the crypts in the cemetery. I can only hope that's where the ringbearer's little body came from."

Morrison swallowed and reached for his radio. "This is the sheriff. Tell crime scene that they're going to have to call in backup from at least four other counties. I need you to radio the tree and park supervisor and have him call me. I need a road cleared ASAP. Have Parker get together the two crime scene trailers, the portable generators, and lots of lights. Tell everyone to cancel plans. It's all hands on deck."

"Everyone, as in . . .?" Dispatch asked.

"As in everyone. All employees. Notify all supervisors that there's a mandatory meeting"—he glanced at his watch—"in two hours."

"Tell them to triple the protection on the two identified targets," Jack said.

Morrison nodded and repeated the request into the radio.

Silence enveloped them and a damp cold sucked the warmth from their skin. As Jack surveyed the dead wedding, his adrenaline died back to a smoldering burn. He turned and walked out of the church, the stench of death following him.

"Where are you going?" Morrison called after him.

"Hunting."

CHAPTER

39

Two police cruisers, an unmarked detective's car, and a crime scene van were parked outside Poole's apartment complex when Jack pulled up.

"Stay here, girl." Jack gave Lady another treat. He left the car running and the air conditioning on. He had a feeling that he was going to need Lady's help again, and he wanted her well-rested.

Officer Tom Kempy stood watch on the steps of the apartment. He smiled and waved as Jack walked up. Married, with three kids, Tom always seemed happy and full of life, but today he was a little paler than normal and spoke quietly.

"Hey, Jack. Is it true? They said you found dozens of bodies in that old chapel."

"Yeah. This guy's as crazy as they come. Who's inside?"

"Castillo and crime scene."

"Good seeing you. Say hi to Amy and the kids." Jack slipped some medical booties over his shoes, the foul odor of decomposition still in his nose.

"Wait," Tom said. "Are you allowed in there?"

"Morrison cleared it." Jack didn't take Tom's questioning personally. "You can call and check."

Tom reached for his radio. "Thanks for understanding."

"I do understand. But I don't have time to wait." Jack walked past him and inside.

"But . . . Jack!" Tom called after him.

Jack headed through the small apartment and straight down the hallway to Castillo, who was standing in a doorway. "What do you have, Ed?"

"We've called the phone company and we're trying to get a ping on Poole's phone. The judge signed off on the warrant and we should get it soon. They located Poole's car. He ditched it. Probably because of the rear window your fiancée smashed."

Jack smiled. "She's got a heck of an arm. Where did they find the car?"

"Dumped behind H&S Auto. They said none of their cars are missing, so we're assuming he's on foot. IT is working on his computer now." Castillo gestured into the room—a simply furnished bedroom with a desk in one corner, where an IT specialist was busily working on the PC.

"Can he pull up Poole's address book?" Jack asked.

"I can't do anything yet," the specialist said, looking back over his shoulder. "I'm mirroring the hard drive. Standard procedure before I can access any files. It should be done in forty-three minutes, give or take."

"Thanks." Jack turned back to Castillo. "Where's Thomas now?"

"At the photography studio interviewing your fiancée and her friends."

"I'm heading over there. I'll be back in forty-three minutes—give or take."

Castillo and the IT guy both laughed.

* * *

Thomas was outside the studio smoking an e-cigarette when Jack pulled up. "You just missed your fiancée," he said. A cloud of vanilla-scented vapor puffed from his mouth as he spoke. "She said she was going to go see your aunt."

Just then Jack's phone beeped with a text from Alice.

AUNT HADDIE'S FRIEND HEARD DISPATCHER REPORT WOMAN IN WEDDING DRESS CHASING CAR. AUNT H KNEW IT WAS ME. IS UPSET. GOING OVER 2 CALM HER DOWN.

Jack laughed.

"Good news?" Thomas asked.

"My fiancée's funny. Our foster mom heard that a woman in a wedding dress was chasing a car, and Alice is surprised that she knew it was her."

"She's a firecracker, all right. She was all riled up."

"Have you already searched inside?" Jack asked.

"We're about to. I wanted to interview the witnesses first, and now I'm waiting on an IT crew to show up. We're stretched thin. We have one crew checking out that camera in the church, another at Poole's apartment, and a third is coming in from Mayfield. They're still half an hour out."

Jack looked down at his phone. "Where was the camera?"

Thomas took another drag off his e-cigarette and exhaled. "Come on. I'll show you." He opened the door, and Jack followed him inside.

"The camera was in the dressing room," Thomas explained as he walked down the hallway. "It was hidden in the smoke detector. Your fiancée's friend bumped the wall and the smoke detector fell apart. Alice noticed an extra wire that she recognized as a data cable."

Thomas stopped outside the dressing room. The smoke detector was hanging against the wall by three wires.

Wow, that was a great catch. Way to go, Alice! Jack smiled just thinking of her.

"Poole's office is down here," Thomas said, waving for Jack to follow.

The office featured wedding photographs covering nearly every inch of wall space, except for the side of the room that had floor-to-ceiling bookshelves. Two loveseats sat facing each other with a coffee table between them. A desk held a computer and two large monitors. Jack peered at the computer equipment.

"Let's not touch anything until IT gets here," Thomas said.

Jack nodded but kept staring at the router. "The only thing plugged into the router is the computer."

Thomas shrugged. "I'm not a computer guy. What does that mean?"

Jack started back down the hallway. "It means that the camera is plugged in somewhere else." He pulled out a pair of gloves. "Do you mind if I follow the cable?"

"Do you know how to do that?"

"I've run cable with Alice before." Jack pointed at the ceiling tiles. "I won't touch anything; I can lift up a ceiling tile and look where the blue cable goes."

"That's fine."

Jack found a chair, took it to the dressing room, and climbed on. He lifted up the ceiling tile and used his phone flashlight to part the darkness; his height made his search rather easy for him. The blue cable led out of the dressing room and down the hall in the direction of Poole's office. Jack repeated the process in the hall, checking every twenty feet to confirm that the same cable continued all the way to Poole's office. He then climbed on a loveseat in the office and peeked up into the ceiling again. Instead of going toward the desk and computer, the cable snaked around to the left—and passed over the top of the bookshelves.

Jack got down and frowned, pinching the bridge of his nose.

"The cable does come in here?" Thomas asked.

Jack shook his head. "It comes through here and runs straight over that wall." He walked over to take a closer look at the shelves.

There were three separate shelving units. They all held framed photographs, but whereas the unit on the left had the frames sitting on the shelves, the middle and right units had the frames mounted to the back of the bookshelf.

"Why are only the photos on these two units mounted?" Jack asked.

Thomas shrugged.

Jack stared along the length of the shelves. "The office used to be much bigger. Poole blocked off part of it with the bookshelves."

He grabbed the middle and right units and pulled. They were hinged together and opened like swinging doors to reveal a hidden room with one chair facing a wall of monitors—Jack counted sixteen—all showing different scenes. The hidden space was aglow from the wall of screens.

Jack pointed at one. "There's the feed from the dressing room."

"We have to catch this guy." Thomas pointed to another monitor, where two little girls, maybe six or seven years old, were swooping up and down on swings in a playground, all smiles, unaware that they were being recorded. "I'm calling the sheriff to notify the child welfare office— Hey, where are you going?" Thomas called after Jack as he walked out of the office.

"Back to Poole's apartment. I have an idea how to find him."

CHAPTER

40

The police were done questioning Boomer, so he offered to drive Alice to the nursing home. Alice left him in the reception area happily reading *People* magazine and chatting up the nursing staff while she crossed to the visiting room.

Aunt Haddie greeted her with a tight hug and held her hand as they sat down together. "You didn't have to come and see me, honey. I can't imagine all that you have to do."

Alice sighed. "You saw for yourself, it's like a three-ring circus that never ends. And then add in my uncle showing up. Plus, getting stalked by a serial killer is never easy."

Aunt Haddie raised an eyebrow and then squeezed her hand. "Alice Campbell, don't joke about such things."

Alice bit her lip. *What was I thinking, blurting that out to Aunt Haddie? Nice way to calm her down.*

She tried to sound lighthearted, raising her voice. "Honestly, my biggest worry is that Jack won't show up for the wedding," Alice admitted.

"Nonsense! He'll be there. You had that boy the minute you set your green eyes on him."

"I think you have it the wrong way around. I've never loved anyone but him."

Aunt Haddie shook her head and smiled. "He may not have realized it then, and neither did I, but *you* knew. And you know what they say: an acorn doesn't become an oak overnight. Some of the best things in life get better with time to grow. And love is one of those things. That boy has a deep love for you, and you know how fiercely loyal he is. You realize that he loves you more than himself?"

Alice blushed. She didn't know for sure, but she knew the feeling, because that's how she felt about Jack.

Could he really love me back the same way?

Alice kissed Aunt Haddie on the cheek and delicately explained why she'd been running down the street in her wedding dress.

"I had an uneasy feeling about that photographer . . . I was hoping I was wrong." Aunt Haddie scowled. "I certainly never imagined that he was a killer, but there was always something off about that man."

"I didn't see it either. But he wouldn't have had to go far to put the note and flowers in Bobbie G.'s car." Alice crossed her arms. She didn't want to explain to Aunt Haddie how scared and angry she was that Poole had been watching her in the dressing room and left that horrible message for her. Not to mention that pictures of her in varying stages of undress could have made their way onto the internet.

Aunt Haddie leaned over and gave Alice another hug. "Don't you worry about that man, Alice. Jackie will get him."

"I know he will." Alice forced a smile.

"You're selling your happy appearance a little too hard." Aunt Haddie winked. "Don't worry about upsetting me. Out with it. What else is wrong?"

Alice sighed. She never could hide anything from Aunt Haddie. "I just want to make sure that I'm doing the right thing. I'm . . . hesitant."

"About marrying Jackie?"

Alice nodded.

Aunt Haddie looked like she'd swallowed a bug. "That boy would give his right arm for you. He's such a hard worker. Kind. Loyal. True. He'll make a fine husband."

"It's not Jack. It's me. Everything you said about Jack is a hundred and ten percent true."

Aunt Haddie gave her a wink. "Did I mention handsome?"

Alice felt tears coming on. "I just don't know . . . How can he be happy settling for me? You know everything that happened when I was young—losing my family, then getting molested . . . Maybe I'm just too broken."

Aunt Haddie pulled Alice in and held her tightly to her chest. All the pressure of the wedding, the stalker, and finding her family . . . Alice finally let it overwhelm her, and she sobbed in Aunt Haddie's arms. She felt like a little girl again, but she couldn't seem to stop the flow of tears. Aunt Haddie just rocked her in her arms and stroked her head.

After several minutes, Alice sniffled and sat up. Aunt Haddie handed her a tissue box, and Alice blew her nose and looked at her hands. "I came over here so you wouldn't worry about me, and now look—"

Aunt Haddie gently put her hand under Alice's chin so Alice had no other choice but to meet her gaze.

"You are too special for words, my child. I know you have a hard time seeing it, so believe an old woman. You are one of a kind."

"Sometimes that's not a good thing," Alice sniffled.

Aunt Haddie laughed, and everyone in the room turned their heads toward the sound of it—bright, loud, and real. Aunt Haddie waved back at them like she was in a parade and welcomed the attention.

"What's so funny?" Alice grabbed another tissue.

"I never met two people who needed each other more or complemented each other better. Don't you listen to the world, darling. Everyone says you have to be independent and stand on your own. That part is true. But the world also tells you that you don't need anyone else. And that's a lie. We're stronger together. Stronger with friends we can talk to. We're stronger with family and those we can count on. And if you find someone who can stand back to back and fight with you? You're unbreakable."

Alice's smile wavered like a candle in the wind, flickering and about to go out. "But Jack's so . . . Jack. Look at me. I fall apart."

Aunt Haddie laughed again. Alice scowled, which only made Aunt Haddie laugh harder.

"I'm just a dainty little thing that falls to pieces," Aunt Haddie said in a high voice. She grabbed a tissue to wipe her eyes.

"Are you making fun of me?"

"Never." Aunt Haddie reached out and took her hand. "Well, maybe a little." She gave Alice's hand a light squeeze. "I'm just trying to show you how silly you're being. You have so much going on that you have every right to a good cry. I expected one long before this. That's why I went with you to the photography studio."

"Great. So, you do think I'm a crier."

"Everyone needs to cry now and then. It's healthy." Aunt Haddie lifted Alice's chin. "But you're no dainty little thing. You're my fierce little lion."

Alice rolled her eyes and wiped the smudged mascara from her cheeks. "I sure don't feel like a lion."

Aunt Haddie called over to three women sitting near the window. "Ellie? What did you say when you heard the police scanner?"

The old woman smiled. "As soon as I heard that a woman in a wedding dress was chasing a car down the street, I said to myself, that must be your Alice."

Aunt Haddie chuckled and waved. "Thank you." She turned back to Alice. "Not a lion? You tell me how many other women would chase a killer down the street in bare feet and a wedding dress."

Alice blushed.

Aunt Haddie took Alice's hands in hers. "Trust me when I say this. If you and Jack are broken, then God has brought you together to make you both stronger."

Alice smiled. "Thank you."

"Now do me a favor?"

Alice nodded. "Of course, Aunt Haddie."

"Go help Jack catch that creep."

CHAPTER

41

Jack parked the Charger outside Poole's apartment. Officer Kempy was standing on the sidewalk trying to answer the questions of an inquisitive couple walking their dog. Jack gave him a sympathetic wave. He'd been there before. When people see police camped outside their door, they have a right to be nervous and wonder what's going on. You can't tell them too much, because the accused and victims have privacy rights, too. But soon enough, Poole's sick story would be on the news all across the state.

"Hey, Jack," Castillo called from the bedroom doorway as Jack walked inside. "I heard you hit the jackpot."

Jack tried not to make a face. He wouldn't call Poole's hidden office a jackpot. More like a toxic waste dump. "Thomas is waiting on IT. How about your guy? Did he get into the computer yet?"

In answer to his question, the IT man walked out of Poole's bedroom shaking his head. "The drive is encrypted. If we can get anything, it's going to take a while. I did find a number of USB sticks that aren't encrypted, but so far they're just client pictures."

"Does Poole have any paper address books? Mail?" Jack asked. "We need to find friends or relatives that he would go to."

"I think the guy is one hundred percent digital," Castillo said. "The only paper I've found is for the printer, and it's photo paper."

"Have you pulled a list of family? Anyone local?"

Castillo shook his head. "Brother and mother in Washington State. No idea about friends."

"Have you canvassed the neighborhood?"

"Not yet. I'm still looking through drawers."

Jack exhaled and forced a polite smile. "That's great. While you do that, I'm going to start canvassing."

Castillo crossed his arms. "I don't know about that, Jack."

"There's nothing not to know." Jack started for the door. "The sheriff deputized me. It's legal."

Castillo started to say something more, but Jack didn't give him the chance. He shut the door behind him and hurried down the stairs. He didn't need Castillo's permission.

And even if I do, I'm not stopping to get it.

"Jack!" Alice called from down the sidewalk.

Jack turned at the sound of her voice, and she broke into a run and leapt into his arms. He held her tightly and kissed her hair, drinking in everything about her. Her being close made him feel stronger.

"I can't tell you how much I wish I could have seen you in your wedding dress chucking a rock at Poole's car," Jack said with a laugh.

"I should have thrown it harder." Alice brushed back her hair. "I was aiming at the back of his head."

Jack didn't want to let her go, so he kept his arms around her. He laughed harder. "What are you doing here?"

"I was thinking." Her face became serious. "We're a team. We work together."

"What about all the wedding planning?"

"Isn't that why you have a wedding planner? I told Erica to handle anything else that comes up. All the important stuff is already done. And if it's not . . . well, too bad. I've got work to do."

"Looking for the guy who's trying to kill you isn't the safest place for you," Jack said.

Alice grabbed his shirt, pulled him lower, and kissed him. "With you is the safest place for me. Besides, someone has to watch your butt."

"You want to watch my butt?" Jack raised an eyebrow.

Alice blushed. "You know what I mean."

Jack laughed. "I'm going to canvass the neighborhood. Want to join me?"

Alice eyed him suspiciously. "You're not going to try to make me go back to Shawna's?"

"Make you? Aunt Haddie gave me some really good advice when I told her I was going to marry you. She said the most important thing in dealing with you is never try to make you do anything, just ask. The truth is, I'd appreciate your help."

Alice beamed. She held up her fist with her thumb up—their own version of a fist bump. "Let's do this."

At the apartment next door, a young woman opened the door. She was dressed in hospital scrubs and looked tired. "Can I help you?"

"My name is Jack Stratton, and this is Alice Campbell. We're working with the sheriff, and we have a few questions about your neighbor, Philip Poole."

The woman gave him a weary, tight smile and stepped to the side. "Of course. Please come in. I don't know how much I'll be able to tell you, though."

Jack and Alice walked in and took a seat on the couch in the living room in front of an open window. A pile of mail was stacked on the coffee table in front of them, next to a dead houseplant covered in dust.

"I'm Amy Paterson." She sat on a high-backed chair across from them. "I'm a shift nurse at the hospital and I'm currently going to school too."

"We appreciate your time," Jack said. "What can you tell me about your neighbor?"

"I'm afraid not too much. As you can see from my poor plants, I'm not home often. And it's really a hi, bye, have-a-nice-day type of relationship. I didn't even know his last name until you told me just now."

Jack pointed outside. "Each unit has two parking spaces. Did Philip have one or two cars?"

"One. A blue sports car."

"Do you remember him having friends over? Any other cars parked there?"

Amy closed her eyes and nodded. "I think I've seen another car parked next to his a couple of times, but I couldn't even tell you what kind."

"Color? Make? Anything?" Jack pressed.

Amy shrugged. "No idea."

Alice pointed at the window. "You have a little security camera."

Amy scowled. "Package thieves. I had two taken from right in front of the door. I got the camera to scare them away."

"Does the camera also catch the parking spaces?" Alice asked.

Jack had to fight the urge to kiss Alice then and there. "You're brilliant."

Alice blushed.

"It might." Amy stood up. "I haven't looked at it in weeks." She took out her phone and opened an app. Alice moved over to stand beside her, and Jack looked over her shoulder.

"I'm not really too familiar with the software," Amy admitted.

"Would you mind if I take a look?" Alice asked.

Amy handed Alice her phone, and with a few flicks of her fingers, Alice brought up the camera view. Sure enough, it captured the front steps and several parking spaces, including Amy's and Poole's.

Jack held onto Alice's shoulders as she scrolled through the footage. Every time he felt her warm skin beneath his touch, the vision of death and insanity he had left in the old church receded a couple of inches.

Alice scrolled down a few days and stopped when Amy pointed at the screen. "That's it." A green Honda was parked next to Poole's sports car. "I've seen it there several times."

"Is it all right with you if I send a copy of this video to myself?" Alice asked.

"Of course." Amy's eyebrows rose. "Do you mind if I ask what he did?" Alice looked at Jack.

"I'm afraid I can't go into that," he said. "But I will say this: if you see him, or anyone else entering his apartment, do not approach, and call the police immediately."

Amy nodded.

Jack took out his own phone and called the station. "This is Jack Stratton. I need you to run a vehicle report for me."

CHAPTER

42

Jack glanced at Alice, who sat beside him in the Charger. "Did I mention that you're a genius?"

"Yes, several times. But you can tell me again." Alice slid over and leaned against him and let out a sigh.

"You're beautiful and brilliant." He kissed her, keeping one eye open and focused on the house down the street with the green Honda parked out front.

Alice followed Jack's gaze and sat up straight, suddenly rigid. "Why haven't you called the police yet? Are you sure he's here?"

"I'd give it four-to-one odds. Philip's got no car, and the police are watching the bus station and the trains. He's a weird guy, so I'm hoping he doesn't have a lot of friends that would help him out. If Thomas shows up with a bunch of cruisers, he'll scare Philip off."

With the back of his hand, Jack knocked on Alice's chest. There was a solid thud.

"Hey!" Alice smacked his hand away. "Inappropriate."

"I was just making sure you had your bulletproof vest on."

"You can ask instead of getting handsy."

"We're about to get married. I want to do a lot more than get handsy."

Alice's face flamed red.

Lady stood up, stuck her head over the seat back, and nudged Alice's shoulder.

"Ow!" Alice bumped into the door. "Easy." She rubbed behind Lady's ears, her thick fur shedding in the car.

"She misses you," Jack said. "We both do."

Alice leaned forward to kiss Jack, but Lady nudged her with her head again. "Okay. I'll give you a treat, but first I get to kiss Jack."

When they pulled apart, both a little breathless, Jack pointed to the house. "Someone's looking out the front window."

The curtain was pulled back and someone scanned the street. With the reflection on the window, Jack couldn't be certain who it was.

Alice sat bolt upright. "There's a guy coming out."

A chubby man walked down the front steps of the house and scanned up and down the street like a frightened bird.

Jack pulled Alice close and kissed her. "Stop staring," he mumbled.

She nodded slightly and kissed him back. The man got into the green Honda and started it up.

"Wait," Jack cautioned as he held Alice close and gently kissed her again. "Let's see where he goes."

Jack smiled as the Honda backed up and drove around to the side of the house.

"Why are you smiling? Why did he move the car twenty feet?"

"If Poole is inside, the last thing he wants to do is go out the front door."

A few minutes later, the chubby man reappeared with a man in a baseball hat carrying a duffel bag and a tripod.

"See the camera equipment?" Jack grinned. "That's our cue. Dial 911. Lady, the chase is on."

Lady barked excitedly as she sat down.

Alice dialed 911 and put her phone on speaker.

"911, what is your emergency?"

"This is Detective Jack Stratton. I need all available units to 35 White Pine. I've got Philip Poole." As the Charger streaked toward the house, Jack ran down the plan once more. "Open your door, but don't move around the car. There are two of them, and if you move, I'll look back at you and take my eyes off them."

"I won't move unless you tell me," Alice said. "You're running the show."

Jack nodded. "Lady, get ready."

Lady huffed and panted.

The man in the baseball hat was closing the trunk when the Charger skidded to a stop, blocking in the Honda. The man's head jerked up at the sound of skidding tires, and Jack saw the surprised face of Philip Poole.

Jack pressed Lady's release button as he jumped out of the car, his gun aimed at Poole's chest.

Alice's door opened behind him and Lady's claws clicked off the cement.

"Freeze!" Jack ordered. "Police! Hands where I can see them!" A thrill shot through him as he realized how much he'd missed saying those words.

The chubby man got out of the car. When he saw Jack, his hands shot over his head so fast that he dropped his car keys and they bounced off his balding head. Poole started to run for the house, but Lady sprinted in front of him and cut him off.

Snarling and barking like a hungry wolf, she was truly terrifying. Poole shrieked and tried to run the other way, but Lady quickly circled him.

"Stop!" Jack moved sideways, keeping his gun trained on Poole.

Poole stopped moving, but he was still screaming in fear.

"Lady, no speak."

Lady stopped barking. She planted her feet, her fur sticking up, making her look even larger. She bared her teeth and a low rumble emanated from deep in her chest. It sounded like a freight train going by.

"Driver, interlace your fingers behind your head and get down on your knees," Jack ordered.

The chubby man complied; his red cheeks puffed out.

"Lie on your face. Arms out from your sides and feet spread wide."

Poole's hands started to lower.

"Raise your hands!" Alice shouted.

Jack smiled. "You'd better do it, Poole, or she'll shoot you, and then the dog will eat you."

Lady growled and chomped the air. Poole's hands shot back up and he awkwardly kept them up as he knelt and then lay on the ground.

Sirens sounded from every direction. Jack frisked him and slapped cuffs on his wrists. When he yanked Poole to his feet, he couldn't stop smiling.

It felt great to be back.

CHAPTER

43

"Good work," Morrison said, addressing Thomas and Jack equally as they walked into his office. "They're processing Poole now, and then you can interview him, Frank."

"I want to be in on that," Jack said.

"There's an observation room." Thomas crossed his arms and looked to the sheriff. "We've already muddied the legal waters enough by having a consultant present during so much of the investigation."

Morrison stood up behind his desk. "He's not a consultant, remember? He's a detective. I deputized him."

Jack turned to face Thomas. "Look, I'm willing to let you steal credit for catching the guy—"

"Steal? I'm the one who officially arrested him." Thomas tapped his own chest with his thumb.

"After I found him and had him in handcuffs. But hey, get your picture in the paper. I don't care. I just want to make certain we got the right guy."

Thomas made a face like he'd bit his own tongue. "What are you talking about, Stratton?"

"Besides the dressing room, Poole's cameras were all set up in playgrounds, school bus stops and the bathroom outside the kid's park. He's a pedophile."

"You're forgetting to mention the camera we found in the church," Thomas said.

We found?

"None of the monitors in Poole's hidden office had a feed from the church," Jack said, speaking directly to Morrison. "That's why I want to be in on the interview. Poole's definitely guilty of a number of crimes, but we need to make certain that he's the killer we're after."

Thomas put his hands on Morrison's desk and leaned forward, towering over him. "Stratton can't let go of his theory that the killer is after women on their wedding anniversaries. He's got blinders on. There's no way I'm letting Stratton into my interview room, I don't care if he's deputized or not. I've gone along with all this so far, but if you push me, Sheriff, I'm going over your head."

Jack knew the look on the sheriff's face. Jack had just lost the argument. In the end it came down to politics, plain and simple.

"Jack, you'll be watching from the interview observation room," Morrison said. "But Frank, I'm going to join you for the interview."

Jack smiled grimly. He had lost that battle, but with Morrison in the room, there was a chance they could still win the war.

* * *

Jack stood in the interview observation room waiting for Morrison and Thomas to bring Poole in. Castillo scowled as he paced back and forth behind Jack. Thomas had insisted that only two people should question Poole, so Morrison had sent Castillo to watch with Jack. It was clear that he wasn't happy with the decision either.

Jack felt bad for Morrison. The last thing the sheriff needed was for Castillo to hold a grudge; things were tense as it was.

"You know why the sheriff asked you to stay out here, don't you, Ed?" Jack asked.

"Because it's a high-profile case." Castillo fumed. "This is a career-maker. I bet they even make a movie about this guy. Bob could have insisted I be in the room."

"Come off it, Ed. You know Bob doesn't care about that stuff."

"Then explain it to me, Stratton."

"Bob's holding you in reserve. You're the backup plan. You're right—the sheriff could have insisted that you be included. But then he'd be putting all his eggs in one basket. He doesn't know what kind of an interviewer Thomas is. But if Thomas strikes out, then Morrison still has you."

Castillo stopped pacing. He thought for a moment, and the scowl faded from his face. "Yeah, the sheriff knows what a good interviewer I am. That makes sense."

Jack's phone buzzed with a text from Alice. She had gone back to Shawna's but was still working the case. Frank Thomas had missed an important detail. Alysa Snyder had renewed her wedding vows a year ago tomorrow. The news made Jack's stomach tighten.

"You okay, Jack?" Castillo asked.

"Tell me that Thomas has an officer watching Alyssa Snyder."

"He does. Why worry? We caught the guy." Castillo shrugged. "Besides, Alyssa Snyder didn't fit your theory. She was married in December."

Jack was about to respond when the interview room door opened and Thomas and Morrison led Poole in. The room had a single table, with two chairs on one side and a stool bolted to the floor on the other.

Poole's eyes were wild, and he was pale. He was shackled hand and foot with a chain running between them. He stared right at Jack, and his eyes narrowed. Even though Jack was certain he couldn't see through the window, it was still creepy.

"I have no idea how that camera got into the dressing room," Poole said as Morrison sat him down opposite Thomas. "It wasn't mine."

"Hold on a second, Philip." Morrison sat down at the table and pressed a button on a metal box. "My name is Sheriff Robert Morrison. With me is Special Agent Frank Thomas. I'm speaking with Philip Poole at eleven thirty-five on April second."

Morrison read a standard interview opening from a card in a monotone voice, including the Miranda rights. Then he laid the card on the table, leaned back in his chair, and held a hand out toward Philip.

"Please tell us about the camera in the dressing room of your studio at 1540 Myrtle Street."

"I have no idea how that camera got there." Philip leaned forward and his chains rattled. "I never knew it was there until that woman . . . assaulted me! She did. She punched me in the nose. And then that crazy—"

"Save it!" Thomas went straight to the hard-guy approach, slamming his hand down on the table. It made Poole jump, and any sense of superiority and confidence melted.

Jack rolled his eyes as Thomas winced.

"We found your little peep room," Thomas continued as he rubbed his hand on his leg. "It was in your office. IT is going through that computer and the one at your apartment. It's over, Poole."

Poole drew in a deep, ragged breath, and he looked at the two men with a wild plea in his eyes. Morrison shifted in his seat, his face unreadable, and Poole suddenly cried out and sagged forward, his head dinging off the metal table.

His sobs grew into a loud wail. "It isn't my fault. I . . . I . . ." He raised his tear-stained face and his crazy eyes were back. "It was Ben! Benson Collier. All that stuff is his."

Morrison slid a tissue box across the table. "Benson Collier owns the house where we arrested you."

"Yeah. All of that stuff is his." Poole blew his nose.

"You're admitting that you and Ben worked together to set up the church?" Thomas asked.

"Oh, that was a smooth transition," Castillo grumbled.

"What church?" Poole asked as he wiped his nose again. Part of the tissue stuck to his chin.

"On Buck Mountain." Thomas pulled his seat closer to the table. "The one where you posed the bodies."

Poole tried to reach his ear with his finger, but because of the chain, his hand only lifted as high as the side of his face. He flicked the tissue off his chin and looked back and forth between Morrison and Thomas, clearly confused.

"We found your hidden room," Morrison said calmly. "We've taken fingerprints from the keyboard, from the monitors, and from the various cameras you had set up in the neighborhood—including the one at the playground. It was helpful to us that you placed those cameras in weatherproof enclosures—they preserved the prints. And those fingerprints are going to match yours, Philip."

Poole started crying again, tears cascading down his face, which was now splotchy and red.

"Why don't you do everyone a favor and tell us why you did it. Maybe we can help," Morrison said.

"I—I don't know why I get these . . . urges," Philip stammered through tears. "I can't help it. But I never touched any of the kids. I just took pictures. I'm sick. I need help."

"This guy didn't do it," Jack said. "He's a pedophile, but he isn't a killer."

"But he's confessing," Castillo said.

"To the pictures. Not to the murders. He doesn't have a clue about all that."

"Is that why you killed the women?" Thomas asked. "Because they grew up?"

"What?" Poole grabbed more tissues, but his face was now a snotty mess. "Women? I didn't kill anyone. I just watch, and . . . take pictures. I swear."

Jack walked forward and pounded twice on the wall. Everyone in the interrogation room jumped.

"Someone's in there!" Poole shouted as he stared wide-eyed at the mirror.

Jack walked out into the hallway and Thomas stormed out to join him, followed by Morrison.

"Are you seriously interrupting my interrogation, Stratton?"

"He didn't kill anyone, which means the real killer is still at large," Jack snapped as he texted Alice the news, fingers flying across the screen.

"We have not determined that yet," said Thomas.

"You need to tell the officers guarding Sara McCorkle and Alyssa Snyder to remain on high alert."

"There's no one watching Snyder." Thomas crossed his arms. "I had to pull him back to look for Poole."

"You left her unguarded?" Jack felt the veins on his neck start to throb.

"She was a low-probability target to begin with. She didn't even fit your own pattern of the anniversaries, remember?" Thomas said.

Jack stared down at his phone, his chest tightening. "She does fit. I just got a text from my fiancée. Alyssa and her husband renewed their vows when he got cancer. That was a year ago tomorrow." Jack turned and started running down the hall.

"Where are you going?" Thomas yelled after him.

Jack rushed out the side door and sprinted for the Charger. Thomas was a fool. Jack just hoped that his mistake didn't get Alyssa Snyder killed.

CHAPTER

44

itting in my car parked across the street from Sara McCorkle's house, it's hard not to get too excited. I thought I'd be more devastated that my grand wedding had been spoiled, but . . . *c'est la vie*. My new wedding will be better.

Minimalistic. Intimate.

Stupid Jack Stratton. It still bothers me that I had to abandon my masterpiece, but I have to focus on my new plans. There isn't much time.

I take out my phone. There's still a policeman inside the house. At least the other ones left. I turn up the police scanner and smile. Of course, I knew Philip was a pervert all along. Now the police think he's responsible for everything and they've let their guard down. It wouldn't have mattered if they hadn't. They can't stop me. But it'll make my job easier.

It's almost too easy now.

They're guarding Sara like I'm going to come into the house with guns blazing. How stupid. How foolish. They think they can keep me out.

I unlock my phone and pull up my camera app. I miss not being able to check on The Wedding, but I'll be able to see my new wedding soon enough. I switch camera views to the ones I hid inside Sara's house. Sara is upstairs in her bedroom. She's yawning. Getting sleepy. It's almost time.

I switch to the camera in the living room—the screen flashes. A pretty picture of Sara's husband asleep on the couch. He's got a bad heart, so the carbon monoxide affected him first. The policeman is yawning, too. He's nodding off in his chair beside the window. He'll be asleep soon.

I love Facebook. People always say where they're going and when they won't be home. When Sara posted that she was going to dinner with her brother and his new girlfriend two weeks ago, I hurried right over. Installing the remote damper on the furnace took less than ten minutes.

Oh, I almost forgot.

I switch cameras over to the one at Alyssa Snyder's home. She's all alone. I turn on the damper for that furnace, too. I'll head over there after I pick up Sara.

The policeman nods off. That's my cue.

I put the car into gear and drive right up to the house. I shut off the damper and take out my gas mask. Carbon monoxide gives me a vicious headache. I'm not in the mood to carry Sara to the car, so I hope she's not completely out yet. It'll be easier to get her to walk out. Then I can stuff her in the trunk.

I check the cameras one last time. Sara's eyes are heavy and her head is getting droopy. She probably thinks she's just tired because of all the stress. But she's still conscious.

Slipping inside the house, I leave the back door open to let out a little of the gas-rich air. I don't want to kill the policeman unless I have to. The husband I couldn't care less about.

As I walk past the living room, neither man stirs. A mirror in the hallway catches my reflection. The gas mask ruins the look of my suit, but it can't be helped. I walk up the stairs and stop in the bedroom doorway.

Sara slowly turns her head to stare at me. A puzzled look crosses her face before her mouth twists into the beginnings of a scream.

I hold a finger in front of my mouth. "Silence," I whisper. "Stand up." I aim the gun at her head, and shockingly, she obeys. How convenient.

"Happy anniversary, Sara."

CHAPTER

45

The Charger's tires screeched and the muscles in Jack's forearms flexed as he clamped his fingers around the steering wheel to power through a turn. He was five minutes out from Alyssa Snyder's house, which made him her best chance. The closest cruiser was more than ten minutes away.

He dialed Alyssa's number again, but the call went straight to voice mail.

Lady barked in the back seat. She was still fired up from catching Poole. She liked to run, and Poole hadn't given her the chance to show off. Jack's radio crackled to life.

"Unit 11, please respond to 173 Cloudy Creek Lane immediately." Jack inhaled sharply. That was Sara McCorkle's address.

"Please reconfirm that request," replied the responding officer.

"Unit 11, you are requested to respond to 173 Cloudy Creek Lane immediately. Officer there is not responsive."

Jack mashed the gas pedal to the floor. The Charger roared through a red light and down Alyssa's street. He pumped the brakes, cut the wheel, and skidded to a stop in the driveway. He pressed the release switch and ran for the front door as he unholstered his weapon.

"To me!" Jack called out to Lady as he raced up the front steps and pounded on the door.

He heard a noise inside. Lady growled. Jack pounded on the door again and peered through the little window beside it. Alyssa Snyder stood at the end of the hallway, leaning against the wall. She had her back to him. Jack tried the doorknob—it was locked. Alyssa turned around, squinting as she looked toward the door.

Jack motioned to her. "Alyssa Snyder? I'm with the police!"

Alyssa nodded, but as she stepped forward, her legs wobbled and she slid down the wall. Jack stepped back and kicked the door open. Alyssa didn't even lift her head as the doorframe splintered and the door slammed against the wall.

Lady sniffed, then clawed the air and barked. That was her signal that she had found a scent. She raced through the living room and disappeared into the kitchen, followed by a loud crash.

"Lady! Stop!" Jack called after her, but it was too late. The huge dog had leapt through the screen door and was racing across the backyard.

Jack rushed over to Alyssa and called for an ambulance.

From somewhere in the backyard, Lady howled. She was on the hunt.

CHAPTER

46

Lady's paws dug into the grass as she lowered her head and sped across the backyard. Her muscles stretched, flexed, and felt wonderful as the ground raced by underneath her. The wind against her face made her eyes water, but she pushed herself even harder in the direction the smell was leading her, the stinky odor from the bottle. Jack had wanted her to find that smell at the death house, and now it was here.

Up ahead, a person was getting into a car.

The smell was bad. Death was bad. The person getting in the car must be bad, too!

The ground became a blur. Lady dug down even deeper and picked up more speed.

Run. Run faster.

She gulped in huge breaths and felt power course through her. Her paws sank into the turf and threw up clods of dirt behind her. Her body stretched in full extension. Blood surged into Lady's muscles, and her sharp canine teeth flashed as the need to protect her owners drove her forward. She lowered her head and concentrated on one thing: speed.

The vehicle pulled out onto the road, reached the end of the street, and stopped. Finding new hope, Lady laid her ears flat back against her head and dug in harder. But just as she narrowed the gap, the vehicle moved again, taking a right onto the main road.

Lady's weight shifted, and she cut into the woods to try to cut off the fleeing vehicle. Branches scraped at her face as she raced through the underbrush and bounded over a log.

I can make it.

She burst onto the road just behind the vehicle and let out a roar that echoed off the trees. The vehicle slowed and stopped.

A loud bang sounded, and Lady yelped as something slammed into her side, knocking her sideways. Pain raced across her chest and her legs tangled together. She tripped and crashed into the dirt.

A cloud of dust stung her nose and eyes. Her chest burned. She roared. That only made it hurt more. She did it again anyway.

The vehicle was moving.

Lady got to her feet. But when she put weight on her front left leg, it wobbled beneath her. Her leg hurt. Her ribs hurt. She whined.

She hopped forward on three legs. A car honked its horn. She stumbled to the side and fell again to the dust, barely daring to breathe through the pain.

Where is Jack? I need him.

Lady closed her eyes.

CHAPTER

47

Stupid Jack Stratton! My hands are shaking. That was too close. I had barely walked in through the back door when Jack started pounding on the front door. I have to get out of here.

I stuff the gun under my seat as best as I can with trembling fingers and scan the road. The gunshot was loud. The last thing I need is to get pulled over with Sara's body in the trunk.

I didn't really want to kill the dog.

That's on Jack, too.

Now what I am going to do? I need another witness.

The ring!

It's not on the passenger seat. Did it fall out? I frantically feel the fabric of the seat, jamming my fingers between the cushion and the seat back. I feel something smooth and metal and pull it out.

I still have it.

I start breathing again.

A horn honks in front of me. I've drifted into the oncoming lane. I quickly yank the car back onto my side of the road. The other driver swerves onto the shoulder, kicking up dirt and dust. He's screaming and swearing and making all sorts of gestures.

I hope he turns around. I hope he follows me.

I'm so angry now I'd love to shoot him in the face. That would help. That would make me feel better. I'd pretend it was Jack.

I check the rearview mirror. The other car kept going. Coward.

I open my hand again and look at my prize. It has to be more than luck. Alyssa must have taken off her precious ring to do the dishes. How sickeningly sweet. She cares so much about this little rock that she removes it and puts it in a special dish so it won't get dirty.

These people make me sick. They don't realize what true art is or what's truly valuable.

A rock?

The thought leaves a bad taste in my mouth.

I didn't want to kill the dog.

Or did I?

The dog's death will hurt Jack especially and I want to hurt him since he's caused me so much pain. All that work . . . I was so close to completing The Wedding, and he ruined it.

But I will complete my piece. I'm almost there. It will be a very intimate ceremony. Alice, Sara, me . . . and one more.

I pull up my notes. Social media is such a gift. Aunt Haddie's nursing home lists all its staff, along with their pictures. They're even so helpful as to list their positions. Looks like Susan Brown is working the front desk today. Cute girl, pleasant face. Young. And she's friends with Alice. I saw her name on the wedding guest list.

My heart starts beating faster as I pull into the parking lot and pick up the other phone. I've never used it, but I need it now.

Texting is hard with shaking fingers, but I manage it. HI SUE, 4GOT 2 TELL U WE NEED AUNT HADDIE 4 REHEARSAL. SRY! PLS HAVE HER READY IN 15. SENDING CAR 4 HER. THX, ALICE

I read it over before hitting send. Then I hold my breath as I wait for the response.

It arrives a moment later: NP :)

A smile spreads across my face.

My little wedding is coming together.

And once I have Aunt Haddie, getting Alice will be easy.

CHAPTER

48

Alyssa Snyder was breathing shallowly but unresponsive. Through the open front door, Jack saw the ambulance crew pull into the driveway and laid Alyssa's head down gently as the EMTs rushed in. Jack recognized both men from his days on the force, though he couldn't remember their names. There was still no sign of the police.

"We have to get you two out of here," one of them said. "Carbon monoxide."

That's what killed Delores Gill.

"How do you know it's carbon monoxide?" Jack asked as they carried Alyssa outside.

"Can't be certain, but the same thing happened at 173 Cloudy Creek Lane. There's another EMT crew over there. They gave us the heads-up just as we arrived here. Apparently both houses are related to a case the cops are working on. You probably know more than I do. How do you feel? Were you in there long?"

"I'm fine," Jack said. "I was only inside a few minutes. Is everyone all right at the other house?"

"Two men are receiving treatment for carbon monoxide poisoning. One's an officer."

They laid Alyssa down in the grass and the EMTs started administering oxygen.

"What about the woman? Sara McCorkle?" Jack asked.

The EMT glanced up and shook his head. "They didn't mention a woman."

Jack dialed Castillo. When he picked up, Jack could hear the sirens in the background. "Ed, it's Jack. The guy came after Alyssa Snyder. I scared him off but . . ." He covered the phone and shouted, "Lady!" then continued, "EMTs are treating Alyssa now. She's okay."

"Well, that's one bit of good news. I'm en route to the McCorkles'. Sara is missing, and her husband and Officer Geer are being treated by EMTs. Was it carbon monoxide at Alyssa's?"

"That's what the EMTs are saying, but only because that's what it was at the McCorkles'. No confirmation." He covered the phone. "Lady!" Jack called out, his voice growing rawer with each scream.

"All right. Listen, I'm pulling in now. I'll call you later." Castillo hung up.

Jack touched the EMT's shoulder. "Can you take it from here?"

He nodded, and Jack bolted around the house to find Lady. It had been nearly ten minutes since she ran off, and he had no idea where she'd gone to. And he wouldn't leave his partner. "Lady!" he shouted.

He jogged to the residential street behind the house. There was no sign of Lady. The main road was off to Jack's right, so he went that way. When he reached the intersection, he spotted a car pulled to the side of the road with its hazard lights on. A middle-aged woman with a white shirt and blue jeans was standing behind it, looking down at something lying on the ground.

Jack broke into a sprint.

The woman looked up as he approached, but Jack barely even noticed her. He couldn't tear his eyes away from Lady.

"It's some kind of police dog, I think," the woman said.

Jack dropped to his knees beside Lady. "Oh, girl. Oh, please."

Lady whined but didn't open her eyes. Jack's hand hovered over her as he scanned her body for injuries. His breath caught in his throat when he saw the bullet impact crater in her Kevlar vest. He couldn't tell if the bullet had gone through or not. He reached out to try to put his fingers under the vest.

Lady's eyes snapped open and her head jerked up. Her jaws chomped the air so close to his face that Jack's hair blew back. The woman beside him shrieked.

"Good girl." Jack's hand shook as he gently touched Lady's head. She whimpered and closed her eyes again, breathing soft, shallow breaths.

"Ma'am, I need you to give me a ride to the vet." Jack was in triage mode and all business, his directives clear and concise.

"Of course." The woman nodded but didn't come any closer.

"Move your car right up next to the dog, and I'll put her in your backseat."

As the woman got in her car, Jack examined the wound. Regardless of whether the bullet had penetrated the vest, Lady's ribs could be broken, so he wanted to move her as little as possible. A broken rib could easily puncture a lung.

The woman backed up her car, and when Jack opened the rear door, he caught the frightened look in her eyes. He had seen it a thousand times on too many faces of soldiers, officers, victims. Jack knew he needed to keep her calm.

"I apologize," he said. "But she's hurt, and she's going to bark a lot. Don't be scared. Just drive." He then started to give her directions to the vet.

"I know where it is. Do you want to lay her down in the backseat?"

"I'm going to hold her."

The woman went pale. "Is that safe?"

For him, it wasn't—in Lady's condition, she might lash out. But it was the safest thing for Lady. It was dangerous enough to lift her once; he didn't want to have to do it again. He'd do his best to keep her immobile.

Jack opened the front passenger-side door and moved the front seat forward as far as it would go. Then he knelt down beside his fallen partner. "This is going to hurt, girl. I'm sorry. I'm trying to help you." He slid his arms underneath her front legs and lifted them up and over his shoulders.

Lady's jaws chomped the air, and she howled in his ear. Jack wrapped his strong arms around her, pulling her toward him as he struggled to stand. His thighs and lower back burned as he hoisted her one hundred twenty pounds and backed toward the back seat. An image of Alice dancing with Lady like this in the living room flashed in his mind.

Alice is going to be heartbroken.

"We're gonna take a ride, Lady," Jack said in a hushed voice before lowering himself onto the edge of the backseat. Then, moving as gently as he could, he leaned back, planted his heels against the bottom of the doorframe, and pushed with all his might, sliding the two of them into the car, like a stretcher into an ambulance.

Lady's whole body shook on top of him. Jack spoke softly, trying to soothe her, as the Good Samaritan came around and closed the car door. He held Lady's harness, trying to keep her immobile and not put any stress on her side, but there was no adjusting to being beneath Lady's weight.

The woman got back in the driver's seat, and the car started forward. At one point they struck a pothole and Lady's jaws clamped down on Jack's hand. Her teeth punctured the skin, and Jack felt like the bones in his hand would snap. But he held on and managed not to scream.

"Easy, Lady. Easy, girl. Let go, please." Lady opened her mouth and whined.

Jack felt the warm and sticky blood running down his arm. He closed his eyes and prayed that this dog he loved—who'd saved his life not once, but twice—would be spared her life, too.

CHAPTER

49

While Shawna, Bobbie G., Boomer, and Kendra celebrated in the living room, Alice sat alone on the bed in Shawna's cramped guest bedroom, staring down at the phone in her hand. This was the second time her call had gone straight to voice mail.

Bobbie G. knocked on the open door. "You okay?"

Alice opened her mouth to respond, but slowly closed it. She wasn't okay. Things didn't feel right. In spite of them catching Philip, she still kept looking over her shoulder as if someone was watching her.

"I can't reach Jack."

Bobbie waved a dismissive hand, crossed his big arms, and leaned against the doorframe with a thud. "You know Jack. He's probably interviewing the guy. Raking him over the coals."

Alice shook her head. "He called earlier. He doesn't think Philip is the killer."

"But he had all those cameras and stuff."

"Jack thinks he's probably a pedophile, but he said statistically, they stick with targeting children. So why would he target adult women on their wedding anniversaries?"

Bobbie's smile faded. "Crap. That makes total sense. Guess the party's over."

"I just want Jack to call."

"He will. Don't tell him I said this, but if anybody can find that guy, Jack can."

"Thanks."

"You want to be alone, or . . . ?"

Alice nodded, and Bobbie backed out of the room and closed the door.

Alice's phone buzzed. It was a group chat message. She didn't recognize the originating number, but Erica's number was included in the group, so she knew it had to be wedding-related.

I HAVE A WEDDING SURPRISE 4 U AND JACK. GO 2 BATHROOM WINDOW 2 SEE PARKING LOT.

A surprise for me and Jack?

Alice got up, gave a little wave to everyone in the living room, went into the bathroom, and closed the door behind her. But before she looked out the window, she stopped, wary, and texted back, WHO IS THIS?

The response came immediately. TRUST ME. U WILL LOVE THIS. SOMEONE WANTS 2 SAY HI 2 THE BLUSHING BRIDE.

OK. HAVE EM' CALL ME.

I'm not sticking my head out a window for someone I don't know.

I CAN SEND VIDEO INSTEAD. 4 UR EYES ONLY. R U ALONE?

YES.

The sender texted a video, along with an emoji of wedding bells. Alice opened it.

It showed Aunt Haddie in the backseat of a car, her head leaning against the window. Her eyes were closed like she was sleeping, a line of drool escaping from the corner of her mouth.

SHE'S WITH ME RIGHT NOW. LOOK.

Alice rushed to the window. There was a sedan parked outside. Aunt Haddie was in the backseat.

Alice's heart dropped like a stone in her chest.

COME OUT THE WINDOW. TELL ANYONE AND UR AUNT DIES.

Alice's blood boiled as she texted back. U HURT HER AND I KILL U.

COME OUT NOW! TICK-TOCK!

Alice stuffed her phone in the waistband of her jeans at the small of her back, stepped on the toilet rim to give her a boost, and climbed out the window onto the fire escape. She knew Jack was going to kill her for doing this, but she had to. If this psycho killed Aunt Haddie, she'd never be able to live with herself.

She quickly descended the ladder, her focus on the car. Someone was in the passenger seat.

They probably have a gun and they're going to order me to drive.

The car was parked facing away from her. Keeping a sharp angle to whoever was sitting in the passenger seat, Alice quickly crossed the parking lot. From behind would be the best position to try to attack. Jack had been teaching her karate, and she'd always had a mean right hook.

Alice's hand balled into a fist. The passenger window was down but the person hadn't turned around yet. Alice lunged forward, grabbing the door with her left hand and swinging around with her right and struck the person in the face. The person slumped over onto the empty driver's seat.

Yet something didn't feel right, and when Alice looked in the car, she understood why. The person in the front seat was a woman. Her eyes were open and gray. And she was clearly dead.

I just punched a corpse.

Pain shot up Alice's spine as the Taser barbs hit her. She pitched forward against the car and fell onto the tar in a heap. Her muscles knotted and constricted, but she could feel the sharp jab of a needle into her thigh.

She tried to lift her head, but someone opened the rear door and grabbed her by the shirt. She caught a glimpse of the polished black shoes and suit pants, but nothing more as he stuffed her in the backseat at Aunt Haddie's feet and closed the door.

Alice wheezed. She gasped for air but still felt like she was suffocating. She wanted to scream, but darkness was sweeping over her.

Was she dying?

No. Please, God. Jack . . .

CHAPTER

50

The Good Samaritan stopped right at the entrance of the Darrington Animal Shelter, a long one-story building set back from the road. Jack stroked Lady's head as the woman circled the car and opened the rear door. Then he hooked his feet on the doorframe and awkwardly scooted himself out until he could lever himself to a sitting position. He did his best not to jostle Lady for fear of further injury, but the poor dog still whimpered, whined, and pressed her muzzle against the side of Jack's face.

"Almost there, girl. Almost there." He turned to the woman. "Thank you for everything."

"I'm glad I could help. I hope they can save her."

The vet's assistant, Lacie, appeared at the door and held it open for Jack. She was in her mid-twenties, with a retro punk look—high-top sneakers, black skirt, silver nose ring, and a short-sleeved, paint-spattered shirt revealing arms covered in tattoos. The last time Jack had seen her, she'd had a blue streak running down the middle of her jet-black hair; now the streak was bright pink.

"What happened to Lady?" Lacie asked. Lady was somewhat of a celebrity at the clinic. Everyone loved the huge dog that Jack and Alice adopted after she helped them find the Giant Killer—the man who killed her former master.

"She's been shot. I can't tell if the vest stopped the bullet."

Lacie gasped. "Follow me." Holding onto Lady's harness, Jack followed Lacie down the hall into the examination room. Lacie helped him lower Lady onto the table. The dog's muzzle twisted up in a snarl and she made a noise somewhere between a whimper and a bark.

"You're hurt!" Lacie said, seeing the blood on Jack's hand. "Did you get shot, too?"

"No. Lady's in a lot of pain. She didn't mean it."

Lacie nodded. "I'll get Ryan."

Lady pushed her head against Jack's chest. Jack stroked her head with his left hand. "It's okay," he said, scratching her favorite place behind her ears.

The door swung open only a moment later, and Lacie came in with Ryan, who ran the animal shelter and clinic. He wore round glasses and had a wavy brown ponytail. Although he was in his early thirties, his khaki pants and blue T-shirt gave him a more youthful appearance.

"What happened?" Ryan asked.

"She's been shot."

Ryan laid a gentle hand on the big dog and spoke softly. "You're gonna be fine, Lady. Let's have a look at you." He gently slipped a muzzle over Lady's snout. Jack hated it, but he understood that Ryan had to protect himself and his staff.

"Have you checked to see if the bullet penetrated the vest?" Ryan asked Jack.

"No. I thought keeping her immobile would be the best thing to do."

"It was. Good job."

Ryan gave Lady a shot in her hindquarters to help relieve her pain. She growled through clenched teeth. Jack wasn't sure if it was from the discomfort of the shot or the indignation of the muzzle.

She's a fighter.

The vet took out a pair of scissors. "It would be best for Lady if I cut off the vest to look at the injury. I know it's expensive but—"

"I don't care about the money. I care about Lady. Cut it off."

Carefully, and with a great deal of effort, Ryan cut off Lady's bulletproof vest. As he lifted the vest out of the way, both he and Jack smiled. There was no exit hole in the Kevlar plate.

"Her ribs could still be broken," Ryan said. "Lacie, why don't you take Lady down to X-ray while I have a look at Jack's hand?"

Lacie patted the big dog as she wheeled her out of the room.

"I'll need to take the vest back so we can retrieve the bullet," Jack said.

"No problem." Ryan pointed at the chair. "Let's get that hand cleaned up. Do you need something for the pain?"

"I can't," Jack said. "I have to keep my head on straight. I need to drive."

The vet examined Jack's hand. "I know Lady is up on her shots, so no worries there. But it looks like you're going to need stitches. I can patch you up until you can get to the hospital."

"That could be a while. I'm working another serial killing."

"I don't know how you do it. I'm glad I'm a vet and not a police officer."

As Ryan started washing Jack's cuts, Jack said, "I'm not going to end up howling at the moon when you're done, am I?"

Ryan chuckled. "Don't worry, I started out as a primary care physician. But I got tired of dealing with insurance companies. Besides, animals make much better patients. They don't come in armed with their self-diagnosis from Dr. Google, demanding that I treat them for whatever malady they've already determined they have."

"You seriously went from a human doctor to a vet?" Jack asked incredulously. "I mean—no offense. I just never heard of anyone doing it."

"Neither did my folks. I thought they were going to explode. My father almost did. He didn't speak to me for a whole year. I still had med school debts, after all, and here I was going back to school, only to make less money on the other side." Ryan picked up some clean cloth. "This is going to hurt."

Jack set his elbow on the table and grimaced. "How's your relationship with him now?"

"Oh, it's great. Unfortunately, it took him having a heart attack to turn the tide on things. After that, he agreed that I should do something that I love, doesn't stress me out, and pays the bills."

Jack ground his teeth as Ryan flushed out the deep puncture wounds. Ryan chuckled. "I'm used to dogs growling at me but not humans."

"Sorry."

"You know, you really are going to need stitches. And that should be done at a hospital."

"Can't you just throw in a couple of stitches yourself? One woman is missing, another was attacked, and the guy is targeting Alice. I'll go to the hospital as soon as I can, but . . ."

"I get it. Is your tetanus up to date?"

"Just got one."

"There's still a high risk of infection. I'll throw in some simple interrupted sutures that will hold the wound closed, but you'll have to get this looked at within a few days. Will you agree to that?"

Jack nodded.

"It's going to hurt."

"More than getting bitten by Chewbacca?"

Ryan laughed. "Actually, maybe a little less."

Ten minutes later, Ryan had finished the stitches and was wrapping Jack's hand when Lacie stuck her head in.

"The X-rays are done. I need you to take a look."

"Be right there."

"I can finish wrapping my hand," Jack said, taking the gauze from Ryan.

"Thanks." Ryan set the tape down before following Lacie out of the room.

Jack finished bandaging his hand and awkwardly taped the end. He stared down at the bulky bandage and frowned. *That's going to go great with a tux.* He pulled out his phone and hit speed dial for Alice.

It went to voice mail.

Come on, Alice. Of all the times not to pick up.

He left a message. "Hey. I know you're doing a lot, but I need to speak with you. Call me. Love you."

Jack stuffed the phone in his pocket and adjusted the gauze.

Ryan returned with mostly good news. "Two of Lady's ribs are cracked. But they're not broken, and there's no lung or organ damage. Normally I might recommend external fixation, which involves pins. However, seeing how Lady is used to wearing a vest, I think we can wrap it. I do want to keep her here for a few days, however."

"Thank you, Ryan. And please thank Lacie for me, too. Can I see Lady?"

"You can, but we gave her a sedative to take the X-rays. She's out cold."

Jack's phone buzzed in his pocket. It was Bobbie G. "Sorry, I need to take this," Jack said. He answered while walking into the hallway. "Hey, man. I've been trying to get ahold of Alice. Can you get her for me?"

There was a long pause. Bobbie cleared his throat and when he spoke, he sounded on the verge of tears. "Jack . . . Alice is gone."

CHAPTER
51

A lice's eyes fluttered open. Wherever she was, it was warm. Stuffy. Surprised she wasn't tied up or in chains, she unconsciously rubbed her wrists and stretched her limbs.

She hadn't expected to wake up at all. Her head pounded.

A dim light filtered in through cracks around a door. She was in a room no bigger than a closet. The only furnishing was a bucket in one corner. The room was otherwise entirely empty.

She sniffed the air. The room smelled . . . old. Like one of those living history museums. So, she was in an older building . . . The face of a dead woman flashed in her memory, and she sat bolt upright.

Aunt Haddie!

The killer had Aunt Haddie. She had been in the back seat. Asleep, or . . .

Please, God, let her have been just sleeping. Please help Aunt Haddie. Please.

Alice's hands flew to her lower back, damp with perspiration. Her phone wasn't there. Not surprising. She noticed that her belt was missing as well, resulting in her pants being a little loose. Her shoelaces were gone, too.

Alice felt sick at the thought of the killer touching her when she was unconscious.

As quietly as she could, she stood up and tried the door. The knob didn't turn. She ran her fanned-out fingers over the door, reading it as if she were trying to read Braille. Waist-high on the door was a rectangular cutout nearly a foot long and six inches high, backed by metal.

It's one of those feeding slots they have in prison doors. I'm in a cell. Panic clutched at her, but she resisted the urge to pound on the door.

She flipped the bucket over and climbed on top. It was too dark to see the ceiling, so she reached up as high as she could, but she couldn't connect with anything above her. She stepped down, and the bucket made a scraping sound against the wood floor.

"Hello?" Aunt Haddie whispered from somewhere in the darkness.

Alice's throat tightened, and she nearly doubled over, like someone had punched her in the gut. Instinctively she moved closer to the sound of Aunt Haddie's voice and pressed her hands against the wall, wishing she could knock it down. "Aunt Haddie. I'm so sorry."

"Lower your voice, baby girl. I'm here. Everything is going to be okay." Aunt Haddie's voice was calm and strong—clearer than Alice had heard her in many months. Alzheimer's was a cruel and unpredictable disease.

Alice began to cry. "I'm so sorry. I'm so sorry. This is all my fault. He took you because of me."

"Don't be silly. There's a reason I'm here. I'm sure of it. And I'd rather be here with you to help you, instead of thinking of you here alone."

Aunt Haddie still had the heart of a mother bear. "How did he catch you?"

"Susan said you were sending someone to pick me up. I waited at the front door, and when the car came, I got into the backseat. I didn't even think about it. There was a man driving. I didn't see his face, because he was turned away, but I immediately noticed his cologne: Proper Modern Gentleman. That was the same cologne my Alton wore every day for fifty years, and for just a second, I thought . . . well, I about went to pieces. I opened my purse to get a tissue and the man handed something back to me. I thought he was handing me a box of tissues, but the thing sparked, and then there was a searing pain. The next thing I knew, I woke up in here."

"That was a Taser." Alice fought to control her voice. "What kind of dirtbag Tasers an old lady?"

"Who are you calling an old lady?" Aunt Haddie chuckled.

"How can you laugh at a time like this? That man is a—"

"I know what kind of man he is. And I know how dark this looks. But we're going to pray, and the good Lord is going to get us out of here."

Tears rolled down Alice's face. She wanted to be strong, but this was just too much. "Aunt Haddie, how's God going to get us out of here? We don't even know where we are and no one else does either."

"God knows where we are. And Jackie's going to be looking. That boy will find us."

"What if he doesn't?"

There was a little pause and Aunt Haddie started humming softly. "There's always the chance that he won't and God calls us home. If that's the case, then you try to concentrate on what a wonderful reunion party it's going to be."

Alice sobbed. She didn't want to die. Not now. She wanted to live. She wanted to scream how unfair it all was. But she knew she didn't have to say a word. Aunt Haddie understood. She had already buried Chandler and Michelle. She had never been able to bear children, but she had loved those two like her own. And she loved Alice and Jack the same way.

"Alice?"

"I'm here."

"Put your hand against the wall."

Alice placed her right hand on the wall, guessing where Aunt Haddie would be placing hers.

"Dear Lord. I know we're in a long line of a great company of your children calling out to you from the darkness of prison, but we also know that you're there for each one of us. You hear us. If it's your will, please show us the way to get out or lead others to us. If it's not to be, give us the strength to bear this burden. Thank you for Alice, and be with her now. In Christ's name, Amen."

Alice let her head sag forward until her forehead touched the wall. She could picture Aunt Haddie on the other side. She'd be sitting on the floor, one hand against the wall, the other lifted to the heavens.

"We're going to get out of this, Alice," Aunt Haddie whispered.

"How do you know?"

"Because this man messed with the wrong family."

Alice's faint smile faded as she heard a door open and footsteps drawing closer.

CHAPTER

52

An officer parted the crowd to let Jack pull the Charger into Shawna's parking lot. Three police cruisers were already there, along with Morrison's car. Jack jumped out of the car and ran over to Bobbie.

"What happened?"

Bobbie was pale and shaking. He pointed up at Shawna's apartment. "Alice went to the bathroom, and the next thing we knew she was gone. Out that window."

Jack's gaze traveled up the fire escape to the open window on the second floor. "Did she say anything to you?"

"Nothing. I spoke to her in the bedroom just before. We were all celebrating about you catching Philip. But she said you didn't think Philip was the guy. Next thing I knew she came out of the bedroom, went straight to the bathroom, and closed the door. After a few minutes, Kendra got up and knocked. When Alice didn't answer, she kicked in the door. We saw the window was open and Alice was gone."

Jack wanted to grab Bobbie and shake him, tell him to calm down, but Bobbie was already so upset, Jack figured smacking him around would only make him worse. He lowered his voice, softening it, coaxing him to remember.

"Bobbie, close your eyes and think. When Alice walked out of the bedroom, did she say anything? Did she do anything?"

Bobbie clamped his eyes closed, his big hands clenching and opening. After a moment he shook his head violently like a dog with a toy. "Nothing. She just . . . wanted you to call." He glared down at the ground.

"Picture Alice walking out of the bedroom," Jack said.

"She opened the door and . . . looked at us. Waved." Bobbie's face scrunched up. "She had her phone—" His eyes snapped open. He looked at Jack hopefully. "Her phone was on. I'm sure of it. The screen was lit."

Did someone call her?

Jack looked over at Kendra, who was speaking with Morrison and Thomas. When Jack caught her eye, she hurried right over, with the sheriff and special agent following right after. It was clear she had been crying. "I'm so sorry, Jack. I never let her out of my sight except when she'd go to the bathroom. The window was locked. There's no way someone got in from outside."

Thomas looked up at the building. "Unless they climbed the fire escape, held a gun on Alice, and forced her to open the window."

Kendra gasped, but Jack shook his head. "Not Alice. If someone did that, she'd make sure Kendra heard her going outside."

Thomas raised an eyebrow. "Why didn't she tip them off that she was in trouble? Why would she sneak out?"

"We need to pull Alice's phone records. Bobbie said Alice was in the bedroom with the phone. Somehow the killer made her sneak out."

"You're saying she willingly went with the guy?" Thomas asked.

"Not willingly, Frank!" Jack snapped. "The guy tricked her or forced her, but somehow he convinced Alice to quietly open the window and climb down the fire escape without alerting anyone. It's the only thing that makes sense. Kendra would have heard Alice otherwise."

Morrison stepped between them. "We have several officers canvassing the apartments. So far, no one heard or saw anything."

"If you're correct," Thomas said, "is there a chance that this has nothing to do with our killer? Maybe it's a bride that got cold feet?"

"You stupid—"

Bobbie and Morrison grabbed Jack before he could swing. Jack was screaming now. The pressure cooker had completely lost its lid and Jack's pent-up rage rushed out.

Kendra led Thomas away as Jack struggled to pull free of Bobbie and Morrison.

"Cool it, Jack! Now!" Morrison shouted directly in Jack's face.

Jack was seething, but he pulled himself together. "I'm sorry, sir, but—"

"Don't apologize." Morrison's face was twisted into a scowl. "That man is a moron."

Bobbie let go of Jack. "Anybody who knows Alice knows she didn't cut out on you."

"Jack!" Marisa called from the sidewalk on the other side of the street. An officer there was blocking her way.

"Let her through," Morrison said. As Marisa hurried over to them, Morrison turned back to Jack. "Trust me, Jack. We're going to do everything we can to find her."

Bobbie and Morrison walked away as Marisa ran up and hugged Jack. "I'm so sorry," she said. "I came as soon as Shawna told me. What happened?"

Jack's rage was still burning white-hot as he began telling Marisa all he knew through clenched teeth. She held his hand and listened patiently. When he was done, their eyes met. What he wanted to see there was a speck of hope, but all he saw was pity. Marisa's truthfulness was one of the things he valued most about their friendship, but right now he wished she would lie to him and tell him everything was going to be fine.

Jack glared down at the pavement. Alice was missing, likely in the grasp of a killer. And he had no clue where she was or what to do next.

A gust of wind blew a discarded candy wrapper across the parking lot. Dozens of little scraps of paper joined the wrapper as it danced across the asphalt. Jack ran over and stamped his foot down, trapping two of the little scraps.

Puzzled, Marisa stepped up beside him. "What is it?"

Jack triumphantly held up the two brightly colored pieces of paper. "Someone fired a Taser. This is Taser confetti. It's for identification."

"You mean you can find out who owns the Taser that fired it?"

"Yes." Jack scanned the parking lot. Morrison was nowhere in sight, but he saw Kendra and raced over to her, holding up the confetti like a prize. "Kendra! It's AFID! There's more of it in the corner. We need to run a trace on it. Where's the sheriff?"

"He went upstairs to set Thomas straight about what he said to you. That fed is an idiot. I get it—he doesn't know you or Alice. But even so, what runaway bride would leave without her purse? Just slip out a window with nothing but the clothes on her back? It's ridic—"

"Her phone!" Jack said suddenly. "She has her phone!" He tried to reach into his pocket with his bandaged hand, and winced. Using his left hand instead, he took out his phone and unlocked it. "Alice put that Friend Find app on our phones so we can always locate each other."

Jack said a quick prayer as the app opened and a "trying to locate" message appeared next to Alice's picture. Kendra and Marisa looked over his shoulder at the screen. All three of them were holding their breath.

The app beeped, and a little red pin appeared on the on-screen map, only two blocks away. A beacon of hope. Jack slapped the Taser confetti into Kendra's hand and ran for the Charger. Marisa ran after him.

"Where are you going?" Kendra shouted. "The sheriff—"

"You tell him," Jack called back. "And give him the confetti!"

As Jack slid behind the wheel, Marisa grabbed for the passenger door handle, but Jack quickly locked the doors. "I'm sorry, Marisa. This is too dangerous."

Marisa bristled. "Alice risked her life for me. Open the door or I'll shoot the window out."

Jack unlocked the door. He believed her—and he had no time to waste arguing.

A cop moved the crowd aside so that Jack could exit. As soon as he was clear, he floored it. Rocketing through traffic, he covered the distance in under a minute. But when he skidded to a stop, his heart sank. The area was a deserted lot. Weeds and clumps of grass had grown up in the foundation of where a building once stood.

He and Marisa climbed out of the car.

"The ping says her phone is here." Jack started toward the chain-link fence that surrounded the lot. He was about to climb over it when Marisa shouted, "I found it."

"Don't touch it!" Jack rushed over.

Lying in the grass was Alice's phone. The screen was smashed, splintered and strewn about the ground.

Jack's own phone began to ring. He started to automatically decline it, then saw it was Aunt Haddie's nursing home.

"This is Jack."

"Hey, Jack, this is Susan. We're just wondering when Alice is going to bring Haddie back?"

Jack's heart started pounding in his chest. "Who picked Aunt Haddie up? Was it Alice?"

"No, it was a man. Alice texted and said she was sending someone over."

"What time did she text?"

"Over two hours ago."

"What phone number did the text come from?"

"Is everything okay?" Susan asked.

Jack's throat tightened. "Susan, what number did the text come from?"

"Hang on a sec." After a pause, Susan read off the number, and Jack wrote it down. He didn't recognize it.

"Isn't that the wedding planner's phone?" Susan asked.

"No. Did you see the driver?"

"Not really. It was a man in a suit. I didn't get a look at his face. Is everything okay?" she asked again, her voice starting to pick up speed and volume.

Jack froze.

It all clicked into place.

The killer had taken Haddie, then used her to get Alice to go outside. If someone held a gun to Alice, she'd fight back, but if they held a gun to Aunt Haddie . . .

"Jack?" Marisa laid a gentle hand on his arm. "Are you all right?"

He shook his head. "He has them both. The killer has Alice and Aunt Haddie."

CHAPTER

53

Alice heard soft footsteps rapidly approaching. Running up the stairs. A door opened. The footsteps grew steadily louder, then stopped just outside Alice's door. She closed her eyes in anticipation, her muscles knots.

Alice stepped back and got into the fighting stance Jack had shown her, preparing to pounce on her attacker the moment he opened the door. She'd gouge his eyes out for hurting Aunt Haddie.

But the door didn't open. The panel in the center slid to one side, and light streamed through a narrow slot. A bottle of water and two protein bars fell through. "Take these."

Alice recognized the soft voice. It was Lenora Soriano, the seamstress for her wedding. Alice lunged forward, her skin scraping against the slot in the door as she jammed her arm through, frantically grabbing for Lenora.

Lenora fell back. Her eyes were wide. She was terrified. "It's not me. I don't want to hurt you. I . . . I . . . ."

"Shh . . . child." It was Aunt Haddie's voice. "Now open the doors so we can talk to you."

"I can't," Lenora sobbed. "Here." Alice heard her open the slot in Aunt Haddie's door and drop something in. Likely the same water and food.

"Lenora," Alice pleaded, "if someone is making you do this, help us! Open the doors, please."

"I can't. They're locked."

"Do you know where the key is?" Alice asked.

"I know where she keeps it."

"Go get it for us," Aunt Haddie said. "And then we can all get out of here."

Lenora shook her head. Her whole body was trembling. "He'll find out. He'll stop me."

"Who will?" Alice asked. "Who's behind all this?"

"Oh, no." Lenora's eyes darted around like a frightened bird. "They're coming back. I have to go!"

"Wait!" Alice called out.

Lenora whispered, "I'll try." Then her footsteps slowly faded into the distance.

Alice resisted the urge to bang on the door in frustration. Tears ran down her cheeks. Whoever was behind this had trapped Lenora, too.

"That poor girl," Aunt Haddie said softly. "Let's pray for her and say grace."

"You're not going to drink the water, are you?" Alice asked.

"We need to keep our strength up," Aunt Haddie said. "Besides, if they wanted to kill us, we'd be dead already."

"Good point." Alice opened her bottle and took a sip. "You picked up on the fact that it's two people? A man and a woman?"

"I didn't," Aunt Haddie said. "But you and Jack are two peas in a pod. You're right, there are two of them, and they have Lenora scared out of her mind. Do you want me to pray, or would you rather?"

"I'm all out of prayers, Aunt Haddie."

"When that happens, that's the time to pray by listening." After a pause, Aunt Haddie said. "Dear Lord, thank you for this food. Please let it not be poisoned or drugged. Watch over Lenora and give her the strength to get the key and get us out of here. In Jesus's name, Amen."

"I thought you said the water was safe. I already took a sip." Alice leaned her head against the wall.

"That teaches you to wait until we're done praying. My mouth is so dry that I think this bottle of water is a little miracle in and of itself. So, don't you even think about not thanking the Lord for it."

"Good point." Alice took another sip.

"What are you thinking about?" Aunt Haddie asked.

"Jack."

"Me too." Aunt Haddie chuckled.

"What's so funny?"

"Whoever those people are, they have no idea the fury they've unleashed on themselves. When that boy finds out we've both been taken, he'll make the demons tremble."

CHAPTER

54

J ack and Marisa beat the police to the nursing home. As the Charger skidded to a stop out front, Susan came running out. She was bawling.

"I never should have let her get into the car without checking the driver's identification. I'm so sorry. Aunt Haddie really wanted to help with the wedding, and so many different people were giving her rides."

"It's not your fault." Jack held the woman by both shoulders. Aunt Haddie was beloved at the nursing home, and he knew Susan really cared for her. "I need you to tell me everything you remember. Start with where you were standing."

"I was still inside. Just inside the door. Aunt Haddie was outside, and the car pulled right up under the awning just about where you're parked. I watched to make sure she got into the car alright."

Jack walked over to the door and looked back at his car. The whole driver's side was covered in shadow.

"Can you tell me anything about the man?"

"He was in a suit and he had a hat on. The kind old men wear."

"Like a fedora?" Jack asked.

"Yes, more or less."

"What about the car? What kind was it?"

"It was red. Four doors. A sedan."

"Do you know the make?"

Susan shook her head. "I'm not good with cars. It wasn't brand new, but it wasn't really old either. I'm so sorry, I know this isn't very helpful."

One of the nursing home staff stepped outside while Susan was talking. Jack recognized the man as Dario. He had an eagle tattoo on his upper arm. "Hey, Jack. Are you guys talking about the car that picked up Haddie?"

"Did you see it?" Jack asked.

"Yep. I was having a smoke." He pointed to a fenced area a good distance away. "I saw Haddie get into a Ford Focus. I remember 'cause my girlfriend's brother is selling one and I was going to ask Haddie how it rode."

"Did you see the driver?"

"Sorry, man. I was pretty far away."

"Are there any cameras out here?"

Susan answered, "Yes. We run a licensed memory care unit, so we have cameras all over, for the safety of our patients. But they're all pointed at the building. There isn't one pointed out here." She wrung her hands as she spoke, eyes darting from cameras to Jack and back again.

Jack pulled out his phone and relayed all the information to Morrison so he could put out an APB on the red Ford Focus.

Jack hung up and stared down at his hands. They were shaking. It wasn't fear causing his tremors, it was rage. He choked down his fury and remembered to thank Susan and Dario before marching back to the Charger. Marisa jogged up beside him.

"What are you going to do now?" she asked.

"I'm going to look for that car."

"Then let me drive." Marisa held out her hand.

"Not a chance."

Jack slid behind the wheel and Marisa got in the passenger seat. As they sped out of the nursing home lot, Jack took out his phone.

"Who are you calling?"

"I'm calling in every favor I have."

CHAPTER
55

Alice's fingernails were bloody, but she'd managed to pry a large splinter of wood out of the floor. It was thin, but it was around seven inches long, and if she aimed it at a fleshy target, it would do the job.

"Alice?" Aunt Haddie whispered. "I want you to promise me something, angel."

"Anything."

"When we get out of these rooms, you need to run."

"I'm not leaving you."

"My old legs will slow you down. You run like the wind and get help, but no matter what, you get out."

Tears ran down Alice's cheeks as she remembered Aunt Haddie's fire drill instructions to her as a child. *Get out of the house and wait at the telephone pole meeting spot. Do not go back inside no matter what. That's the firefighters' job.* Haddie knew that the best chance of survival for her many foster kids was to have them concentrate on getting themselves out of her old house and not die going back in after something or someone. Alice pictured the now-elderly Aunt Haddie sitting on the floor in the next cell, alone in the dark. The same volunteer mom who'd stepped in to love and care for Alice as an abused little orphan was still guiding her through troubled waters.

"Promise me." Aunt Haddie's voice trembled.

Alice had never lied to Aunt Haddie before, but she found herself doing it now. There was no way she'd leave her behind. "I promise." Her fingers tightened on the wood in her hand.

There were two captors. Lenora had mentioned both a "he" and a "she." Alice would take the man by surprise with her weapon. As for the woman—well, Jack had only recently started teaching Alice karate, but what she lacked in skill she'd make up for with extreme violence.

Footsteps sounded in the distance. Alice's legs started shaking but she scrambled to her feet and listened closely.

These footsteps didn't sound like Lenora's. Hard, flat heels clicked off the wood. Shoes, not sneakers.

"Someone's coming," Alice whispered.

The footsteps stopped outside her door. Alice gripped the wood splinter. She'd aim for the throat.

Metal scraped, and the little slide door opened. Light streamed through; it wasn't much, but it made Alice squint. She crouched down.

A man in a suit stood in the hallway. She could only see from his chest down. Alice moved to the side of the door, trying not to make a sound. Maybe if he couldn't see her, he'd crouch down to peer in and she could stab him in the eye through the slit. She'd still be trapped, but Lenora was still out there, and if Alice killed the man, Lenora could get the key . . .

The scent of men's cologne wafted into Alice's cell.

"Alton?" Aunt Haddie shouted, and her door rattled. "Alton, is that you?"

Oh, no . . . not now!

"Alton!" Aunt Haddie pounded on the door. "The closet door is stuck. I can't get out."

The man walked over to Aunt Haddie's door. "Quiet." His voice was a growl.

"Leave her alone! She has Alzheimer's. She thinks you're her husband."

"Who's out there with you, Alton? Stop fooling around and open the door this instant."

Alice heard a key in a lock. "Please!" she shouted. "Please don't hurt her!"

She pressed her eyes to the slot in the door. She could see a few feet down the hallway, but the man was turned away from her, so she still couldn't see his face. She heard Haddie's door open, and then saw her step into the hallway.

"Sometimes you can be such a twit, Alton," Aunt Haddie said, smoothing her dress. "I must have asked you a hundred times to fix that doorknob."

Alice sobbed. Aunt Haddie looked past him at Alice. Their eyes met, just barely, and Aunt Haddie smiled like she had just taken a tray of cookies out of the oven. Then her right hand balled into a fist, and she swung hard. She caught the man on the bottom of his chin and knocked his head up and around. His hat fell off, and at last Alice could see his face.

It was no man.

It was Lenora!

Aunt Haddie followed up with a left jab that knocked Lenora to the floor. Bending over Lenora, Aunt Haddie hit her again, then yanked the key from her hand and hurried to Alice's door.

"You're amazing!" Alice gasped as she finally realized that Aunt Haddie had been faking her memory lapse.

"I was your age once." Aunt Haddie's hands shook as she tried to get the key into the lock.

"Just calm down," Alice said as the key wouldn't go in.

"It's not that." Aunt Haddie shook her head. "It's the wrong key!"

"Watch out!" Alice cried.

Just as Aunt Haddie started to turn away, Lenora slammed into her and Aunt Haddie's head smacked hard against the wood. She slumped to her knees. Lenora grabbed the old woman and bashed her head into the door again.

Screaming in rage, Alice drove her arm through the slot in the door like a spear. Her splinter missed Lenora's stomach but struck her arm, sinking into the flesh. When Lenora shrieked and dropped to her knees, Alice got hold of Lenora's hair.

Lenora grabbed Alice's arm and pulled it through the door slot, scraping skin off, but Alice hung on. Then something jabbed into Alice's arm like a bee sting. Alice pulled her arm back hard, trying to smash Lenora's head into the door. Instead, she fell back onto the floor of her cell. In her hand was a clump of Lenora's hair ripped from her scalp.

Alice's arm trembled and burned. A syringe was sticking out of it. Lenora had injected her with something again. Alice pulled the syringe out and made it to her knees, her vision blurring. "You're dead." She tried to scream, but her voice was a slurred whisper. "Jack is going to find you."

Lenora smiled. "I'm counting on it."

Alice gasped, and everything went dark.

CHAPTER

56

Jack handed Marisa his phone. "While I drive, I need you to go through my contact list. Anyone who lives in Darrington, call and tell them I need them to take to the streets and look for a red Ford Focus. And give me your phone."

"Why?" she asked, already skimming the contacts, her long nails tapping on each name.

"I need to make some calls."

While Marisa pulled up Jack's contacts, Jack used her phone to call Paula at Channel 5. "Paula, it's Jack Stratton. This is urgent." He brought the reporter up to speed on what had happened. "Can you run the description of the car right now?"

"We'll run it as an emergency alert," Paula said. "I have contacts at the affiliate stations. I'll reach out to them as well."

"Thank you. I appreciate it."

Jack's next call was to Kiku. He blew through a red light as he prayed she would answer a call from an unknown number.

"Hello?"

"Kiku, it's Jack." He could hear the desperation in his own voice. "I know you're busy—"

"My work is done. I am on my way."

"A killer has Alice and Aunt Haddie."

"I am so sorry. I am in a plane still more than eight hours away."

Jack ran his hand through his hair and beat the steering wheel with a fist.

"Send me all the information you have. I will come up to speed on the way."

"I will." Jack exhaled.

Eight hours. It will be too late by then. It may be too late now.

"I will pray for them. And for you, my friend," Kiku said.

As Jack hung up, he did the same. He prayed.

Please, God, help me find them.

He turned to Marisa, who was just finishing another call. "I need you to send some of my photographs to this number." He held up the phone so she could see Kiku's number.

"Okay. You have a ton of pictures. Where do you want to start?"

"Everything but the earlier ones, of Alice and me. There's a picture of me with Alice on a carousel . . ." Jack's chest tightened when he thought of that day. When Alice begged to ride a second time, Jack led her to the carousel's pretend horse-drawn carriage, set her down on his lap, and took a rare selfie. He couldn't remember ever being so happy . . .

Marisa reached out and squeezed his arm. Jack cleared his throat. "Start with the photographs after that one. Pictures of the house where we found the bodies, the sketches taped to the wall, the invitation . . ."

An image of the invitation flashed through Jack's mind. He jerked the wheel to the right and skidded to a stop on the side of the road.

"What are you doing?" Marisa asked.

"Give me the phone." Jack grabbed it and scrolled through the photos until he found the one he was looking for. He zoomed in on the wedding invitation.

"The killer had my wedding invitation pinned to the wall. We went through the guest list and everyone who received one. They all still had theirs. But Alice threw an unused box of invitations away."

"So, anyone could have gotten ahold of them," Marisa said. "There's no way of knowing whose it was."

"No, there is! Alice personally handed out invitations to everyone working the wedding." Jack zoomed in and pointed at the screen. "Look—that pin! It has a gold head. It's a dress pin. I got stuck by one when Alice was trying on her wedding dress."

Marisa's eyes widened. "Are you saying it's Lenora?"

Rocks pinged off the undercarriage of the Charger as Jack jammed down the gas.

Please God, help me not be too late.

CHAPTER

57

Alice's eyes slowly fluttered open. The world spun, but she stayed where she was—standing.

What the . . .?

Nausea washed over her and she felt like she was about to vomit.

Yes, she was definitely standing up, and her head was held high, but she couldn't move. She was wearing her wedding dress, stockings, the special-order beaded shoes, and the veil. A bouquet of flowers was tied to her hands, her arms held tightly against her chest. The scent of the flowers made her queasy stomach flip. She strained to move her arms and legs, but her body was trapped in some kind of frame that held her rigidly upright. Even her head was nearly immobilized.

Her gaze darted around the room. Aunt Haddie sat in a chair to her left, wearing a beautiful blue dress and a hat with a long arching feather. She had a box of tissues in her left hand and a tissue clutched in her right. Her chin was lifted but her eyes were closed. A metal rod peeked out underneath her raised arm, and a strap holding her head up was just visible beneath the brim of her hat. Alice breathed a sigh of relief when she saw Aunt Haddie's chest rise and fall.

To Alice's right stood the dead woman that Alice had punched in the car outside Shawna's apartment. Her gray eyes were open and staring right at Alice.

All three of them had been posed like mannequins at one end of an enormous open warehouse. Racks upon racks of fabrics and dresses stretched into the distance. The floor was made of the same thick old boards that had been in Alice's cell. Some paper or film covered the large windows, giving the light from outside a yellowish tint. A framework of thin pipes ran across the ceiling.

"Aunt Haddie," Alice whispered. "Aunt Haddie, wake up!"

Haddie's nose twitched and her eyes snapped open. Panic crossed her face, and she started to struggle.

"Aunt Haddie, it's okay. I'm right here," Alice said. "We're tied up and we can't move."

Aunt Haddie stopped fighting, but she still looked terrified. "Where are we?"

"I think it's the dressmaker's warehouse."

"Is someone next to you?"

Aunt Haddie was trying to see around Alice but couldn't move her head.

"She's dead."

"Oh, Lord help us." Aunt Haddie started struggling again. "What does that crazy girl want with us?"

Alice clamped her eyes closed until they burned. She focused on the darkness, letting a map of information spread in her mind. "It's something to do with weddings. Look how I'm dressed and how you're posed. There's even a unity candle."

"But why?"

"I don't know. But once she's done with whatever this is, we're dead."

Soft footsteps sounded in the distance. Alice strained to look. Lenora came into view, carrying flowers.

"I'm so sorry." Her mouth twisted as she set the flowers around the unity candle. "My parents . . . they're very insistent." She took out a lighter and lit the candle.

"Lenora," Alice said. "You don't have to do this. You can let us go."

Lenora shook her head. "I can't. My parents won't let me. I have to set up the wedding, and they want to see you in your dress."

"Then let us go before they get here," Aunt Haddie said.

"No!" Lenora covered her ears.

"Why are you doing this?" Alice asked.

"I'm not doing anything. It's my father. He's so angry."

"Why?"

Lenora's eyes blazed. "Because of her"—she thrust a finger out toward the dead woman—"and all the others. My parents worked their fingers to the bone to make each and every wedding gown spectacular for the most important day of their lives. Every dress as unique as the bride who wore it. And what do you do?" Lenora stepped so close to Alice that she could feel Lenora's breath on her cheek. "You wear it once. One time, and then it goes into a box. But this . . ." She tapped Alice's diamond engagement ring. "This hunk of hardened coal? This rock? You brides wear it every day for the rest of your lives."

"Alice isn't even married yet!" Aunt Haddie said. "She couldn't have angered your parents."

Lenora smiled serenely. "Not Alice. Alice is special. She's nice. She'll never make my parents angry, because she'll never take the dress off."

"I won't," Alice said. "I'll wear it every single day. I promise. Just give me a chance and—"

"No!" Lenora screamed. "My father gave them all a chance. A year, a decade, fifty years, it didn't matter. None of them wore it again. Not one. I would have killed to have had my father design a wedding gown for me. I would have been proud to wear it. But he said it was bad luck to design a dress for an unengaged woman . . . and now it's too late." Tears streamed down her face. "Do you know how long it takes to make a dress like this?"

"I didn't even want a fancy wedding or a designer dress!" Alice shouted. "I wanted a simple, small wedding. I wanted to wear Aunt Haddie's dress."

Lenora slapped Alice across the face. "You should be honored to wear an original Soriano."

"Why?" Alice scoffed. "It's itchy and makes my butt look big."

Lenora slapped her again.

"Stop it this instant!" Aunt Haddie demanded. "You will not strike her again!"

Lenora slowly turned to glare at Aunt Haddie.

Alice swore.

"Alice!" Aunt Haddie admonished. She met Lenora's scowl with a patient smile. "You and I need to talk, young lady."

Lenora looked down at the floor and shook her head. "No. I'm going to get my mother now. The wedding needs to be perfect." She turned and disappeared into the depths of the warehouse.

"She's completely wacko," Alice said.

"Don't be cruel. She's obviously had some type of breakdown."

"She's way past a breakdown, Aunt Haddie. The wheels have come off her crazy train and it's going over the bridge. Do you know any bride who wore her wedding dress after her wedding day?"

Aunt Haddie shook her head—or tried to.

"This is legit nuts. Going psycho over a bride not wearing her wedding dress more than once is like the piñata maker getting mad that kids bash his papier-mâché sculpture to get the candy. The fact that you only get to wear your bridal gown for one day is part of what makes your wedding day so special. This is just so wrong!" Alice was so angry, the frame holding her rattled and banged against the floor.

"I agree with you, Alice, but you still need to pray for her."

"I'll pray for a piano to fall on her head."

Alice desperately looked around. She couldn't make out anything through the covered windows. For all she knew they were several floors up. And in the middle of nowhere. She screamed anyway.

"HELP!" she shouted as loudly as she could. "HELP US!"

Aunt Haddie joined in.

"Shut up!" Lenora came back wheeling a dolly with another body strapped to it. This one, another woman, had clearly been dead for years. The skin on her face resembled leather, but her bright-green dress was crisp and new, and her golden jewelry sparkled. Lenora wheeled the corpse beside Aunt Haddie. "This is my mother, Marie."

"I don't mean to be rude," Alice said. "But you are aware she's dead . . . right?"

Lenora pulled out a gun.

"She didn't mean that," Aunt Haddie said quickly.

"I sure did!" Alice yelled. "Go ahead and shoot!"

Aunt Haddie's eyes widened. "You think someone will hear the gunshot and come for me!" She frowned at Alice.

The gun wobbled in Lenora's hand. "Be quiet or I'll shoot you both." She pointed the gun at Aunt Haddie. "My father is coming. Say anything and I'll let him deal with you." Lenora stalked off.

Alice waited until Lenora was gone before whispering, "Why did you tell her what I was trying to do?"

"Because you're the one who needs to make it out of here," Aunt Haddie said. "Getting yourself shot so I get rescued makes no sense."

"It does to me."

"Stop being so ridiculous."

Alice rolled her eyes. As she did, she noticed once more the pipes running overhead for a sprinkler system. She looked at the candle. Then at the dead woman standing beside her. They weren't that far apart.

She started slowly rocking.

"What are you doing?" Aunt Haddie asked.

"I have a plan."

"You'd better hurry. When she comes back, she's expecting to have the perfect wedding and then—"

Footsteps sounded in the distance. Flat heels on wood.

Alice looked down at her hands, red and irritated from the bindings. She couldn't move them, but she could still move her fingers. Using her left thumb, she managed to slide her engagement ring down her finger and flick it away. It tinkled onto the floor and rolled somewhere out of view.

"What was that?" Aunt Haddie asked.

"A stall tactic." *I hope.*

Lenora returned. She was once again dressed in a dark blue suit with a white shirt, and her hair was hidden under a fedora. She walked to the dolly where her mother was propped up and kissed the corpse on one cheek, then the other.

Alice's stomach turned.

"That's revolting," Aunt Haddie said.

Lenora turned to them and scowled. "There's nothing revolting about a man loving his wife."

If you closed your eyes, the voice could have been a man's. And suddenly, Alice understood. Dressed like this, Lenora thought she was her father. This was the "he" she had referred to back in their cells. And the "she" was her mother. Lenora believed she was doing their bidding. Except she was them. She was all three.

She was truly insane.

Lenora stepped in front of Alice, and a smile slowly spread across her face. "You, my dear, are the perfect bride. Are you ready for your wedding?"

"No." Alice made a face. "I can't get married without my ring."

"What?" Lenora's voice dropped so low it was a deep growl. She grabbed Alice's hand and her eyes widened. "What happened to your engagement ring? I know you had it on."

"I took it off in my cell. You'd better send your daughter to get it."

"No." Lenora's face hardened. "We'll do without it."

Alice's heart sped up. "But what about the perfect wedding? It can't be perfect without the ring. You know that!"

Lenora swore and started hitting herself in the forehead. "Stupid, stupid, stupid fool, Lenora!" She slapped herself hard across the face. "I'll go get it, Father." She turned to face the opposite direction and her voice changed. "No, I will, stupid girl!" Then she turned and scurried away.

Alice resumed rocking, gradually increasing her momentum, like a pendulum swinging back and forth, until at last she lightly struck the corpse standing next to her. Swallowing her disgust, she kept rocking and hit the corpse harder. The woman teetered, but didn't fall.

Alice gave one final push and slammed into the corpse. This time it fell, knocking into the unity candle. Together the candle and corpse fell to the floor.

As Alice came to rest, she found herself looking away from both Aunt Haddie and the woman's corpse. "Did it work?" she asked.

"Oh, no . . ." Aunt Haddie gasped. "Alice, she's on fire!"

Alice exhaled. "That's what we want. It will set off the sprinklers and the fire alarm."

"When do they go off?" Aunt Haddie asked, her voice rising.

Alice sniffed. She could smell smoke behind her and was starting to feel some heat.

"She's going up like a pile of dry kindling!" Aunt Haddie's chair scraped on the floor. "You'd better try to move, baby. It's spreading."

A cloud of black smoke crept along the ceiling. Alice strained forward and pushed with her toes. She managed to hop a couple of inches. Clenching her jaw, she did it again, wobbling at the end of the jump. Sweat made her skin glow and refracted the fire's light.

She could see Aunt Haddie now, pushing back with her toes. The chair scraped on the floor, but it barely moved an inch.

"Oh, good Lord." Aunt Haddie's eyes were wide.

Alice hopped again. Behind her, there was a whooshing sound and a blast of scorching heat.

Lenora burst through the door. "No!" She raced through the warehouse screaming as if a part of herself was dying. "Not my dresses!" She scooped up an armful of wedding dresses off one of the racks. The hem of one was burning brightly. As she fled down the long warehouse, pieces of the burning dress broke away into flying fiery embers, starting dozens of little fires all over.

"There's no alarm, Alice!" Aunt Haddie said.

"There should be! And the smoke should have set off the sprinkler system." Alice hopped again, but this time, she went too far. She wobbled on the landing, tipped forward, and crashed to the floor, her side taking most of the impact.

A huge cloud of black smoke now covered the ceiling.

Aunt Haddie was coughing. A deep, dry cough, it rattled her entire body.

Flames licked at Alice's feet. She tried to roll, but couldn't.

Aunt Haddie closed her eyes and began to pray.

Alice crushed the flowers in her hand. She was supposed to get married in this dress, but now it would be her death shroud. Her plan had backfired. And now she'd killed Aunt Haddie, too.

Even if Jack knew where they were, there was no saving them now.

CHAPTER

58

The Charger's tires squealed as it rounded the corner. Marisa clung to the roof handle as Jack straightened out the steering wheel and jammed the gas pedal to the floor.

"Jack, look!" Marisa pointed at the three-story warehouse that loomed ahead. Black smoke billowed out of the top-floor windows.

A quick internet search by Marisa had told Jack he had two choices—Lorenzo Soriano's shop downtown or the warehouse where they kept the fabrics and dress templates, and shipped out all over the world. Jack had already called Morrison, but with the police stretched out all over the county, who knew when backup would arrive.

"Call 911. Wait for the fire department and tell them I went in." Jack opened his door as the Charger skidded to a stop, jumped out, and bolted toward the burning building.

As he reached the huge front door, broken glass rained down from a window shattering above. The door was locked, so he stepped back and kicked it. The wooden casing splintered and the old door broke inward.

"Alice!" Jack shouted as he ran for the staircase.

The fire breaking out here, now, was too much of a coincidence to be random. Jack prayed that somehow Alice was behind the blaze and it wasn't the killer using the flames to hide his tracks and destroy any evidence.

"Alice!" he shouted again and again as he took the stairs three at a time. The air got worse the higher he climbed, and an acrid stench of burning synthetics stung his nose and eyes, but he kept shouting.

Just as Jack reached the third floor, Alice's terrified cry rose above the roar of the fire. "Jack!"

"I'm here!" he bellowed. "I'm coming!"

A cloud of black smoke already covered the ceiling. In an effort to stay below it, Jack hunched as low as he could and ran forward in a crouch. The smoke wafted into his throat, making it a dry tomb, and he coughed and wheezed as he moved. He found himself in a large room full of flaming clothing stretching off in every direction, giving the black smoke an amber glow.

He almost tripped over Alice's body on the floor. She was strapped to some metal contraption, and flames were only yards from her feet.

Jack pulled at her straps, but with his bandaged hand it was no use. Instead he grabbed her and hefted her upright. The metal frame doubled her weight, but his adrenaline was surging, and he barely noticed it. He grabbed one of the straps with his good hand and wrapped his arm around Alice's waist.

"Get—Aunt Haddie!" Alice said through coughs.

"Where is she?"

"Right here, Jackie!" Aunt Haddie's voice was weak. She was tied to a chair that was tipped over and facing away from him. The smoke was so thick he could barely see her.

Jack righted the chair, tipped it back, and dragged her over to Alice. He was unable to grab Alice with his bad hand, so he wrapped his arm around Alice's waist and, tuning out the pain, dragged them both toward the stairs. He'd taken only two steps before Alice's stand caught on the uneven floorboards and nearly tipped over.

"Take Alice, Jackie. Take her and come back for me," Aunt Haddie coughed.

"No!" Alice shouted. "Jack, take Aunt Haddie."

The smoke was getting thicker by the second. Jack's eyes burned, and sweat rolled down his face. Again, he tried to get them both; he wasn't about to choose between them. He tipped Alice toward him and managed to hook his arm on Haddie's chair back. This time he made it three steps before Alice's stand slipped. Jack pivoted his weight to try to keep hold of her, and all three of them ended up crashing to the floor. Flames roared all around them.

"Jackie, please listen to me!" Aunt Haddie begged. "Leave me!"

Tears ran down Alice's cheeks. "Jack! Don't you dare. You can't leave Aunt Haddie to burn. You can't!"

Jack's heart was breaking. He couldn't get them both out. They'd never make it.

Please, God.

Somewhere, glass shattered from the heat. The smoke rushed in that direction for a moment, but Jack's hope was quickly gutted as the increased oxygen only fed the flames.

"Let me go, Jackie. I've lived the life I was meant to. I want to go home and be with my Alton, Chandler, and Michelle."

"No!" Alice coughed as she struggled against the straps. "Don't leave her, Jack. I could never live like that."

Jack again started dragging them both backward. Aunt Haddie's chair caught on a rack of clothes. Gritting his teeth, Jack yanked her free.

"Now you listen to me! Both of you," Aunt Haddie wheezed. "I've lost two babies. I can't lose you too. Please, Jackie! Please!"

Jack tore at his gauzed hand with his teeth, freeing his fingers. Screaming with a mix of rage and pain, he hooked his injured hand under the loop of Alice's lashed-together wrists and tightened his grip around the back of Aunt Haddie's chair.

Like a lumberjack dragging two logs, he leaned forward, dragging Alice and Aunt Haddie down the crowded aisle, burning dresses washing waves of heat over them from both sides. Alice's frame and Haddie's chair caught against racks and floorboards. Jack's lungs burned and his vision blurred. He strained, pulled, and yanked. Each step was a fight. And he was losing. Every breath was getting shallower.

Alice and Aunt Haddie had stopped pleading. They were just struggling to keep breathing now. Jack stumbled and fell to his knees. The stairs were so close, but his leg muscles were deprived of oxygen, and he felt like he was stuck in mud.

"Jack!" Marisa emerged from the smoke and leapt over a burning box. She looked as fierce as the female gladiator statues that used to adorn her tattoo parlor. "I'll get Haddie!"

She took hold of Aunt Haddie's chair and started to drag it toward the stairs. Jack dug down deep within himself and managed to get to his feet. He grabbed Alice and stumbled after Marisa.

A monstrous racket behind them announced that the ceiling was crashing down. A wave of heat and flames washed over them just as Jack yanked Alice clear of the fire and down the stairs.

From somewhere above them floated a woman's pitiful wail, cut off by a single gunshot.

* * *

The four of them dropped to the ground outside like shipwreck victims coming ashore. The sound of sirens filled the air. Firefighters rushed to their aid, moving them to safety on the far side of the parking lot. Jack knelt between Alice and Aunt Haddie as the EMTs administered oxygen and cut them free of their restraints.

A second ambulance team was treating Marisa. She met Jack's gaze and gave him a weak thumbs-up. Jack returned the gesture. It was a feeble way to thank her for saving all of their lives, but there was nothing he could ever say or do to repay her. The gift she'd given him was priceless.

The EMTs loaded Alice and Aunt Haddie onto stretchers. But when an EMT tried to evaluate Jack, he waved him off. Stampeding bulls couldn't keep him from riding with Alice and Haddie to the hospital.

282 - CHRISTOPHER GREYSON

He squeezed Alice's hand. She reached up and pulled her oxygen mask to the side. Jack leaned down and kissed her sooty cheek.

She pulled him closer and whispered, "I knew you'd come for us."

Jack gave her a crooked grin. "The hard part's over. Now we just have to survive the wedding."

CHAPTER

59

When the doctor finished bandaging Jack's hand—she'd had to redo the stitches, too, as Jack had managed to pull out every last one in the fire—Jack wiggled his unwrapped ring finger. "Thanks for leaving this one free."

The doctor smiled. "I'm happy Alice will be able to put a ring on it. But you're going to need to keep it elevated and ice it every couple of hours to keep it from swelling."

"I will." Jack held his other hand up in a Boy Scout salute. "How's Alice?"

"She's eager to go home, but I got her to agree to stay overnight for observation by placing her in the same room as Haddie. Considering how strong Haddie's vitals are, I would expect them both to be released tomorrow."

"That's fantastic news. How is Marisa?"

"You know with HIPAA, I can't give you specifics, but I think they're about ready to release her."

"Thanks again, Doc." Jack shook her hand and hurried out of the room.

A nurse called after him about making a follow-up appointment, but her words barely even registered. Jack's focus was on Marisa, who was standing in the hallway, her dress smudged with soot and grime. She looked like a sexy chimney sweep, her tousled hair adding to the ensemble. Her Mona Lisa smile appeared.

"How are you?" they both asked in unison.

Marisa laughed until she coughed. "I feel like I've been sitting in a smoking lounge for a long weekend. You?"

"Same." Jack held up his bandaged hand. "At least I can still get a ring on it."

Maria's smile vanished. "And that's a good thing?"

"Marisa . . ."

She stepped forward and took his good hand. "Bad joke. Really." Her brown eyes met his, but there was something different about them now. There was something missing.

She leaned forward and kissed his cheek. The corner of her mouth brushed against his, but she didn't linger, and though the kiss felt nice, Jack didn't feel the magnetic pull to lean into it. He rocked back on his heels to look at this beautiful, strong woman who had given him so much.

Whenever she had looked at him before, Jack had felt as if she were searching his face for some hidden answer. The problem was, Jack had never known what the question was. What did she want to know? Or what did she want him to know? As long as he'd known Marisa, she remained an enigma.

Marisa smiled. It was big and genuine, but her eyes glistened. "When I first heard you were getting married, I thought . . . well, a lot of things can happen. And I thought maybe there was still hope for you and me. But when I saw your face in that warehouse, I knew I had lost you. I wasn't surprised that you were willing to run into Hell to save Alice—you're a born protector. But when I came in after you, I saw it in your eyes: you would have chosen to die with her rather than live without her. You love her."

Jack nodded. "I do."

"Believe it or not, I'm happy for you. For you both. You're a good man, Jack Stratton."

"Jack!" a man called out from down the hall.

Jack turned to see a tall, handsome man with wavy brown hair and an expensive gray suit jogging toward him. There was no mistaking Pierce Weston.

"How's Alice? I came as soon as I could."

Jack's head tipped to the side. There had been a time—before Jack saved Pierce's life and they became friends—when Pierce was romantically interested in Alice. Now, his question pricked Jack's jealousy. A small taste of what Alice was sure to have felt with Marisa's appearance.

"I'm fine. Thanks, Pierce."

Pierce waved his hands dismissively. "I can see you're fine."

Jack held up his bandaged hand.

"Maybe not totally fine," Pierce conceded. "But Erica called and said Alice was nearly killed."

"By your seamstress."

"She's not my seamstress. I just hired her."

"Which makes her . . ." Jack moved his hand in a circle trying to get Pierce to admit the truth.

"Technically, I hired her father."

Jack rolled his eyes. "I hope you have learned the value of a good background check."

"Come on, Jack! The woman was completely unglued! She was impersonating her father; I doubt a background check would have saved me from hiring her." Pierce winced like he'd bit down on an olive with a pit. "There is one more employment issue that's come up—Erica."

Jack rolled his eyes. "She's probably freaking out that the dress is ruined and—"

"She quit," Pierce said. "I tried to double what I was paying her, but she said no one could pay her enough. She's already flying back to California."

Jack ran his hand down his face.

"I can find a replacement," Pierce offered, taking out his phone.

"Nope." Jack crookedly grinned. "I know the perfect Replacement. Alice will be delighted to take charge and let the whole thing ride."

"I'll help her, and I'm sure the bridesmaids will too," Marisa offered then looked at Pierce. "Don't feel so bad. Jack has a way of making some people run away screaming," she said jokingly.

Pierce turned to Marisa, and his deep-green eyes widened. Jack understood. She had that effect on most men.

"Pierce, this is Marisa Vitagliano. Marisa, Pierce Weston."

Pierce did a double take. "Not the Marisa who lives in Hope Falls?"

Marisa shook his hand. "The same."

Jack leaned toward Pierce and gave him a sympathetic look. "She's the beautiful lady I thought might show you around town."

Jack was surprised that Pierce didn't smack himself in the head, but he did look like he wanted to kick himself. "I didn't— I thought— I'm so sorry." His shoulders slumped.

"As I told your secretary," Marisa said confidently, "not a problem."

"Actually . . ." Pierce cleared his throat. "I've managed to free up some time on my calendar after Jack's wedding, and I was hoping . . . your kind offer was still available?"

Marisa crossed her arms and looked the handsome billionaire right in the eye. "And what's the reason for this sudden turnaround?"

Pierce swallowed and looked down at the floor like a shy schoolboy. Jack let Pierce squirm for a moment. He'd have to have a talk with his friend. The one attribute that Marisa valued more than anything was honesty.

"Two things, I imagine," Jack said. "The first is, he saw you."

Marisa bristled. The last thing she wanted was a man who was attracted solely to her looks.

"But that's my fault," Jack continued. "I was kinda kidding Pierce about the royal tour of Hope Falls and I might have described you as a cross between Danny DeVito and Maleficent."

Pierce nodded—a little too rapidly. "Exactly. Jack's such a kidder."

"The other reason is, I've been trying to sell him on Hope Falls," Jack said, "and he's finally realizing he needs to get to know the place."

Marisa eyed Jack suspiciously, but he didn't flinch. Both of the things he'd said were technically true. Though one was much truer than the other. Sure, Hope Falls was a great place, but Jack knew that after one look at Marisa, any single guy would be crazy not to want her to show them around. He also knew that deep down, Pierce and Marisa were two beautiful but wounded people who together might find some healing.

"Well," Marisa turned her head away from Jack and gave Pierce a smile. "I'll have to check my schedule."

"Okay," Pierce said, looking relieved. "That would be great." He flashed Jack a grin.

"Right now, I'm going back to my hotel to get some rest," Marisa said. "I'll see you both at the rehearsal dinner. It's still on, right, Jack?"

"Oh yeah," Jack said. "After all the effort she's put in, Alice said she'd kill the first person who tried to cancel the wedding. Pierce, you're welcome to try."

"No thanks." Pierce shook his head.

Jack caught Pierce's eye and tipped his head toward Marisa.

Pierce widened his eyes, as if to say, *What?*

Jack had to hide his smile. Pierce might be a computer genius but the boy billionaire was clueless with women. "Thanks again for coming by, Pierce," he said. Jack was the furthest thing from a hugger, but he pulled Pierce close, patted his back, and whispered, "Offer her a ride, idiot."

"Do you need a ride?" Pierce almost shouted.

Marisa gave Jack a sidelong glance.

Jack smiled knowingly. "I can assure you that whatever he's driving beats any taxi or limousine."

Marisa nodded. "Thank you. I'll take that ride."

Pierce lit up. "Great, but I want to check on Alice first."

"She's good," Jack said quickly. "Really, she needs sleep."

"Are you sure?"

"Positive." Jack gave him a thumbs-up with his good hand. He trusted Alice, but still, he'd feel much better about having the handsome billionaire around after Jack and Alice were married.

As Pierce and Marisa headed off together, Jack's phone buzzed in his pocket.

"Hello, Sheriff."

"Hi, Jack. How's everyone doing?"

Jack knew the call was more than a friendly courtesy. Morrison wanted to schedule interviews. Although Detective Castillo and Special Agent Thomas had already done initial interviews, the sheriff would still need to conduct follow-ups.

"Marisa is heading back to her hotel, and they're keeping Alice and Aunt Haddie overnight for observation. Would it be possible to reinterview them in the morning?"

"I can't see why not. How are you holding up?"

"Fine." It was an automatic response. Really, he felt like he'd been hit by a truck. "Did you find Lenora Soriano?"

"We've found her body. She shot herself. We also found a partially mummified body downstairs that looks to be that of her father. He's been dead for years."

"Alice said Lenora's mother had been dead for a while too."

"Well, we'll have to wait for the ME before we can positively identify the mother's body, since it was in the middle of the fire. But I don't doubt it was really her. I've spoken with Lenora's doctors—she's been institutionalized several times. The last one was in New Hampshire. That's when she stole Carson Murray's ID."

"Is there any evidence of an accomplice?"

"None. We turned up piles of sketchbooks and journals in her living area on the bottom floor. Ed's going through them now. They're manifestos, really. She felt that brides disrespected her father and mother by wearing their custom wedding gowns only one time, on their wedding day. After her parents died, she was making the dresses herself and posing as the great Lorenzo. She felt she could somehow right things by giving her parents a 'forever bride.' That was going to be Alice—the one bride who never took the dress off."

Jack rubbed his eyes. He was dead on his feet and fading fast. "I appreciate the update, sir."

"One more thing. I'm posting a guard outside Alice's hospital room—just in case. Mostly so you'll go home and get some sleep."

"I'm fine, sir. I was planning on staying here anyway."

"Under no circumstances. You need to rest, Jack. Do I need to remind you that you're getting married the day after tomorrow?"

"No, sir. Thank you."

"Go get some sleep, son."

Morrison hung up, and Jack stopped by the nurses' station en route to Alice's room to check on her and Aunt Haddie. The nurses said they were both sleeping, and told him to go home and get some rest or they'd likely need to find a bed for him too. Jack didn't stand a chance of sleeping without seeing them both. He nodded to his old work colleague posted outside their room and pushed the heavy door open as quietly as he could. There, side by side in adjacent hospital beds and in matching medical gowns, slept two of the dearest people in Jack's world. Jack felt a tsunami of gratitude wash over his tired body. *Thank you, God.* He slipped out as quietly as he entered.

And with Officer Tom Darcy standing guard, Jack headed for the exit.

On the way to his car, he called the vet.

"Lady is fine, Jack," Lacie answered.

"Hi, Lacie. I was going to stop by—"

"Please don't." Lacie exhaled. "Your landlady just left, and she wouldn't stop sneaking Lady homemade dog treats. What Lady needs most is rest."

"Thanks for watching out for her."

"I'm also looking out for you. You sound exhausted."

"I am," he confessed, rubbing his eyes with his good hand, attempting to banish the impeding headache with sheer determination.

"Well, you'd better rest. You have a big day coming up."

"Will we see you there?"

"I wouldn't miss it for the world."

Satisfied that all the women in his life were safe, Jack headed home, desperate for sleep. With the killer dead, what else could go wrong?

CHAPTER

60

J ack snuck up the stairs to his apartment, unlocked the door, and quietly closed it behind him. He loved Mrs. Stevens, but if she heard him come in, she was sure to come up and want to know everything. And he could barely keep his eyes open.

He walked into the kitchen, opened the refrigerator, and took out a bottle of water. He drained the entire bottle as he pulled out his wallet, keys, and gun and put them on the counter. His hand throbbed. He grabbed a bottle of aspirin from the cabinet, took two, and opened the refrigerator to get another water.

When he turned around, an old man was strolling out of Alice's bedroom. He'd seen a picture of Alice's great-uncle on her phone but he didn't expect him to be here now.

Jack slowly lowered the water bottle. "Hey… Alex, right? How'd you get in?"

"Alice gave me a key." Alex walked over to the counter. "You must be Jack. I thought you were both still in the hospital."

"They released me, but they wanted to keep Alice for observation. She should be home tomorrow. Did she call you?" Jack took a swig of water from his bottle.

How could she? She didn't have her phone.

Alex didn't answer Jack's question. "You must be excited about the wedding. And Alice said you're going to the Bahamas for your honeymoon. I'm surprised you can afford it on a bounty hunter's salary."

Jack stepped closer to the counter and his gun.

Alex shook his head as he took a .38 from his pocket and leveled it at Jack's chest. "Toss the bottle in the sink and raise your hands."

Jack thought about throwing the bottle at Alex, but the half-empty plastic bottle would hardly even be a distraction. He flipped the bottle into the sink and raised his hands. "What are you doing, Alex?" Jack's tired mind couldn't think of a reason for Alice's great-uncle to do this sudden one-eighty.

Alex's eyes hardened. "Tell me where my brother is."

"Alice's grandfather? I don't have a clue."

"You're lying." Alex aimed the gun at Jack's head. "There's no way you two could afford such a grand wedding on your own. My brother must be paying for it. Where is he?"

Jack rolled his eyes. "You've got to be kidding me. Look, we wanted a simple wedding. We have this friend named Pierce Weston and he—"

"Do you think I'm a fool? No mere 'friend' would spend that kind of money on someone else's wedding."

"Unless he's a billionaire, which Pierce is. We saved his life and his company, so he feels indebted to us. I knew we should have turned him down, but he insisted. This whole—"

"Save your lies!" Alex waved his pistol toward the living room. "Move."

Jack didn't move. "I'm serious. Look Pierce up. I'll get him on the phone if you want to talk to him."

"I want to know where my brother is. Now move." Alex stepped back, the pistol steady in his hand, a weapon he was clearly comfortable with. When Jack walked past him toward the living room, Alex pistol-whipped him and pain exploded through Jack's already throbbing head. Groaning, he dropped to his knees, his right hand instinctively moving to the back of his head.

Alex yelled something, but because of the ringing in his ears, Jack couldn't understand what he said. The cold barrel of the gun pressed against the base of Jack's skull.

"Where is he?" Alex bellowed.

Jack gritted his teeth. Alex clearly wasn't going to believe him that he truly had no idea where Alice's grandfather was. And if he didn't give Alex an answer, the old man seemed more than prepared to put a bullet in the back of Jack's battered head.

Alex stood behind him on his left, the gun pressing against Jack's skin. Jack exhaled slowly as he prepared to spin to the right and try to disarm Alex. It was a long shot that he could move before the old man pulled the trigger, but it was the only chance he had.

The front door opened.

Yana stood frozen in the doorway, a look of horror on her face. "What are you doing?"

"He knows where my brother is. He knows. Shut the door."

"I have no idea what he's talking about," Jack said.

"He's lying!" Alex snapped. "There's no way a bounty hunter could afford this extravagant wedding."

"Pierce Weston is paying for it, Yana. Google him," Jack said.

"Papa . . ." Yana stepped into the apartment and closed the door behind her. "Please put the gun down."

"I need that money," Alex growled. "He knows where it is."

"There is no money, Papa. That story was just . . . a story." A tear ran down Yana's cheek. "Put the gun down. Think of Kaya Kukla. If you kill Jack, you'll be killing her, too."

Alex cocked the revolver, his breathing fast and heavy.

"Papa . . ." Yana's voice was just above a whisper.

The sound of the gunshot filled the apartment.

Jack's ears were ringing from both the gunshot and the blow to his head. Still on his knees, he wiped blood off the side of his face with the back of his hand.

The gun slipped from Yana's hands and bounced off the floor. "I just wanted to scare him . . . so that he would stop."

Any thought Jack had of giving Alex CPR was dismissed when he turned to look at the man lying on the floor. The bullet had struck Alex in the head. He was clearly dead. Yana covered her face with her hands.

Jack made it to his feet, stepped over the body, and draped an arm across her shoulders. She sobbed as he turned her around and led her out into the hallway.

Mrs. Stevens, her red hair jutting out in all directions, huffed and puffed her way to the top of the stairs. "Jack, are you all right?" she panted. "I heard a gunshot and called the police."

Jack moved in front of Mrs. Stevens so she wouldn't see the blood and the body. "Mrs. Stevens, please wait for the police at the front door. We'll wait here. Tell the officers that I'm up here and the scene is under control."

"Under control," Mrs. Stevens repeated. "Under control." Nodding, she turned and went back down the stairs.

"Yana . . ." Jack held both of her shoulders. "Where did you get that gun?"

"You should help my father," Yana whispered.

"Yana?" Jack lifted her chin so she looked into his eyes. "The police are coming. Where did you get that gun?"

"Papa had it in the trunk. He took the one in the glove compartment when we got here. But I didn't really think . . ."

"Yana, the police are coming. You need to tell them it was your father's gun. It's illegal for you to have one."

Yana shrugged. "They can ask Papa. He'll tell them the truth." Her eyes widened. "Where's the ambulance?"

Jack's stomach turned. There was never an easy way to tell a person that someone they loved had died. "Your father is dead."

Yana nodded, but from the glazed look in her eyes, he didn't know if his words even registered. He had seen people react this way before, their body accepting the news before the mind.

Despite the tragedy that had just occurred, this woman had saved his life. Jack pictured Alex's cold stare. He was certain the man would have killed him.

"Yana." Jack gave her shoulders a shake. "Don't say anything to the police. I'll talk to them."

Yana shook her head. "I'll tell them the truth. It was an accident."

"It was, but you're shaken up. Tell them you want a lawyer and that's all. I'll explain what happened. You need to say that you want a lawyer. Yana, do you understand?"

Sirens grew louder as the first police cars approached the building.

Yana leaned against the wall and slowly slid down until she was sitting on the carpet.

Jack rubbed his eyes. There would be so many questions. The last thing he wanted was for this to become a double tragedy, and for Yana to lose her freedom. But no matter what Jack tried to do for her now, jail or no jail, how could anyone ever feel free again after killing their own father?

CHAPTER

62

The nervous groom stood in the small room at the back of the church, peeking out the door. He couldn't breathe. He felt as though he was going to pass out. As he scanned the packed pews, he saw the faces of everyone dear to him.

His father came up behind him and placed a reassuring hand on his shoulder. "Well, Jack, it's almost time. How are you holding up?"

"I think I'm going to throw up. Getting shot at is easier than this."

Ted Stratton chuckled. "Trust me, if you're still hiding in here after you see Alice, I'll hold you back from running out that door."

"Then I'll go for the window," Jack shot back.

"Relax. All you have to do is walk out there, say a few words, and put the ring on her finger."

Jack's mouth dropped open and he frantically felt his pockets. "I'm a dead man! The ring. I left it at the apartment!"

Ted closed his eyes. "I hate to say it, but maybe you really needed that wedding planner. You're toast."

Jack ran into the hall, heading for the nearest exit. But high heels in front of him brought him up short. Thankfully, it wasn't Alice; she would kill him if his first glance of her in her dress was in the hallway and not the aisle. Instead, a familiar exotic beauty stood before him, accompanied by a handsome but stern-looking Asian man in an expensive custom suit.

"Hello, Detective." Kiku smiled, her pearly but pointed eyeteeth in sharp contrast to her signature red lipstick.

"Stratton." Takeo Nakumora curtly nodded. His raven hair was so black, the highlights were midnight-blue.

"It's so good to see you." Jack gave Kiku a quick hug. She smelled like cherry blossom and felt like silk. "Can I ask you for a huge favor?"

Takeo cleared his throat, and Jack quickly let go of Kiku. "I forgot the rings in my apartment. Can you please break every traffic law and—"

Kiku held out her hand and opened her palm. Jack exhaled loudly when he saw the ring box.

"Alice knows you too well. You are a very fortunate man, Jack Stratton."

Jack went to snatch the box out of her hand but Kiku easily moved her hand out of the way.

"Alice has a surprise for you. I have been instructed to bring them to her."

"You still saved me." Jack kissed her cheek, a wave of relief sweeping over him.

"I would stop pushing your luck," Takeo said. His voice had a sharp bite. "Getting married on April fourth is already bad luck."

Jack grinned roguishly. "Good thing I don't believe in luck."

Kiku smiled and reached for Takeo's hand, which had balled into a fist. She gently stroked the back of it until he opened his fingers and clasped her porcelain hand.

The church organ started playing, and Jack swallowed.

Kiku's smile faded and she whispered, "Jack, you should know Alice's grandfather is alive, and men are looking for him."

"I know. But do we have to do this now?"

Ted came up behind Jack. "Sorry to interrupt, but . . . did you hear the organ? That's your cue."

Jack's eyes went wide and he stood perfectly still.

A Cheshire Cat grin appeared on Kiku's face. "I watched you take on many armed men and your hand did not shake. But now, you are scared?"

Jack nodded. "Actually, I am."

Takeo chuckled.

Kiku leaned close and whispered in Jack's ear, "Do not be a fool. It is written that he who finds a wife finds a good thing and obtains favor from the Lord. And Alice is a priceless jewel. Go. We will talk after the ceremony."

Ted placed both hands on his son's shoulders, turned him around, and nudged him toward the door. "I'm proud of you, Jack. You're going to make a wonderful husband." He opened the door and gave Jack a little push.

Pastor Warren Braxton was there to greet Jack, and walked him to his designated spot. The church was decked out in righteous splendor. The long pews were filled with family and friends, all there to support him and Alice in their time of commitment and celebration. White banners and veils were suspended from the ceiling, Erica's final touches to what Jack felt had been her life's mission. He had to admit, she'd done a superb job.

His groomsmen—Bobbie G., Boomer, Finn, and Mac—were lined up in their black tuxedos and waiting for him. Each member of the motley crew looked relieved to see Jack join them at the altar.

"Jack, my man!" Boomer said, and launched into his usual complicated set of first-bumping and hand-clapping that ended only when Jack grabbed Boomer's wrist and dragged him forward for a shoulder bump. Jack chuckled, grateful for the comic relief.

He would have given anything to have Chandler here with him. In life and in death, Chandler would always be his best friend, brother, and best man. He looked at the spot in the front row that he and Alice had agreed would be reserved for Chandler. An American flag had been draped over the back of the pew, and on the seat, facing Jack, was a picture of Chandler in his dress uniform. Beside it sat a clear jar full of Oreo cookies—Chandler's favorite.

They were a sweet reminder to Jack and Alice that the Chandler they knew and loved was so much more than the serious soldier in the military photo who gave his young life in service to his country.

In the next seat over sat a picture of Michelle, Chandler's sister, Jack's foster sister, and Alice's best friend and maid of honor. A White Rocks Eastern College pennant hung above the photo. Michelle would have graduated this year had she not been murdered. The photo Alice had selected showed Michelle sitting on the hood of her blue Honda Civic with a bright smile. It was the best and last picture ever taken of her.

Jack gazed into Chandler's and Michelle's warm, dark-brown eyes, grateful to have had their love and friendship. And thankful that Alice was so very thoughtful. They had agreed to reserve seats for their departed brother and sister, but Alice had done so much more. This was truly special.

There was one more departed relative in attendance. Next to Jack's birth mother, Patty, was an empty chair with a photograph of Jack's father, Steven. It was his school photo. Jack smiled, once again taken aback by how much he looked like him. Steven's mother, Mary Ritter, Jack's only grandmother, sat on his other side.

He wished that Alice's cousin Yana could have attended the wedding. It would have meant a lot to Alice, but given that Yana had just shot and killed her father, it was impossible. Another knot in the tattered tapestry of Alice's life.

Jack gave a nod of thanks to his benefactor and friend, Pierce Weston, sitting in the second row, next to Marisa in a sharp blue dress. He saw his brothers and sisters in blue filling the back four rows, including Sheriff Morrison, Detective Castillo, Kendra, and even Murphy.

He smiled and waved at his adoptive mother, Laura, sitting next to his birth mother, Patty. Ted sat on Laura's other side, and beside him, an open seat was saved for Aunt Haddie, who would be walking Alice down the aisle. In some ways, in spite of his horrible childhood, Jack was uniquely blessed. Between Patty, Laura, Aunt Haddie, and

Mary Ritter, he felt like he had four mothers now. And at this moment, the three who were watching him motioned for him to straighten up and close his mouth, which he suspected had been hanging open since he walked into the church. He smiled and obeyed, fighting the urge to fidget with his tie.

The organ began to play an unexpected tune: Snoopy's song from *Peanuts*. Jack's gaze snapped to the double doors at the back of the sanctuary as they flew open wide and all one hundred and twenty pounds of Lady bounded toward him with a heart-shaped ring pillow strapped to her enormous back. Now the music choice made sense. Mrs. Stevens followed along behind, holding Lady's leash, her face as red as her hair as she fought in vain to slow the wild ringbearer's procession.

Jack knelt to swiftly untie the rings from the satin pillow, but not fast enough to avoid a sloppy lick up the side of his face.

Boomer let out an, "Aw, man. That's not the smooch you've been waiting for."

The wave of giggles from the attendees came to a halt when the organist began to play the "*Wedding March*."

"Please rise for the bride," said the pastor, and the wedding guests stood in unison.

Two women appeared. Aunt Haddie was crying and smiling at the same time.

But Jack had eyes only for Alice. At the sight of her, time stopped. She took his breath away. He hadn't asked what she was going to wear since the gown designed by her would-be killer had been cut from her body by the paramedics after the psychotic "wedding" in the warehouse. But she had made the perfect choice.

Alice was wearing Aunt Haddie's wedding dress. Jack recognized it from the photo Aunt Haddie kept next to her bed. It had been altered to fit Alice's petite frame. Her shoulder-length brown hair fell loose in shining waves, and instead of the chapel veil she had planned to wear, she had opted for a simple ring of spring flowers. Tucked into it was her mother's butterfly pin. She looked like she stepped out of an ethereal painting.

Jack had never seen a woman look so beautiful. He felt like her smile was giving him the strength of a thousand suns. His heart felt so full, he thought it might burst.

She held her head high and stepped slowly down the aisle towards him as the music played.

Jack felt like he was flying and Alice was the only one in the sky with him. He knew that the church was filled with friends and family, but he saw only her.

Haddie took her seat as Alice stepped to Jack's side. He took her hand, and something hard pressed against his leg. He glanced down, puzzled. Alice looked at him with scared green eyes that swelled with love. "I got nervous you might run, so I brought my Taser," she whispered.

Jack let his head roll back and he laughed. His four mothers were shushing him, but he couldn't stop. He laughed loud and long. Alice starting giggling too, and then she was laughing as hard as him. Soon the whole church was filled with laughter.

Jack pulled Alice close. He knew he wasn't supposed to kiss the bride until after the ceremony, but he didn't care. He pressed his lips to hers and gave it everything he had.

Lenora had it all wrong. Weddings weren't about designer dresses and pageantry. They were a celebration of two people coming together with their family and friends before God to publicly declare their love and commitment and begin a new life together as one.

Jack held Alice's chin and peered into her emerald eyes. "I love you, Alice Samantha Campbell. And I always will."

"I love you more." She kissed him. "Let's go catch that happily ever after."

CHAPTER

63

Yana swayed in the back of the gray sedan as it wove through the airport traffic. Without turning, the driver handed a phone back to her. The large mountain of a man hadn't said a single word to her. Not when he picked her up, not on the ride. That wasn't a good sign.

The phone buzzed like an angry wasp. Once. Twice. Yana held it on her open palm, but there was no way to avoid the sting to come.

The driver stared into the rearview mirror, sending a clear message to answer the burner phone.

Yana obeyed. "Hello?"

"Explain," Anatoli Belilovski said in Russian.

"Alex was a careless idiot." Yana's voice was full of sharp condemnation.

"Give me facts," the gruff voice demanded.

"Alex became impatient and tried to go for the information directly. It turned out we were mistaken. The granddaughter's friend was paying for the wedding. Pierce Weston."

"I am aware of who he is. Continue." Anatoli's voice was a low rumble. Even though he was in his sixties, he terrified her. "Is there now a problem with the police?"

"No. Stratton told them it was self-defense. They let me go."

There was silence on the other end of the phone. She began to fear Anatoli had hung up, then she picked up on his quiet breathing.

"Alice still trusts me," she said. "I told her that I would contact her after I buried my father."

"And she believed you?"

"Yes. She thinks I saved Stratton's life. She wants me to come back. She trusts me, and is blissfully unaware of the danger she is in."

Anatoli grunted. "There may be no reason for you to return. If the source of funds for the lavish wedding has been explained, it no longer stands to reason to think Andrew's granddaughter is in contact with him."

"Clearly, she is not. Nor do Alice and Jack know where he is. Otherwise Jack would not have his federal contacts trying to locate him."

"Then again, I ask, why return if they have no information we need?"

"Because Andrew will find her. I'm certain of it. It was the Americans looking for Andrew that alerted us that Alice was alive. It will alert Andrew as well. And when he finds out his granddaughter is still alive, he will come for her."

"And we will be there. Where is the granddaughter going on her honeymoon?"

"The Bahamas."

"We will wait until they return. If you are correct, Alice will reach out to you. It is good she trusts you."

"She does. But she has a new husband at her side. He has proven that he would die to protect her. He is a real-life superhero."

"He is no superman—he bleeds like the rest of us. But you are right. It is time to get rid of Jack Stratton."

DON'T MISS OUT ON ANY OF THE DETECTIVE JACK STRATTON MYSTERY-THRILLER SERIES!

The Detective Jack Stratton Mystery-Thriller Series, authored by *Wall Street Journal* bestselling writer Christopher Greyson, has 5,000+ five-star reviews and over a million readers and counting. If you'd love to read another page-turning thriller with mystery, humor, and a dash of romance, pick up the next book in the highly acclaimed series today:

And Then She Was GONE

A hometown hero with a heart of gold, Jack Stratton was raised in a whorehouse by his prostitute mother. When his foster mother asks him to look into a missing girl's disappearance, Jack quickly gets drawn into a baffling mystery. As Jack digs deeper, everyone becomes a suspect—including himself. Caught between the criminals and the cops, can Jack discover the truth in time to save the girl? Or will he become the next victim?

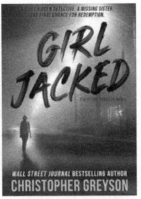

GIRL JACKED

Guilt has driven a wedge between Jack and the family he loves. When Jack, now a police officer, hears the news that his foster sister Michelle is missing, it cuts straight to his core. Forced to confront the demons from his past, Jack must take action, find Michelle, and bring her home... or die trying.

JACK KNIFED

Constant nightmares have forced Jack to seek answers about his rough childhood and the dark secrets hidden there. The mystery surrounding Jack's birth father leads Jack to investigate the twenty-seven-year-old murder case in Hope Falls.

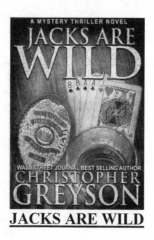

JACKS ARE WILD

When Jack's sexy old flame disappears, no one thinks it's suspicious except Jack and one unbalanced witness. He knows that Marisa has a past, and if it ever caught up with her—it would be deadly. The trail leads him into all sorts of trouble—landing him smack in the middle of an all-out mob war between the Italian Mafia and the Japanese Yakuza.

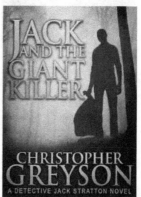

JACK AND THE GIANT KILLER

While recovering from a gunshot wound, Jack gets a seemingly harmless private investigation job—locate the owner of a lost dog—Jack begrudgingly assists. Little does he know it will place him directly in the crosshairs of a merciless serial killer.

DATA JACK

When Replacement gets a job setting up a computer network for a jet-setting software tycoon things turn deadly for her and Jack. Can Jack and Alice stop a pack of ruthless criminals before they can Data Jack?

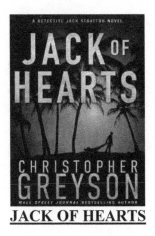

JACK OF HEARTS

Jack Stratton is heading south for some fun in the sun. Already nervous about introducing his girlfriend, Jack is still waiting for Alice's answer to his marriage proposal. Now, Jack finds it's up to him to stop a crazed killer, save his parents, and win the hand of the girl he loves—but if he survives, will it be Jack who ends up with a broken heart?

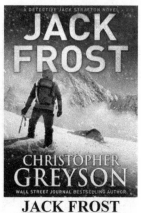

JACK FROST

Jack has a new assignment: to investigate the suspicious death of
a soundman on the hit TV show *Planet Survival*. What started
out as a game is now a deadly competition for survival. As the
temperature drops and the body count rises, what will get them
first? The mountain or the killer?

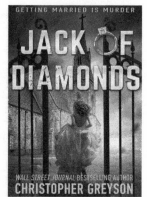

JACK OF DIAMONDS

All Jack Stratton wants to do is get married to the woman he
loves—and make it through the wedding. As Jack and Alice fight
a deadly killer, their long, happy future together seems like it's
just inches from slipping away. This time, "till death do us part"
might just be a bit too accurate.

Also available:

Epic Fantasy

PURE OF HEART

Psychological Thriller

THE GIRL WHO LIVED

Hear your favorite characters come to life in audio versions.
Audio Books now available on Audible!
You could win a brand new HD KINDLE FIRE TABLET
when you go to **ChristopherGreyson.com**
No purchase necessary. It's my way of thanking readers.

INTRODUCING
THE ADVENTURES OF FINN AND ANNIE

Finnian Church chased his boyhood dream of following in his father's law-enforcing footsteps by way of the United States Armed Forces. As soon as he finished his tour of duty, Finn planned to report to the police academy. But the winds of war have a way of changing a man's plans. Finn returned home a decorated war hero, but without a leg. Disillusioned but undaunted, it wasn't long before he discovered a way to keep his ambitions alive and earn a living as an insurance investigator.

Finn finds himself in need of a videographer to document the accident scenes. Into his orderly business and simple life walks Annie Summers. A lovely free spirit and single mother of two, Annie has a physical challenge of her own—she's been completely deaf since childhood.

Finn and Annie find themselves tested and growing in ways they never imagined. Join this unlikely duo as they investigate their way through murder, arson, theft, embezzlement, and maybe even love, seeking to distinguish between truth and lies, scammers and victims.

Don't miss out, pickup the whole collection on Amazon today!

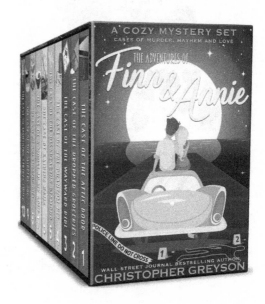

ACKNOWLEDGMENTS

I would like to thank all the wonderful readers out there. It is you who make the literary world what it is today—a place of dreams filled with tales of adventure! To all of you who have spread word of my novels via social media (Facebook and Twitter) and who have taken the time to go back and write a great review, I say THANK YOU! Your efforts keep the characters alive and give me the encouragement and time to keep writing. I can't thank YOU enough.

Word of mouth is crucial for any author to succeed. If you enjoyed the novel, please consider leaving a review at Amazon, even if it is only a line or two; it would make all the difference and I would appreciate it very much.

I would also like to thank my amazing wife for standing beside me every step of the way on this journey. My thanks also go out to my two awesome kids—Laura and Christopher, my dear mother and the rest of my family. Finally, thank you to my wonderful team, Maia McViney, Michael Mishoe, my fantastic editors—David Gatewood of Lone Trout Editing, Charlie Wilson of Landmark Editorial, and the unbelievably helpful beta readers!

ABOUT THE AUTHOR

My name is Christopher Greyson, and I am a storyteller.

Since I was a little boy, I have dreamt of what mystery was around the next corner, or what quest lay over the hill. If I couldn't find an adventure, one usually found me, and now I weave those tales into my stories. I am blessed to have written the bestselling Detective Jack Stratton Mystery-Thriller Series. The collection includes *And Then She Was GONE, Girl Jacked, Jack Knifed, Jacks Are Wild, Jack and the Giant Killer, Data Jack, Jack of Hearts, Jack Frost,* and *Jack of Diamonds.* I have also penned the bestselling psychological thriller, *The Girl Who Lived* and a special collection of mysteries, *The Adventures of Finn and Annie.*

My love for tales of mystery and adventure began with my grandfather, a decorated World War I hero. I will never forget being introduced to his friend, a WWI pilot who flew across the skies at the same time as the feared, legendary Red Baron. My love of reading and storytelling eventually led me to write *Pure of Heart,* a young adult fantasy that I released in 2014.

I love to hear from my readers. Please visit ChristopherGreyson.com, where you can become a preferred reader and enjoy additional FREE *Adventures of Finn and Annie,* advanced notifications of book releases and more! Thank you for reading my novels. I hope my stories have brightened your day.

Sincerely,

CPSIA information can be obtained
at www.ICGtesting.com
Printed in the USA
BVHW031809291219
568070BV00005B/18/P

9 781683 990932